MOSS GATE

THE JACK OF MAGIC BOOK 2

MOSS GATE

ALEX LINWOOD

GREENLEES
PUBLISHING

This is a work of fiction. Names, characters, organizations, places, events, and incidents are either products of the author's imagination or are used fictitiously. Any resemblance to actual persons, living or dead, or actual events is purely coincidental.

Copyright © 2019 by Alex Linwood

All rights reserved.

No part of this book may be reproduced in any form or by any electronic or mechanical means, including information storage and retrieval systems, without written permission from the publisher, except for the use of brief quotations in a book review.

Published by Greenlees Publishing, contact@greenleespublishing.com

ISBN-13: 978-1-951098-10-0

Cover design by Dominic Forbes

*For my Family
and
other Magic Users*

The musical note of a bird call coming in through an open window contrasted sharply to the dark and dusty classroom in front of Portia. She sighed heavily. Spring had arrived, and it was torturous to be inside. All the excitement of battling for a place in the Magic Academy last fall was forgotten. What she wanted right now was to be out in the sun under a cloudless sky. The light green grass outside the window pulled her eyes away from the chalkboard. She imagined herself lying on the soft new growth and basking in the sun.

"Student Portia, may we ask the favor of your presence?" Professor Aelric Terfel asked from the front of the class, one eyebrow up. He rapped his pointer on the board for emphasis.

Portia looked guiltily at Professor Aelric and nodded, sliding down into her seat. Twitters of laughter bubbled up from the back of the class. Portia knew Magisend and her friends enjoyed her embarrassment. She glanced over and saw that even her own friends Ella and Mia were trying to hide grins. Portia relaxed, relenting into a small smile of her own. It was understandably hard to be inside on such a beautiful day, no matter how much she loved school. There were few things to recommend her previous life as a thief, but being outside all the time was one of them. Her life was much different now.

"Excellent, so glad you could join us," Aelric continued. "You are all in for a special treat." Aelric looked around at the rest of the class. "The queen has decreed that more detailed research of our earliest history is required by all students. You will be allowed access to books the previous classes have not been given." He looked at the class intently. "As I'm sure you are all aware by now, I believe that all privileges should be repaid with hard work, if not earned ahead of time by earnest efforts. But this privilege has been extended in advance, so you will have to earn it now."

The class groaned. It had been a difficult year in Professor Aelric's history class. Portia thought she was the only one who really enjoyed learning about the Kingdom's history. Most of the noble students had tutors of their own growing up, teaching them more history than they had ever wanted to know. The remaining students would have much rather practiced their magical skills—and played pranks on each other with them—than studied the dusky tomes in the library. But Portia spent as much time there as she could. It was a whole new world to her—one that, by all rights, she should never have been able to see. Few orphans were ever admitted to the Magic Academy.

"Enough," Aelric chided. "You would do well to

remember this is a privilege. You are to be allowed entrance into the Special Library—The Building of Mages."

Magisend Lucy gasped, shock on her face. Portia turned around to look at her enemy. Magisend Lucy Gwynn was one of the few nobles in the class, and one of the most educated. She was from the House Riddlepit, the second most powerful house in the Kingdom.

"Only special librarians and historians are allowed in that building... and the Royal House," Magisend protested.

"And now this year's history classes," Aelric continued, giving Magisend a severe look to prohibit any further interruptions. "There will be students from other classes in the building as well as yourselves. Please do not disturb any of the normal research that is conducted there. You have a unique privilege as students. No other year in my recollection has done this." Aelric stared at the class, his arms folded, his frown evidence of his disapproval of these unusual arrangements. "You will be expected to familiarize yourselves with the library. You will get special access cards that are not to be shared. They will be magically keyed to you individually. Your first task is to write a three-thousand-word report on the earliest history of humankind based on the books in that library. This report is due Monday. I must caution that this is your background report for all further in-depth study of the time. I suggest you do it well because you will not have time to make up for any deficiencies as we continue. We will be moving through the materials quickly."

Special Library? Unique Access? Portia's heart soared. This was true excitement. Judging by the muttering from the other students, Portia figured she was the only one who thought this way. Her happiness could not be contained. Not only was she getting an education at the elite institution, but more of an education than the usual Magic Academy student received. A small part of her worried for the reason behind this change—her presence as a unique Jack of Magic, one of only three in the history of the Kingdom—but even that nebulous fear was not enough to erase all the thrill at this new opportunity.

The class ended, and Portia left with Ella and Mia. Ella turned to her and said with a giggle, "It's so cute how much you love school. I don't think I've ever met anyone like you. I'm guessing that you want to go that library as soon as our last class is over." Ella flipped her blonde hair back and gave a mock sigh of exasperation. She seemed to know everyone on campus, so for her to say she didn't know anyone like Portia was quite the statement.

Mia turned away, her red hair hiding her own laughter.

Portia took her friends' ribbing in stride. For all their teasing, she knew they were on her side. Ella and Mia had spent countless hours tutoring her that year to help her catch up with the rest of the students.

"Of course I do. And you two are coming with me," Portia said, not bothering to wait for an answer before she walked off to her next class. "Meet me outside the main library after fifth period," she called out as she walked away.

Mia and Ella erupted into laughter behind her. Portia knew they would be there.

The rest of the day dragged on. Portia tried to concentrate

on her classes, but it was difficult, knowing what adventure awaited them in just a few hours. Today was one of her least favorite classes, music. After six months, she was just starting to get the hang of the complex rhythms required for some pieces they learned. She still didn't understand why they had to learn music in the Magic Academy but trusted that there was a reason, even if no one could explain it to her.

When her last class was finally over, Portia rushed over to the library where Mia and Ella were already waiting. The main library was an imposing building made of the same magical blue stone that was used for every hall on campus. Four large pillars spanned across its impressive face, and the entryway was two stories tall.

But the building they were going to was not the main library. It was no larger than a small cottage, nestled to one side of the main library and behind an iron fence with a large gate. Portia had never thought much of the building, guessing it was a maintenance shed or the former home of a caretaker. She had not realized its significance. That must be part of how it was kept safe, she realized when she looked at its humble appearance.

"This is the Building of Mages?" Portia asked, peering through the iron bars.

"Apparently so," Ella said, her voice calm, as it always was. "Shall we?"

Mia walked up to the gate, holding the access card Aelric had given her up to the large lock that held the iron gate shut. A soft click sounded and the lock slipped open, releasing the gate to swing out slowly. Mia entered. When Ella tried to follow, the gate swung shut of its own volition before she could enter. It locked again with a resounding clank. Portia whistled in appreciation. Both Ella and Portia had to press their own cards up to the lock before the gate would allow each to enter. Portia tried to open the gate from the inside and it swung open easily. It was only locked if they tried to enter from the outside. It reassured her somewhat that they were not locked in.

They walked down a gravel path to the entrance. Unlike the other buildings on campus where the stone was cut into neat blocks, this one had oddly shaped and sized blue stones pieced together tightly to form the walls, seemingly without mortar. Portia felt a knot of disappointment in her stomach at the building's small size—how many books could it hold? It wasn't much larger than two dorm rooms put together.

But when they entered the front door she sucked in a gasp of shock. The inside was cavernous, the ceiling soaring four stories above them. Balconies and doors ringed the large room on all four floors. Elation gripped Portia. Hopefully each door contained an entire room of books.

The main room was filled with tables and chairs, some occupied with blue-robed Academy scholars and a few students Portia recognized from their year. Surrounding the open space were walls of bookshelves filled—and in some cases overfilled—with stacked books and scrolls. There were even books piled on the floor. A central workstation, elevated ten feet up, overlooked the vast space. A tiny woman sat behind the counter, her fingers tented as she gazed at Portia, Ella, and Mia, waiting for them to approach.

"How can this be?" Portia asked. She felt a little dizzy from the shock of the difference of size between the inside and the outside of the building.

Ella looked around calmly. Nothing ever seemed to faze her. "I've heard of this before but never been able to see it for myself."

"This building?" Portia asked.

"No, the magic of dimensions. I think that's what it's called. Dimensions... Space... Something like that. It's very rare magic. There are few who can do it—and it requires energy to maintain it. Which is why it's rarely used."

"I thought it was prohibited," Mia said, puzzlement in her voice. Mia was one of the students from a noble house. She knew more than most new students since she'd had the privilege of tutors in her youth. But apparently even the tutors didn't know everything. Or maybe it was because she was from House Kelynack, which was not as powerful as the other houses. Portia wondered if all knowledge was shared equally between the houses.

"I don't know about that," Ella said, "but I have heard whispers about it in my village growing up. It's hard to know what is truth and what isn't with the gossip. Mia, you would know better than both of us."

Mia looked around. "Apparently not."

"Why would it be prohibited?" Portia asked Mia. It seemed like such a useful magic to her. You could hide almost anything anywhere in plain sight.

"Could you imagine what would happen if the magic was not maintained?" Mia responded, waving at the huge space in front of them. "This entire building would pop into the surrounding space. I bet it's large enough to crush the library outside as well as all the other surrounding buildings."

"Would it crush them? Or just appear inside them?" Portia asked. She couldn't imagine what would happen if two buildings tried to occupy the same area at the same time.

Mia shrugged her shoulders. She didn't know either.

A small shiver went down Portia's spine at the thought of what might happen if the magic ceased working while they were inside the building, or even inside the main library or the other nearby buildings. Apparently, the knowledge they were going to get here did not come without some form of danger. She breathed in deeply to calm herself. She had faced worse, and no one else within the building seem concerned. She would not think about it.

They approached the librarian in the center of the building who nodded at them, a welcoming smile on her face. "It is so exciting to see new faces in here," she whispered to them conspiratorially. She looked around then straightened up and said more formally, "Welcome to the Building of Mages. May I see your cards?"

The three girls pushed over the cards they had received from Aelric in history class. The woman nodded at each one and gave each a small red stamp in the corner.

Portia couldn't contain her excitement. "Can we go anywhere?" She gestured around the room and at the visible doors on the surrounding balconies.

"No," the librarian said, then softened at Portia's look of disappointment, "but nearly everywhere. Your card will open locks where you are allowed." She patted Portia's hand reassuringly then leaned in to whisper, "You will not be disappointed."

Portia cheered up at that. She reminded herself to not be too greedy. It was amazing enough that she was here at all. And she knew she should work hard—especially as a Jack of Magic. If what Queen Lorica and King Consort Aldis had told her last winter was truth, she needed every bit of knowledge on her side. Somehow, a Jack of Magic was a defender of the kingdoms—human kingdoms anyhow. Perhaps more... There was so much she didn't know about.

Ella pulled at Portia's sleeve. "Come on, let's get to work. We're having a roast tonight, and I'm starving." Portia laughed. Ella was the only girl she knew who could eat more than she did.

"Wait, we have to know where we're going," Mia said, turning to the librarian, but before she could ask a question, the librarian simply pointed to the back corner. Portia saw other students working at the tables there and pulling books from the shelves. They were not the first students to arrive. Others were there also doing homework for Aelric's class.

Portia, Ella, and Mia split up to explore the stacks of books behind the tables in the back corner. The shelves held books of all different sizes, some originally black, brown, or red, but now faded to various shades of yellow and tan. Portia selected a small yellow book with a hand-tied binding off the top shelf near the very back. It was hard to see, but Portia knew it was there. It had called out to her. When she grabbed hold of it, it fit perfectly in her hand.

She flipped it open and scanned the table of contents. The stylized handwritten lettering was hard to read, but she was still able to make out what it said. Each chapter was the name of a noble house. She recognized the names Riddlepit, Ladock, Kelynack, Hayle, and Coverack, but the first name, Callac, was unfamiliar. It was listed before all others, which confused her.

Turning the pages, she saw lists of names and family trees drawn out. There was even a sketch or two of people, but so poorly done as to not be recognizable, even if the people sketched were still alive. She guessed this was a history of the noble houses from ages ago. She flipped to the front, but there was no date on the book. Each family tree started from an event called The Splintering.

She paged the first section of family trees, those listed under the name Callac. The trees were just as large as in the other sections. This had been a healthy house with many members. There was no indication of anything happening to them. This confused her greatly since she had never heard of a noble house by that name.

She wandered through the stacks holding the book until she found Mia, who was examining the contents of a large book of maps. "Mia, I don't understand what this book is saying. It looks like it references six noble houses."

Mia looked up, confused, then puzzlement crossed her face. "It's in that book?"

"It lists another noble house—at least I think that's what it's saying—by the name of Callac."

Mia's mouth made a small oh. She held out her hand for

the book and Portia gave it to her. She flipped through the book and landed on the first page of the Callac family tree. "I can't believe a book references that house. In the official library."

"Why wouldn't it? Who was that house? Are they still... around?" Portia asked, her curiosity piqued.

"No, they are not around." Mia hesitated. She started to talk then stopped herself with a soft grunt and just stared at the book some more.

"Come on, Mia, you have to tell me more. Why are you surprised they're listed in this book? And more so, how do you know anything about them if they're not supposed to be in books?" Portia folded her arms and stood in front of Mia.

Mia sighed and then gave the book back to Portia. "The House Coverack decreed long ago that the House of Callac was never to be written or spoken of. But as a member of a noble house, I was aware of them, if for no other reason than to make sure I did not speak of them, especially at court." At the others' questioning looks, Mia sighed. "They had no choice after I found an accidental reference to them in an old text. They got rid of the book too, before I thought to save it."

This surprised Portia. She had only met the queen and king consort once, but they seemed in favor of sharing information, not hiding it. She reminded herself once again how little she knew. She had been in the city for just over a year, but sometimes it felt like she had just arrived yesterday. There were so many traditions and verbal pieces of knowledge she did not know—especially as a commoner. And especially as an orphan.

"They were the original royal house," Mia continued. "They were the house that led us to this world. Something happened though. I don't know what—no one has ever been able to tell me—and they lost all their power and position. I was always curious, but any time I asked for more information, it brought such upset and consternation from my tutors that I learned never to speak of the subject. My parents were even more upset when I asked about the house. They had told me that was all they knew and then asked me to never speak of it again."

"They were the royal house?"

"Yes. House Coverack took over when they disappeared."

"That doesn't make any sense," Portia said, her face scrunched up. "If they were so powerful as to lead everyone here, how could they just vanish like that?"

Mia shrugged her shoulders. She didn't have an answer. She picked up the book of maps again and started reading it. She paused and then looked up at Portia again. "Don't tell anyone I told you this. And whatever you do, don't put the House of Callac into your report. I don't know how this book got here, or why it was allowed to remain, but it will be taken from you if you breathe a word of this to anyone, of that I'm sure."

Portia looked down at the book with a new sense of having found a treasure. The last thing she wanted to do was lose it. Especially if so much of their history was verbal and whole houses had been written out. She looked at the surrounding books with a sense of consternation. How much of what was here was true, and how much was rewritten history? For the first time, she felt skepticism towards the Academy. It was unpleasant to learn that not everything was as she had hoped—ethical, honest, knowledgeable. She nodded at Mia, who waved her away, now engrossed in her study of the maps.

Richard and Liam joined them after about an hour. Their history class had also been assigned the essay. Richard looked like his usual self—dark hair messily arranged because he honestly didn't care—and Liam had slicked-back blond hair with purple tips that perfectly matched his purple tunic. Portia didn't think the twins could be any more different. Ella still had not wrested the secret of Liam's changing hair from him, much to her unending consternation.

The twins headed straight for the cabinets of legal briefs. An interest in the dry intricacies of the law was one of the few things they held in common. Portia was glad they were not being forced to do reports in teams. Or at least not in a team with them.

Ella strode by, her fingertips touching each book at hand level as she walked. "Ready to go, Portia? My stomach tells me it's nearly suppertime."

Portia nodded. Laughter from behind her caught her attention. Richard and Liam were laughing over a large drawing spread over one of the tables. They had found something more amusing than law reports.

Ella looked over at the twins, curious as well. "Shall we see what they have?" she asked, not bothering to wait for a response. Portia trailed after her to see what they were looking at.

"Ella, you won't believe this, but this is a planning map of the city. Or a replanning map. There was another city here first, and apparently the planners were not impressed with how things were laid out," Liam said, shaking his head and laughing. "I don't know if they weren't allowed to speak their mind in person or what, but they certainly took it upon themselves to say what they really thought here."

"How curious," Ella said as she leaned in to look at the map.

Richard shook his head. He was less amused than Liam, but even he, the more serious one, had a small smile on his face. Portia peeked over his shoulder to see what he was looking at. Tiny lettering on the side of an architectural drawing listed the dimensions for a hallway, and then the comment: 'needs to be five feet wide, minimum, because we are not all as skinny as Devorak.'

"Maybe Devorak was an official measure of width," Portia said.

Liam laughed. "I doubt it. My guess is Devorak was the boss who never bothered to look at the plans drawn up by underlings. You'd be amazed how many bosses are like that."

Portia looked at Liam in surprise. He was a student just as she was. What would he know of bosses? She looked down at the map again. It was filled with little comments in tiny handwriting. Mia joined in and crowded around the maps as well.

Ella sighed, bored. "I'll leave you to this." She wandered off into the stacks again when it was clear Mia and Portia were not going to leave just yet.

Eventually, Portia's stomach growled so loudly that all four of them heard. Her face turned red. "Perhaps it *is* time to go," she said. Richard and Liam laughed loudly. Portia was grateful that Mia at least turned away politely.

Ella returned as they were putting away their materials. She had a tiny book with her, its cover bright purple despite its age. It was handstitched and fit within her palm. "Look at this beautiful little thing. It's like a piece of jewelry."

Portia took the book from her. It was much heavier than it appeared. "No jewelry I'd like to wear. Is it full of rocks?" She flipped it open but couldn't understand anything within it. The script curved and flowed as if a different language. Beautiful gold foil drawings of the first letter of each chapter graced its pages. She looked up at Ella. "What does it say?"

"No idea. I just thought it was pretty. Can we finally go eat now?" Ella asked, a hint of irritation in her voice.

"Yes, yes, yes," Liam said, "Portia's stomach agrees with you." He started giggling all over again.

"Do you want this book?" Portia asked Ella, who shook her head.

"No. I just thought it was pretty. I'll put it back."

"No need. I want to look at it some more. Perhaps they'll let me take it back to the house."

Portia brought the two books to the librarian. The same tiny woman was at the station in the middle of the room. "Can I take these with me?" she asked.

The woman took the books. Opening the yellow one, the book about the noble houses, her eyebrows rose. She stared at Portia. "Did you read this one?"

"No, not really," Portia said. She had only skimmed it— she hadn't really *read* it. Hopefully, that was close enough to the truth. Portia's ears burned a bit, but thankfully her face did not turn red and betray her less than truthfulness to the librarian.

The librarian pursed her lips. "This one is not removable from the library." At Portia's disappointed look, she continued. "You may read it here. But do so in a corner, please. For my sake."

Portia wondered what that was about. At least she was not forbidden from reading it—not openly in any case.

Taking the second book, the one that was in the foreign language, the librarian checked the inside cover. "Interesting. Most books here are prohibited from leaving the building, but for some reason this one has nothing against it inscribed inside. This is highly unusual. But since it is not prohibited, I will let you take it. Just be careful, my student friend; it looks extremely old."

The woman wrote out a small card with the name of the book. She took Portia's access card and copied something from it onto the card.

Portia took the book back. "Do you know what language it's written in? I don't recognize it." Portia didn't bother to explain that there were few languages she would recognize.

The librarian opened the book to the middle and stared at its contents, her brows pulling together. "I don't know," she said. She waved over another blue-robed attendant to examine the book. The attendant also didn't know. The librarian shrugged her shoulders and handed the book back to Portia. "Ask your teachers. One of them might know."

Portia thought Hilda, a professor and the pyromancy

house leader, would be a perfect person to ask. If she got lucky, she might even be able to have a conversation with her tonight.

Portia rushed to catch up with her friends, who were already walking out the door. She didn't notice Magisend getting up from the table where she was studying until it was too late. They collided, books scattering to the floor.

"Watch it, *commoner*," the girl said, drawing herself up.

Portia sighed. She had thought they were beyond that. Magisend was from the Noble House Riddlepit that Portia had robbed prior to entering the Academy. Worse, she had specifically robbed Magisend and got caught in the process. She despaired of Magisend ever letting it go. "I'm so sorry. I didn't do it on purpose."

"I should hope not," Magisend said, but her indignation softened at Portia's apology. The angry fire left her eyes.

"Of course not. I meant it when I said we should at least get along," Portia said, trying to soften Magisend towards her even further.

It worked. Magisend looked slightly ashamed. "I suppose I should not have called you a commoner."

"Don't worry about it. It's true. I am a commoner." Being indignant about it would do nothing to help her navigate the school. Getting along with Magisend, though, that would help a great deal. Portia wanted all the friends she could get.

Her response surprised Magisend. It also loosened her tongue. "It has nothing to do with you... My temper, I mean. I just hate this festival so much. It shouldn't be allowed in Coverack."

"Festival?"

"Spring Festival. I don't want to talk about it." Magisend looked down at the books at her feet. She gasped softly and reached for Portia's purple book—the book in the foreign language that no one knew. Holding it, she flipped through it and then looked up at Portia with glittering eyes. "Where did you get this?" Magisend's face flickered between excitement, fear, and a third emotion Portia could not place.

Portia gestured to the far corner where they had been studying. She wasn't sure exactly where Ella had found the book but thought it was from that area. "I checked that one out," Portia said, pointing to the purple book.

Magisend shook her head. She wasn't going to try take the book from Portia, thank the mages. She shoved the book back at Portia and then hurried off to the far corner Portia had indicated, leaving Portia to watch, her mouth hanging open at Magisend's sudden rush.

2

Hilda was not in the house that evening. Portia was disappointed but decided to get up early the next morning to find someone to help her with the book before classes. One of her professors had to know about the language in the book. For some reason she couldn't explain, it felt important—too important to wait for the next afternoon.

It was also unusual for Professor Hilda Griffiths to not be in the house in the evening. She was normally present for a few hours each evening to check on her pyromancy students and offer informal advice. This was especially important to the new students, most of whom were away from home for the first time. Hilda's absence added to Portia's sense of unease. Portia did not sleep well that night.

The campus was beautiful in the morning. Fog clung to the grass in patches, burning off before the sun in the few exposed spots between the long shadows of the buildings. Portia made her way to the pyromancy building and Hilda's classroom. She found Hilda preparing for the day's lessons, distributing glass tubes and stands on each desk.

"Good morning," Portia said, knocking gently on the doorframe to get Hilda's attention. "We missed you last night."

Hilda looked away and cleared her throat. "Ah, yes, sorry about that. Things, you know."

Where were you? Portia thought but didn't dare ask. Hilda had always been so generous and helpful, the last thing Portia wanted to do was to pry. "I was hoping you could help me with something. It's not from our class, but still I thought you might know." Portia held out the purple book to Hilda while entering the room.

Hilda turned, looked at the book, and raised one eyebrow. Taking the book from Portia, she opened it and scanned the pages. She shook her head. "I'm sorry. I don't know anything about this."

"Do you know what language it's in?"

"No. It's nothing I've ever seen before." Hilda handed the book back to Portia and looked at her closely. "How are you doing? I haven't asked you in a while. I know you have a lot of pressure on you."

"I'm doing okay. Ella and Mia are still helping me catch up. It's been a lot, but I think I'm almost there. It's not nearly as stressful as fall term." Portia was grateful to get a bit more sleep these days. Between her classes and Mia and Ella's additional tutoring help, she figured she'd studied four hours more a day than most of the students. But it had been worth it to fill in some of her knowledge gaps from her years on the street as an orphan in Valencia.

"That's good," Hilda said, nodding, "but what about your special studies, the ones Mia and Ella are not supposed to know about? We need you versed in all sorts of magic—a skillset no other student, or anyone else in fact, is capable of. Professor Aelric has not given me an update recently."

"I think I'm picking things up well enough. At least the number of complaints from Professor Aelric has dropped," Portia said with a small laugh. Professor Aelric was a tough taskmaster but a thorough teacher. Portia was grateful for all that he was sharing with her.

"Well, that's good," Hilda said, smiling. She was well aware of Professor Aelric's prickly temperament. "I'm sorry I can't help you with the book—perhaps he can. There are also professors on campus who specialize in language if he doesn't know."

"Okay, thanks," Portia said. Hilda nodded and resumed her tasks in the classroom. Portia left and went to find Professor Aelric in the history building.

She was in luck. Professor Aelric was at his desk, eating soup from a small bowl. She knocked on the door tentatively to get his attention. A flicker of irritation crossed his face before he smoothed it, controlling his reaction at having his breakfast interrupted.

He motioned her to enter. "Well, don't just stand there, come in. I clearly am not to have a peaceful repast this morning."

Portia's cheeks flushed. Even though she knew he was prickly to everyone, it was hard to not feel like she had done something particularly wrong. Even so, her own stomach growled. The roll she had grabbed on the way out the door was long gone, and lunch was not for some time. She walked into the room and pulled the purple book out of her bag. "I'm sorry to bother you, but I was hoping you would know something about this." She held it out to him.

He looked at the book then slowly looked up at Portia. "This is something history related, I take it?"

"I think so." She walked closer, bringing the book to him.

He took the book from her and opened it. His eyebrows slowly rose as he looked at it, turning page after page of the thin volume. "Where did you get this?"

"From the library—the special one."

"And they let you walk out the door with this?" he asked, his voice soft, while he continued to examine the contents.

She wasn't sure if that was a rhetorical question but thought it safer to answer anyway. "They did. The librarian said there was nothing prohibiting it. I think she was a little surprised herself."

"I bet. This is a very interesting find." His eyes never left the book.

"Do you know the language?" she asked. The way he was holding the book made her wonder if she was going to get it back again. Perhaps it was a mistake she was allowed to take it in the first place.

"I do, though I never thought to see it in a book brought to me by a student. How can I help you with this?" he asked, finally bringing his attention back to her face.

"I want to know what it says," Portia said, fidgeting a bit. "I thought it would be good for my report." She remembered his admonishment about honesty after the incident with Deyelna and her minions over the winter and quickly added, "And I'm really curious."

Aelric nodded approval at her blunt statements. "As am I, I must confess. Since I know this language, I will translate it and satisfy both of our curiosities. I'll have it done in a few days. I will let you know in class. Until then, please go. My breakfast is growing cold." He put the book down on the desk, indicating their discussion was over.

Portia walked to the door, loathe to leave the book behind but having no other choice if she wished to know its contents. It was going to be a long couple of days.

"Oh, I almost forgot," he said, his voice stopping her as she reached the doorframe, "have you gone to the Spring Festival yet?"

She turned to face him. "No, I haven't."

"I suggest you do so. Things are done much differently in Coverack than in Valencia. Consider it a homework assignment. You, in particular, need to understand these things." He resumed eating his soup. No other words were forthcoming.

Portia nodded and left the classroom. She had never heard of a festival being assigned as homework, but then again there was so much she had not heard of before. Perhaps others would go with her and explain some things she didn't understand.

Classes dragged on that day. Portia blamed it on her empty stomach. She vowed to never have such a light breakfast again, not if she could help it. It was a shorter day, and most of her classmates planned to go to the Library of Mages to get some work done before supper.

She arrived to find Mia and Ella already there working at one of the long tables. Mia was industriously copying from a book while Ella conversed with some students at a nearby table, drawing irritated looks of other library patrons. Ella made it a point to make friends wherever she went. The hardest challenge she would ever face, Portia decided, would be to sit still and not talk for longer than thirty minutes. She valued her roommate greatly, but at times the noise was too much even for Portia. Mia seemed to be doing exceptionally well ignoring the conversation and focusing on her own task.

"Good afternoon, housemates," Portia greeted her friends. "Do you know about the Spring Festival? I would like to go—"

This drew Ella's immediate attention. "Spring Festival? Is that already going on? We *must* go. Today. Tell me it's going on today, Portia, tell me."

Portia's eyebrow's knit together. "I'm not sure. I think so." She realized she hadn't confirmed the dates and wasn't sure how to do so.

"It is," Mia said, without looking up from her paper.

Ella clapped her hands together excitedly, drawing even more irritated looks from other patrons. She noticed the looks and stopped clapping, her face reddening. "We must go today," she whispered to Portia and Mia, nearly as loud as her normal talking voice.

Mia put down her pen with a sigh. She knew as well as Portia that once Ella had a notion in her head, it was nearly impossible to dissuade her. They were going to the festival that day.

Just then, Richard and Liam entered the front doors and weaved their way through the tables towards the group of girls.

"Greetings, ladies," Liam said, a broad grin on his face. His hair was black today with white tips, pushed into a Mohawk rising several inches in the air. Portia wondered if he ever got tired of fussing with his hair. He rarely wore the same style for longer than a week. Today he looked much different from how he did even yesterday. When did he have time to make these changes?

His twin brother, Richard, merely nodded his greetings. He was as opposite to his brother as could be imagined. While they were both tall, Richard was retiring and Liam an extrovert. Richard consistently had the same shaggy brown hairstyle and conservative clothes, and Liam often looked like a rooster or peacock showing off his prized plumage. Despite their differences, they were rarely apart.

"Liam and Richard, we're going to the Spring Festival today!" Ella told them, brooking no argument.

"Wonderful! Excellent! Much more exciting than this boring homework," Liam said, on board with the idea immediately.

Richard, however, was not so enthused. "We just got here. And our reports are due in a few days..."

Mia nodded agreement, tucking a strand of her red hair behind her ear. She too was a conscientious student and would have stayed the rest of the day working in the library.

"Nonsense," Ella said, rising and pulling on Mia's arm to draw her to her feet. "We have plenty of time for silly reports. Let's go."

Liam clapped Richard on the shoulder and then turned him to face the door again. He didn't bother responding to Richard's protest. Richard looked down in resignation and dutifully marched towards the exit, followed by the rest of the group. Portia felt a bit sorry for him, but not sorry enough to argue for the group not to go. It was homework for her anyway, and she'd much rather go with her friends than alone.

The festival itself was located off campus, near the central marketplace that was close to the seawall. It was close enough to walk. Other students had the same idea, so they joined a stream of fellow students leaving campus and heading towards the market streets.

Portia could smell the food several blocks away. Lunch had not fully banished her hunger left over from such a scanty breakfast, and she was glad of the coins in her purse. When they reached the market, she saw festival booths tucked in amongst the normal stalls and scattered in the normally empty grassy area by the seawall. The crowds were thick. It seemed like half the countryside had come into the city to either sell something or seek entertainment at the gathering. Cloaks of various colors gave away that travelers had come from far and wide.

"I have to eat something," Portia said to Mia and Ella.

Mia snorted under her breath. Portia knew Mia was well used to her appetite, only outdone by Ella on the girls' side of the pyromancy house.

"I know just the thing," Ella said, pulling Portia towards a vendor that had a long line in front of it. The smell of grease and sugar wafted from the stall. Portia did not argue.

The fried dough balls were perfect—hot, chewy, and not too sweet. Portia could not stop herself from eating too fast and burned her tongue, but it was well worth it. They served nothing like this on campus.

The twins joined them, bringing the three girls glasses of mead and holding their own cups. They wandered through the festival together, seeing what other treats vendors had brought. Most of the food smelled delicious, but there were a few things that made Portia recoil. A sign over one booth said, 'Duck Eyes, five for a copper'.

"They aren't really serving duck eyes, are they?" she asked. It must be a euphemism for an unusual dish.

Mia nodded. "Yes, it really is duck eyes. It's not a savory dish—I know because my father insisted we try all new things in my training." She glanced at Portia's expression, amused. "Unfortunately, that was one of them."

For the first time in her life, Portia was glad she had been an orphan and not a noble. At least no one had forced her to eat anything she did not want to.

Beyond the central core of food vendors there was a ring of games, both of luck and of skill. Normally quiet, Richard excelled at one game that involved throwing balls at glass bottles, winning so many times that he refused the prizes the glum vendor offered. The vendor was so grateful he gave Richard extra balls and allowed him to continue his streak until he was too tired for further play.

Liam laughed and clapped Richard on the shoulders when he was done and then stepped up to the counter. He bested Richard by five throws, also refusing additional prizes from the vendor after the first. Other students from the Academy lined up to try their luck, seeing the twins' success and thinking it was an easy game. Portia heard cries of disappointment after they walked away when those students found out after the first throw that it was not so simple. She thought the vendor stood to make a great deal of money and probably should have paid Richard and Liam for bringing people to his stall.

Even Ella and Mia won prizes tossing rings on bottles. Portia tried as well but failed miserably, the rings falling between the bottles or to the side. Anywhere but where she intended them to go. She was too cheap to spend more than a copper trying and so resigned herself to walking along as the only one in her group without a prize tucked in her belt.

Liam noticed her lack of a prize. Coming up next to her, he put his arm around her. "What? You can't hang out with us without some sort of prize. It's a house rule!"

"No, it's fine," Portia protested, but Liam was already gone. Portia bit her lip. She wanted to stop him but knew it was probably futile. He could be as stubborn as Ella. Giving up the idea, she followed the rest of the group.

A few moments later, Liam reappeared at her side holding out a small locket. She gave a small smile. He held up one finger at her lukewarm response then spun the locket. An image of a bird in flight appeared as the locket spun. Portia gasped in delight.

"I did good, right?" he asked, a wicked smile on his face.

"You did," Portia said, mesmerized by the beautiful piece of art. It was not something she expected as a fair prize.

"It's yours." He grabbed her hand, putting the locket into it.

"I can't," Portia said, but Liam only shrugged and ran up to join his brother. It was ironic that she was so bad at games when supposedly she was the unique Jack of Magic and was told she was destined to save the kingdom. She couldn't even win a prize at a festival game. But at least she had friends.

They continued on, going further into the festival. It was so large that it took over a good section of the city.

"What's that?" Portia asked the group, noticing for the first time an open square beyond the games where colored fog and flashes of light were drifting upwards from the ground.

Ella glanced over then clapped her hands excitedly. "Oh, magic demonstrations! We have to go." She hooked her arms in Mia's and Portia's, dragging them towards the open square with Richard and Liam following closely behind.

"Magic demonstrations? Don't we see everything at school?" Portia asked, confused.

"No, no. This is different. These are people with magic so rare we would only read about it in the books in school. We would never be so lucky as to see all the different types of magic in person," Ella said, excitement shining in her eyes. "The Academy has access to some of this magic, but it can't afford to keep these people on full-time. They make far more money traveling the country and showing off than they would in some stuffy school."

Portia looked sharply at Ella at the word 'stuffy'. She knew Ella was just as grateful to be at the Academy as she was.

Ella saw Portia's scowl and squeezed her arm. "You know what I mean. School is great and all, and I love it, but wait until you see these folks. Then you'll understand."

Mia nodded solemnly at Portia from the other side of Ella. She would know more than any of them. Portia felt a bit of excitement as they approached the square.

There were individual performers scattered in the large square, each surrounded by a group watching. Portia and her friends had to peer between people's shoulders to see what was going on. One large group of observers was gathering on the far side, so they hurried over there to see what the fuss was about.

An elderly man was digging rocks from the hard-packed earth. He had two fist-size rocks at his feet and was using a small shovel to dig out a third. He arranged the rocks in a row in front of him and then looked up and around at his observers. He did this slowly, dramatically. He knew how to work his audience and wanted their full attention. The surrounding people quieted expectantly as the old man waited for their full attention.

Slowly, he walked to the end rock and held his palm over it. At first nothing seemed to happen, then the rock glowed, at first subtly then a more intense red. The glow morphed into a yellow and white color, the rock itself melting into a puddle on the hard-packed earth. Steam rose from it. Even from ten feet away Portia could feel the heat emanating from it. The old man had turned the rock into lava.

He repeated the task with the other two rocks, maintaining the super-heated state of the first one. Finally, he had three small puddles of liquid rock. Raising his hands, the puddles lifted off the ground and were suspended in the air at his chest height. Slowly, they started to rotate until it looked like he was juggling lava. The crowd whistled and cheered, clapping in appreciation. The old man beamed in their adulation. He then winked at the crowd and held up his right hand to get their attention. Making a twisting motion with his right hand, he changed the trajectory of the lava, causing it to all join briefly in the shape of a horse then break apart again, once again in three chunks. He did this repeatedly, every time in the shape of a different animal, much to the crowd's approval.

Portia had never seen such power exhibited in pyromancy —for that was surely what it was.

"Do you think anyone at the school could create that much heat in their pyromancy?" she asked Ella quietly, not wanting to draw the attention of others or their ire for disturbing the show.

"Not many, I'd say," Ella said, chewing her lip. "Though, where I'm really puzzled is how he can move them with so much control through the air. I'd give much to be able to do that. I feel like I'm throwing globes of mud with my magic, but he has such minute control over the shapes and effects of his magic."

Portia nodded. She had not thought of that. When she was doing her light mote magic, she only had control over the general direction where they went and roughly how many there were based more on her strength than anything else. She could not control the path of the single mote, much less masses of them simultaneously. This man possessed a great deal of mental strength and discipline.

Liam, standing on the other side of Ella, looked over at Portia and whispered, "Someday I'll be that good, just you see."

Richard shook his head at Liam's bravado. Mia simply stared, entranced, at the show. Portia knew that of all the pyromancers, Mia was the closest to having that intensity of strength. But Mia was a quiet one, not prone to bragging.

The group peeled off from that display, curious to see what else was there. The next was a young woman who had cryomancy as her power. She too had great control, sending out streaks of ice and simultaneously having the streaks themselves shrink down into complex structures, swirls and curlicues, and intricate carvings the most skilled woodworker would be jealous of—all while continuously projecting new ice.

Portia edged closer, trying to see the details on the ice carvings. She regretted it when another section of ice twirled around her waist unexpectedly as the young woman quickly formed small rivers of carved ice that touched the ground in sections and then soared up and whirled around her and the other observers. The young woman worked so quickly that an individual spectator could barely react before the ice formed itself around them and moved on. Her control of the growing ice never wavered, and not a single observer was touched as it streaked by, its speed creating cold puffs of air.

Soon, the woman's display area was a tangle of ice and people. The woman laughed, clearly enjoying herself and the surprised and shocked looks on the people observing her. The young woman abruptly halted her work and then raised her hands and snapped her fingers. All the ice instantly collapsed and broke apart into tiny fragments the size of snowflakes, falling to the ground and freeing the observers who had been trapped within swirls. The crowd cheered and clapped.

Portia stepped back to join the rest of her group. As much as she appreciated the skill of the magic user, it made her uncomfortable to be within the display itself. It brought back bad memories of having ice used against her by the bullies in the Academy that past winter. And she appreciated that something could always go wrong. It would be wise to not make herself vulnerable to such an instance.

A few displays over, Portia noticed something she had never seen before. Or rather people she had never seen before. They were slender and willowy, much thinner than the average human and perhaps just a little shorter. At first, she had thought they were children, but looking closer she realized they were adult males and females, some with gray hair and wrinkles. They had pointed ears and heart-shaped faces.

Portia nudged Ella and motioned to the group. "Who are they?"

Ella looked over and her face lit up with excitement. "Elves! How exciting! I remember elves at a festival once when I was just a child but haven't seen them since. What a treat. Their magic is so different."

Elves? Portia wanted to ask what was so different, but Ella had already taken off in the direction of the elves. Portia looked over at Mia and shrugged her shoulders and they followed Ella. Richard and Liam talked excitedly behind her. She was not the only one who had not seen elves before.

When they joined the ring of observers, they found that a lone elf was standing in the center of the circle. Her clothes were beautiful and delicate in shades of green and brown. The Elven woman had large orange eyes that stared from one observer to the next. She started singing a beautiful tune, her vocal range sometimes going so high Portia wasn't sure if she could hear it at all. Behind her, several elves played on percussion instruments, beating out a complex rhythm Portia recognized from her music class. Surprised, she began to understand, perhaps belatedly, the reason for such an esoteric topic being required at the Academy.

Around the Elven woman the grass visibly grew, slowly at first and then with speed. Further from the elf, the growth turned into small trees that sprouted quickly, the tender shoots and bright green leaves spreading and darkening as the trees rose into the air. The circle around the woman widened, making room for the display. Gasps of delight wafted up from the crowd.

Portia noticed that when the elf's singing increased in tempo, so too did the speed of the growth. Her magic was coming from the music—or perhaps from her singing. It was so unique.

Portia felt a strong desire to learn how to do this magic. It was so beautiful. She vowed to do better in her music classes.

Mia was next to her, tapping her foot to the beat of the

song. Mia had always excelled in music classes; at least that was what she told Portia since they had not shared one of those classes yet.

Portia leaned in and whispered in her ear, "Do you know how this is done?"

Mia shook her head and continued watching the display. Richard and Liam's mouths hung open slightly as they watched. Portia guessed they didn't know how it was done either. She vowed to ask the elf as soon as the display was over.

Just as the trees in the outer ring display had reached full maturity, five elves burst into the center of the circle, startling the singing elf. Her song faltered, and the display stopped changing. The elf eyed the newcomers and then bowed gracefully and retreated away from the center of the circle. The woodland display created with her magic remained.

The largest of the elves, dressed entirely in black cloth that matched the blackness of his hair and his flashing dark eyes, stepped forward and held up his hand. "We come sharing important news." He looked around, making sure he had everyone's attention. "The Splintering is once again upon the world. Beware. Preparations must be made."

The crowd tittered uncertainly. *The Splintering?* Portia gasped, recognizing the term from the book from the library. The elf in black crossed his arms and glared at the crowd. He opened his mouth to explain further but was interrupted by half a dozen city guards bursting into the circle and surrounding the elves. One guard grabbed the Elven woman who had created the display, and she squeaked in surprise as he yanked her forward by the arm and shoved her towards the five elves in the center of the circle. The display itself abruptly vanished.

The captain of the city guard, a tall lanky man dressed in the gold and purple uniform of Coverack, approached the elf in black and gave a small bow. "I'm sorry, sir, but I must ask you to stop this preaching."

The elf in black drew himself up in indignation, puffing his chest out and flashing his dark eyes at the captain.

The captain nodded slightly, acknowledging the elf's ire and changing his tactic. He spoke more deferentially. "May we request you accompany us to the palace? This appears to be a matter for the queen. I believe you would agree. Let us not further bother these gentlefolk." The captain gave the elf a meaningful look, clearly wishing him to agree and graciously remove himself and his companions from the display area.

Understanding came to the elf, and he nodded slowly. "The queen, yes, that is the appropriate audience."

The captain bowed again and motioned towards the palace. The elf in black walked out of the circle, his head held high. The crowd murmured in disappointment as the city guards and elves left the area, walking out of the circle of onlookers and towards the royal castle.

Portia watched them leave, frustrated that she would not be able to learn more about their magic. She was curious about what a Splintering was and what preparations needed to be made.

"Well, that was interesting," Ella said dryly. "Do you suppose we'll ever find out what that was about?"

Richard looked after them thoughtfully. "I'm not sure I want to know. It didn't sound good."

Liam elbowed Richard. "Why jump to such bad conclusions? It could be something exciting." Richard did not bother giving Liam an answer, and Liam took the hint and left him alone.

"Oh, I would so love to learn that magic," Portia said. This drew surprised looks from the entire group. Portia looked back questioningly. "What did I say?"

"Humans can't do elf magic, silly," Ella said, rubbing her belly. "Let's go back. I feel supper calling." Mia laughed at Ella's obsession with food.

"But wouldn't that be great to have elf magic?" Liam said, a look of envy in his eyes. "They can see magic nodes. Try laying a surprise for them... That's not gonna happen. It would be a handy tool to have for sure."

Portia agreed. But the part about humans not being able to do Elven magic bothered her. "Is there a rule against using elf magic?" she asked as they started back to the campus.

Mia quietly spoke up next to her. "No rule. Humans just are not... able. They simply can't do it."

Portia frowned at that news.

3

Portia was exhausted that night. Between rising early to find someone to look at the purple book and going to the festival, it had been a long day. She was grateful when supper was over and she could retreat to her room and get ready for bed. She didn't normally retire so early, but it seemed like a good idea.

But it was not to be. A knock on her open door alerted her to a Royal Guard standing outside. She jumped at the unexpected presence. Hilda or someone else in charge at the Academy must know about this, or else the guard never would have been able to pass through the portal to the Pyromancy house. Still, it unsettled her. She would have felt better if he had been escorted by someone she knew.

She tried to hide her discomfort. "Can I help you?"

"I'm sorry to disturb you, Miss," he said, giving her a small bow. "I know it's late, but there is an urgent matter, and Queen Lorica requires your presence immediately. I'm to escort you to the castle. Professor Griffiths has given me this note for you." He held out a small folded piece of paper with a heavy wax seal on it.

Portia took the letter, her neck and fingers tingling from magic as she touched it. The thick seal, imprinted with the symbol of fire, was beautiful but decorative. The real barrier against tampering was the magic that keyed this letter to her and her alone. At least that was how it normally worked. No one else but the addressee should be able to open it and read its contents. If others tried, the letter would be blank, or in the case of extremely sensitive correspondence, would burn itself to ash immediately. Few possessed the magic needed to protect written correspondence beyond those few practitioners at the Academy, so the letter's presence along with the guard having passed through the portal reassured her that this was not a ruse.

She sucked in her breath and slid a few fingers under the flap of the envelope, pulling the letter open. Indeed it was from Professor Hilda Griffiths, saying only that she was to accompany the guard immediately to the castle. Portia threw the letter on her bed and nodded at the guard. She grabbed her outer coat and the bag she always kept with her and walked to the door.

The guard had a carriage and a team of four horses waiting at the edge of the Academy grounds. It was short work to reach the castle.

As always, Portia was struck by the beauty of the Royal House. The shimmering purple stone was difficult to see at night, especially against the backdrop of the sea, but during the day it reminded her of an exotic flower. She had only been there a few times, which she acknowledged was more than most would ever experience, and she was still in awe that her life had changed so much. Two years ago, she never would've imagined herself in the presence of the queen and king consort, much less required for a discussion.

When they passed through the long hall of portraits of prior kings and queens, she was gratified to see Professor Hilda and Professor Aelric waiting for her outside the throne room. She hoped they would let her know what was going on. She was nervous enough as it was in front of the queen.

Hilda walked towards her, a warm smile on her face. She grabbed Portia's hands within her own. It was as if she could read Portia's thoughts. "Don't worry, we're here too. She's discussing something with her advisors. They'll call us in a minute."

The admonishment to not worry had the opposite effect—now Portia *was* worried. Why would Hilda think to mention it otherwise?

Portia's ruminations were interrupted by Professor Aelric approaching her. "That book was very interesting. Once I started working on it, I found it difficult to concentrate on much else. So, lucky you, I finished it early. Frankly, as a professor of history, I am somewhat appalled at myself for not having known of its existence, as well as the failure of the library staff to bring it to my attention. Are you sure it was just lying on the shelf?"

"I think so. I wasn't the one who found it."

"Interesting. In any event, I have finished translating it.

You may pick up the translation in the morning. We will have time to discuss it further," Aelric said with a small sniff. He wandered away to look at the portraits while they waited to be called.

Portia turned her attention back to Hilda. "Do you know what this is all about? It's so late for an audience."

Hilda's face mirrored her own confusion. "I don't dare venture a guess. But I know you worry, so I want to reassure you." Hilda gave a small laugh. Portia couldn't help giggling a little herself. It felt good to be known so well. But that meant Hilda's reassurance couldn't mean much if she didn't know the reason for the summons either.

The door to the throne room opened abruptly. Hilda and Portia straightened up, drawing their faces into serious looks, while Aelric turned from the paintings and quickly walked back to the throne room door. A guard stepped out and nodded at the three. "The queen will see you now."

He stepped back and motioned for them to enter. The room was much emptier than the last time Portia had been there. The crowds of nobles were not there. Only a few advisors, King Consort Aldis, a scribe in the corner and, of course, Queen Lorica. Guards stood at every door and two on either side of the dais.

Portia, Aelric, and Hilda approached the throne. Portia had been practicing her curtsy but still felt awkward. Hilda's motions were much smoother, and Aelric managed to maintain his dignity while bowing.

The queen motioned at the guard standing in front of a door to the side of the throne room. He opened the door, and much to Portia's surprise the elves she had seen earlier at the festival entered the throne room. The elf in black bowed to the queen.

Queen Lorica nodded, and an advisor stepped forward to address Portia and her professors.

"A matter of much urgency has come to the attention of the Kingdom. These elves," the advisor said, motioning to the small group who had entered from the side door, "are from Rocabarra."

Portia knew Rocabarra from her history class. It was the Elven kingdom to the northwest of Haulstatt. It was quite far away. She wondered at their journeying to Coverack.

Queen Lorica interrupted, impatient at the languid words of the advisor. "This envoy comes bearing news that might warrant the attention of our Jack." She motioned for the elf group to step forward and speak.

To Portia's surprise, the elf in black stepped back and bowed, while a female elf, dressed in flowing robes of various shades of blue, stepped forward. She curtsied to the queen, as well as to Portia and the professors. "My name is Lady Harper of the Meadows. I'm the leader of this convoy. We have been sent here by King Magnus of Rocabarra to bring serious news that needs the attention of both our countries. The Splintering is at hand. The fate of the world is in the balance of our actions. We must act now."

The Splintering. The same thing they had talked about at the festival, Portia thought. She looked to the queen and then at Hilda and Aelric. Their faces betrayed no shock. There was no clue from them as to the seriousness of what the elf was saying.

Lady Harper waited for a response. When none was forthcoming, she hesitated then spoke again. "Your Majesty, perhaps I can share our understanding of the Splintering? Would that be useful?"

Queen Lorica nodded. "It would. Please proceed."

"The Splintering is our name for the event that has happened every several thousand years in the history of our world. The first mention in our books brings the elves to this world, but we have been told this was not the first event. The dwarves have recorded previous events but are reluctant, or unwilling, to share further details with us. The second Splintering in our written history brought humans to this world, pushing the elves and dwarves further afield." Lady Harper looked uncomfortable then pushed on. "Just as the Elves pushed the Dwarves out before that time."

Portia's mouth fell open into a small circle. So this was the human origin story that Professor Aelric had been teaching. But it sounded so different coming from another. The displacement of others was not something of note in their class, at least in the way he had taught it. What else was not thought of as worthy of the academy's teaching? Did the elves have information as to where the humans, or even the elves, had come from? Surely they were not just created from thin air to appear in this world.

"What do splinters look like?" Portia asked, forgetting herself.

Hilda's surprised look and Aelric's scowl reminded her

that she should be following court manners and waiting to be asked a question. The queen didn't look upset, though, instead turning to the elf and awaiting the answer to Portia's question. The king consort was also interested, leaning forward in his seat.

Lady Harper hesitated for a moment, then answered. "We do not know. There are no sketches or other indications in our records. It is written of as being a chaotic time, and we feel lucky to have the information that we do have. We do know if the current splintering is not healed quickly that others, beings unknown to ourselves might come into this world and cause havoc."

"It is good then that you warned us," Queen Lorica said. "How may we assist in this matter that must affect us both?"

"We need access," Lady Harper said. She gave the queen a deferential nod.

"Access?"

"To the sea, Your Majesty." Her expression was grave. "Humans are the only race whose lands border the sea. Our records indicate the Splintering has only occurred over water. If others come through, then humans will be the first to bear the brunt of any untoward events. We have also sent an envoy to the dwarves, imploring that they share any information they have in this dire time."

"And when do you expect a response?" Queen Lorica asked.

"We hope for a response by summer. We have had poor luck in obtaining information from the dwarves in the past. It may be that they ignore our envoy and we are on our own."

Lady Harper looked down, then up again at the queen, considering her next words. "I will be forthcoming with you. We are offering our help in a selfish desire for an alliance. We fear that if the splinter is not stopped in time whoever—or whatever—joins our world through it will overwhelm us all. We need access for our mages to prevent it, and if not, for our warriors to fight any possible invaders."

The throne room was silent at this pronouncement.

Queen Lorica nodded. "Your honesty does your kingdom justice." She looked at the elf, her eyes hooded slightly, and her lips pursed. "However, letting an army onto our lands for such a vague pronouncement does not seem wise."

Lady Harper cleared her throat. "That is understandable, Your Majesty, but I assure you that only Elven magic can heal the splinters."

No one spoke for a moment. The scratching of a quill on parchment resonated through the room as the scribe recorded the meeting.

"How convenient that only elves can do this magic. Why cannot humans?" the queen asked, an edge to her voice. "And how did the dwarves manage before the coming of elves?"

The elf's face turned red at this last statement. "We do not know how the dwarves managed in their time. As we have mentioned," Lady Harper said with a grimace, "the dwarves have not been forthcoming. We have not found them reliable in a crisis. We should do much better with an alliance between elves and humans."

"And the question of humans and this magic?" the queen asked a second time, her eyes narrowing.

"I cannot explain why, but in all our experiences we have found no human that could perform our magic. There is no analogous human magic."—

"I see," said the queen, in a noncommittal tone. "I shall have to consider this."

Lady Harper's face hardened at these words. A delay was not welcome.

"In the meantime, I have reason to believe that one of our own *may* be able to perform this critical magic." Queen Lorica smoothed her gown, then rested her gaze on Lady Harper. "You will test her—and teach her if she is able."

Lady Harper stilled. She considered the queen carefully. "We need to heal the splinter, and with haste. The longer it is open, the wider it becomes, and the more vulnerable this world is to any who might want to explore it or make it their own. It is imperative we are granted access—"

Queen Lorica held up her hand, stopping any further words from Lady Harper. "Yes, you have told me as such, and I have told you, you *will* test our Jack. We will take no further action until that is completed." The queen pointed to Portia, who shrank under the angry stare of the watching elf. "And as you told me earlier, the splinter is not yet open, correct? Then we have time. I will not allow others alone to defend our kingdom. We have a champion, and we will use her." She motioned her advisor to step forward.

He addressed Lady Harper. "We will provide you with whatever you need to test our Jack."

Several emotions crossed Lady Harper's face—indignation, frustration, and impatience—before she finally settled her visage into a calm smile. "I see. I must remind you that we have little time."

"As we are aware," the advisor said with a knowing smile. "Please let us know how we may speed things along."

Lady Harper grudgingly nodded acknowledgment. She turned to Portia. "You are the champion? A Jack?"

Aelric stepped forward at this, answering for Portia. "A Jack of Magic can do magic from all branches. They are not limited by one branch of magic, or even one single type of magic, as is the case for nearly all humans. Portia is one of three known Jacks in the history of our entire kingdom, the first herself creating the magic that allowed for Jack. It is written in our history books that these Jacks only occur when they are desperately needed by our kingdom."

Queen Lorica interrupted. "This is why we are not surprised by the news you bring us this day. We have been expecting something ever since Portia's existence was discovered." Aelric nodded acknowledgment and stepped back.

Lady Harper took this in, considering it. She turned to Portia and raised an eyebrow. "Is your name also Jack, or is that merely your title?"

Portia shook her head shyly. "My name is Portia. I don't think 'Jack' is an official title."

"Portia, then. It is apparently our task to see if you can learn this magic. It is an arduous type of magic, and you would have to come to our land to learn to heal a splinter since none of our convoy members are versed in it. But before you make the journey, you must pass the basic tests to see if you can even do any elf magic at all. These *basic* tests are our current task," Lady Harper said, her tone indicating she thought it would be a waste of time, but she had no choice. The queen had left her with none.

A lump formed in Portia's throat. What if the Academy was wrong about her being a Jack? What would happen to her? She already felt unsure in her position, and the events of last winter and Deyelna's death at her hands weighed heavily on her conscience. Now another test loomed in her future. Another opportunity for them to find her lacking. Sweat broke out along her back and neck, but she spoke of none of this, instead merely nodding at Lady Harper. She had no choice. She had to prove herself yet once again.

Lady Harper turned to address the advisor. "We need some rooms to prepare for the tests."

The advisor nodded. "You will be given a spare ballroom and the three adjoining chambers. Is that sufficient?"

"It is. Thank you." Lady Harper turned to Portia and gave a small bow. "We can begin as soon as the rooms are ready."

Hilda stepped forward, blocking Lady Harper from leaving. "We would like to supervise these tests. We are responsible for our student's well-being."

Lady Harper looked coldly at Hilda. "That will not be possible. It might affect the tests."

Queen Lorica tilted her head at that response. "Are these tests dangerous?"

"Only if she fails," Lady Harper responded. "But there is no other way."

Her words did not reassure Portia.

Once again, the sound of writing was the only noise in the throne room.

"Then we will proceed," Queen Lorica said, breaking the quiet.

The queen dismissed the elves with a flick of her fingers. The advisor that had spoken led the elves towards a set of side doors that two guards held opened, several of them peering curiously at Portia as they passed. She felt her cheeks flame at their attention.

Once the advisor and elves had exited, Hilda turned to Portia, a soft look in her eye. "Are you ready for this?"

Portia swallowed nervously. She spoke quietly, not wanting the queen to hear. "Would it be possible to do these tests tomorrow? I'm not avoiding them. I'm just so very tired. It's been a long day."

Queen Lorica yawned. "Yes, yes, tomorrow. That is soon enough."

Portia jumped nervously at having been heard. King Consort Aldis leaned over to whisper in the ear of a different advisor.

Portia realized she was staring at the king and turned away to find Aelric gazing at her intently. He put his hand on her arm and leaned in intently. "You can do this. But please, whatever you do, try not to kill them."

After a quick inhale and a wave of shock that passed over her scalp, Portia realized he was joking. He gave her a small wink. She exhaled with a little snort and immediately felt better.

She was so distracted thinking about the tests to take place on the following day that she barely saw any of the city on the carriage ride home. Her eyes didn't register the variety of shops, nor did she enjoy the speed of the rare ride in the royal carriage, something that would have normally thrilled her. The elf had mentioned that if she passed, she would have to go to the Elven kingdom of Rocabarra to learn the magic. She had heard so little about the kingdom, only that there was an uneasy peace between elves and humans. What would their cities be like? Would she be welcome? Were there other humans there? She had never seen an elf in Valencia, and only in the festival while in Coverack, even after living there for a year. It was an unusual occurrence.

When she arrived back in her room, she had barely enough energy to change into her nightdress, her head bobbing in exhaustion. Ella was already asleep in her bunk. Luckily, she slept deeply, and Portia did not have to worry too much about waking her. Even so, she kept the lights low and changed quickly.

She'd just pulled back the covers to slip into bed when a loud knock sounded at the door. Portia rushed to the door and pulled it open, ready to scold whoever was disturbing them so late. She recognized the palace guard just in time to stop herself and bit her lip in concern at his presence.

He gave her a small bow and then spoke softly, having seen the sleeping form in the bunk behind Portia. "Sorry once again to disturb you, Miss, but I've been instructed to tell you that you are expected at the palace at noon tomorrow. A carriage will await you in front of the main building on the Academy grounds."

"Very well, thank you," Portia said.

The guard gave a small bow again and turned and exited in the direction of the portal back to the Academy. She wondered if he knew the true location of the Pyromancy house or if that was kept secret from even the palace guards to protect the students. Perhaps he did know the location of the house, but he would not ride a royal mount to it and risk drawing attention and giving away its value to the palace.

———

THE NEXT MORNING, Portia woke to the sounds of Ella getting ready. She had hoped to sleep in, but her body's adaption to her normal school schedule and the incessant chatter of her roommate talking to herself would not allow that. She sat up, her head groggy with exhaustion.

Ella noticed Portia stirring. "Good morning, roomie. It promises to be a beautiful sunny day."

Portia grunted under her breath and pulled back the covers to rise. She adored having Ella as a roommate except for the early mornings when Ella bubbled and shone with energy while Portia slogged away until her mind woke up more fully in a few hours. She was grateful the tests with the elves were not planned for 8 a.m.

Ella went off to find breakfast. Portia opened her personal trunk and pulled out her old bag of clothing and effects, as well as Elyas's small bag. She held up her old, worn breeches and doublet—clothes she had retained from her days as an orphan on the street. They were the attire of a boy and not a proper young lady of the Academy, but she knew she would feel more comfortable in them. There was something reassuring about having breeches and not a kirtle.

She pulled on her clothes, grateful to find they still fit, mostly. The breeches were just a hair short but the doublet and tunic, oversized to begin with, fit perfectly. She pulled on an old jacket over it all. She did not want to worry about ruining any of her current finery since she had no way to replace them. Thieving was forbidden to her as a student and she had no other way to raise coin. She refused to waste her remaining silver and copper replacing ruined clothes.

Opening Elyas's faded yellow leather pouch, she pulled out a small locket with engravings of Elyas and his daughter, Chenna. She knew he had treated her just as if she had been his daughter; sometimes she looked at the engraving and imagined her face on it as well. He had been planning on getting one done for her to keep but had never gotten around to it before his untimely death. As it was, holding the image of his face warmed her heart and gave her strength to face the uncomfortable tasks she had ahead of her that day. She knew he would not want her to give up nor to despair in the face of seemingly insurmountable challenges. He had believed in her, something she valued immensely. She held the locket tightly and imagined him giving her words of encouragement.

The breakfast bell rang. Portia had to hurry if she wanted to eat. She tucked the engraving safely back into Elyas's pouch and added the locket Liam had given her to the bag. Then she shoved the two bags back into her trunk and shut it.

"What are you wearing!" Ella asked, her voice rising in

dismay as Portia entered the breakfast hall. She looked at Portia wide-eyed. Her voice had been loud enough to draw attention from all those supping that morning, and they turned curious eyes to stare at Portia. A few gasps and a small giggle reached Portia's ears, which were turning red from embarrassment. Her clothing would not have been that unusual in Valencia, and now she felt keenly just how far away she was from the city she had grown up in.

Ella continued to stare until Mia, who was sitting next to her, gave her a sharp elbow while she was studiously eating her oatmeal. Ella didn't take the hint, continuing to stare until Mia elbowed her again, much harder this time, whereupon Ella rubbed her arm and transferred her irritated look to Mia. Portia scooped some eggs onto a plate and made a mental note to do Mia a favor, any favor, as soon as possible.

She brought her tray of food over to join them. Ella scanned Portia's outfit up and down, scandalized. She leaned in and whispered loudly to Portia, "What *are* you wearing?"

Portia looked down at her outfit casually and then put her attention to buttering her toast. "It looks like clothes," she said, taking a large bite.

"Yes, but *what* clothes? Those are not the clothes of an Academy student! You look... You look... like a page. And a poorly dressed one at that." Ella's lip curled in distaste.

At this, both Mia and Portia burst out laughing.

Ella turned to Mia and gave her a scathing look. "I don't understand why you're laughing. You're a noble. No one in your house would dress like this. *You* would never dress like this."

Mia turned to Ella and spoke quietly. "No, I would never have been allowed to dress like that. I can give you twenty different rules I had to follow about what to wear, when and how, and all for reasons that made little to no sense to me. I've had enough of such rules. It is one of the reasons I am so grateful to be here at the Academy and away from that dreadful, hidebound routine." Mia's eyes flicked to Portia and then back to Ella. "Perhaps the important question is *why* has Portia changed her style of clothing so dramatically."

Ella took this in and then turned to stare at Portia again. Portia faced their questioning eyes, wondering if one would actually speak the words. Ella gave a deep sigh and gave in. "Okay, why are you wearing those clothes?"

"I have an important test today. I want to feel comfortable," she said.

"We have a test today?" Ella said, suddenly concerned. She had forgotten about more than one test with her focus on social life at the Academy. Portia knew Ella could not risk forgetting about another test and face the possibility of being booted out and condemned to her old life in the boring village she had grown up in. Ella said it was boring enough to bore boredom, whatever that meant.

Portia realized she might have made a mistake by telling them about a special test. Neither one knew about her special magical abilities or that the king and queen had deemed her a Jack of Magic. She was one of three people in the known history of humans to be able to do all types of magic, only limited so far by what she had been shown as possible. Certainly no other human would be tested for an ability to do elf magic. Beyond the palace, she only knew there were a few in the Academy that knew of her existence, including Professor Hilda and Professor Aelric. Mia and Ella were definitely not supposed to know.

"Not a class test," Portia said quickly, shoving the rest of the bread in her mouth and scooping in the eggs to follow. She needed to finish her breakfast and get out of there before she said something she shouldn't.

Ella was not going to let it go as easily as that. "Well, what test then?"

"Some ancient sword technique Professor Aelric had found in the archives. You know how much I love history and swords."

Ella immediately lost interest. She did not understand Portia's obsession with history, much less any sort of weapons. "Oh, thank the mages. I cannot be unprepared for a test again," she said, stacking her dishes on her tray and rising to leave. The end breakfast bell would soon sound, and they all had to go to class.

Mia looked at Portia skeptically while stacking her own plates but did not say anything. Portia looked down, avoiding her scrutiny and hoping Mia would just go and not linger to inquire further. As quiet as Mia was most of the time, Portia feared that she knew and saw much more than she let on.

She breathed a small sigh of relief as Mia rose and followed Ella to the tray rack. Portia pretended to be drinking the rest of her broth, trying to kill some time so she wouldn't have to walk to class with the other two girls. It was bad enough she had the first period with them in Professor

Aelric's history class. But at least there would be little opportunity for further questioning from them while Aelric lectured. Hopefully, neither would ask Professor Aelric himself about Portia's special test.

Portia sighed. Perhaps she should have asked for permission to skip the entire day's lectures. Instead, she felt like she had to go to her morning classes and then, after a busy morning, go face whatever the elves had waiting for her. Sleeping would have been much better preparation.

4

The carriage had been waiting exactly where the guard said it would be. Portia went to the Hall of Portraits. The royal advisor who had led the elves away the previous night was already there and waiting for her. He brought her to a large ballroom which was guarded by two burly guards who stared straight forward. The advisor motioned for her to enter the door the guards held open, but he didn't follow. Instead, the doors were shut with a resounding thud, leaving Portia in the cavernous ballroom.

There was a row of elves at the far side of the room sitting behind a long table. There were three portal doors set up next to the table. They were oval and appeared to hang in the air, unlike the doors in the courtyard for the different houses, which were square and normal except that they weren't attached to anything visible other than their frames.

The elves sat quietly staring at her. She walked towards

them, a little unnerved by their silence. Uncertain what to do next, she stopped about twenty feet away.

Lady Harper sat at the end of the table, dressed in all white leather. Portia thought the leather pieces almost looked like armor. She suddenly was glad to not be meeting Lady Harper alone in a dark alley. She rose and came around the table to Portia. "Welcome. Everything is prepared. Are you ready?"

Portia could only nod.

"We need you to answer verbally before we can continue," Lady Harper said.

"Yes. I am ready."

"Excellent. Your professors tell us you are familiar with portals. We have created portals to three worlds constructed for the tests. One world for each test you will perform, or at least attempt. If you fail a test, you will not be permitted to go on to the next one. You must complete all tests to pass the challenge," Lady Harper said, her voice even but her eyes flashing. Portia wondered if it was anger or indignation that the elves must go through this with Portia.

Something Lady Harper said tickled at her mind. She said they created worlds. That was different from simply creating a portal to a different location. Could she really mean that's what they had done? "How... How do you create worlds?"

Lady Harper squinted at her, a flicker of irritation crossing her face, but she answered the question nonetheless. "It is part of the Splinter magic. We know how to heal a splinter; thus we also know how to make one. We simply create a world and then open a splinter to it. The worlds we have created are not large, but they are large enough for the tests. It takes a great deal of magic to maintain these worlds."

This explanation confused Portia. How could anything that existed not be a part of this world? Her mind hurt trying to figure out the puzzle. At Lady Harper's intense gaze, she gave up. If she passed, maybe she could ask again. But she did not want to press the issue further now, instead filing it away in her mind as something to learn more about later if she was allowed to go into the kingdom of the elves.

"Okay," Portia said, nodding.

One of the other elves stood and came to join Lady Harper and Portia. He exchanged a look with Lady Harper, and she nodded at the first door. He held his hand out for Portia and led her to the first door on the left. Portia stood in front of it, uncertain what to do.

Over her shoulder she could hear Lady Harper clear her throat. "You need to enter each door—we call them gates—and complete the task on the other side then return."

"What if I can't do it?" Portia asked. Her hands were trembling. She focused on her breathing and tried to calm herself.

"Then you can't come back," Lady Harper said, her voice impassive.

Portia whirled around to face Lady Harper. "What do you mean I can't come back? Am I dead?"

"No. But you will not be able to exit." Lady Harper tilted her head questioningly. Portia wondered if she was waiting for her to say she wouldn't do it.

"But if I can't come back... and it takes a lot of energy to maintain these worlds... then..." *I'll die.* The words stuck in Portia's throat.

"Yes, exactly. At one point, we will stop maintaining the worlds. They have only been created for this test."

Silence hung in the ballroom. Portia wished desperately she could talk to Professor Hilda or Professor Aelric. Or even the queen. She couldn't believe they would want her to face a mortal trial.

"The queen and king know," Lady Harper said, her voice low.

"But..." Portia didn't know what to say. This felt like too much to ask of her. And if the queen knew, why wouldn't she have warned her? Perhaps they were afraid she would not dare attempt the test. Portia swallowed. She had to make a decision. If she was too afraid to attempt the test, then there was still a chance the elves could heal the splinter and save them all. But there was also a chance they could not. There was a reason she was here. There was a reason she had been given the powers of a Jack. Perhaps this was a test of the strength of her belief as much as a test of her skills.

Portia trembled. She had to decide. Finally, she shook out her arms, trying to banish her shakiness. She spoke louder than she intended to. "Fine. I want to finish this." Portia's stomach roiled with anxiety. Her heart hurt at the thought of failing and never seeing her friends again. But she was not going to let that stop her. She could not. She turned and faced the door.

Murmurs of approval from the other elves surprised Portia, but she refused to look at them, instead grabbing the portal door handle and opening it. She stepped through it before she could think about it a moment longer and lose her nerve.

The portal opened directly onto a path leading through a woods. She heard the door shut behind her, but when she turned to look there was nothing but the path itself going off into the distance. She stood there for a moment, listening, but the woods were disconcertingly quiet. The air was absent of birdsong or the scurrying noises of small creatures running through the leaves on the forest floor. No sound at all. She shivered involuntarily.

Turning back to face her original direction, she walked down the path, her footsteps unnaturally loud. Portia gritted her teeth and forced herself to keep going. Her ears tingled with the effort to hear any sound, especially any from behind her. But there was nothing. Portia forced herself to not hold her breath.

The path led to a small clearing. In the center was a fence with a set of scales on top. The trays on each side were empty and the scale rested, perfectly balanced. Twelve red balls sat in a row on the fence top next to the scales. Portia went closer to investigate.

As she drew closer to the fence, a figure shimmered into existence. It was an elf, dressed all in shimmering gold robes. Portia couldn't tell how old she was. She smiled at Portia.

"Hello," Portia said, shoving her hands into her pockets.

The figure merely nodded in return.

Was this part of the test? Did she have to figure out what the test was as well as perform it? Irritation flickered on the edge of Portia's mind, but she pushed back. She would not think clearly if she was upset. She must remain calm above all else.

"Please tell me what the task is," Portia said, pushing on.

The figure nodded again and spoke. "Out of these twelve balls, all are the same weight save one: That one is heavier than the rest. You need that ball, and you need to find it, but you may only use the scales three times."

This was not the sort of test Portia was expecting. How could she find the single heavier ball of twelve identical looking ones and yet only use the scales three times? She would rather have had a duel than this.

Portia stared at the balls. They all looked the same. The first task was to change that. She used fire magic to engrave numbers on each ball, one through twelve, so she could distinguish them. She was a bit surprised her fire magic worked. She added asking about that to her list of questions for Lady Harper if she survived this task.

She walked to pick up the end ball but the elf in white stepped quickly in front of her and stopped her. "No, you may not touch them. I will handle them for you."

Portia chewed her lip. She must use strategy correctly the first time. She doubted they would give her several attempts. Three tries with the scale, and that was it.

The odd thing about the test was that it was not testing magic at all. Did the elves have so little faith in her they just wanted her to fail on the logic test? It didn't make sense to her, but she had to pass, so she forced herself to concentrate.

"Put balls one through four on one side, and five through eight on the other," Portia said.

The elf stared at Portia with a serious expression. She did not move. "Are you sure you do not want to put all the balls on the scale?" she asked, tilting her head slightly.

Portia's heart pounded at this question. Was she missing something? She didn't like the fact that the elf was questioning her—especially since she couldn't be sure if she was trying to help, or hurt, Portia's chances of solving the puzzle. She felt much the same she had in Deyelna's presence. But then Portia realized that was the clue she needed—Deyelna had never tried to help her, only hurt her chances, so if she felt the same way here, then her instincts were telling her the elf was not working in her favor. Portia sucked in her breath—she could not let the question undermine her confidence.

She lifted her chin up and spoke loudly. "Yes. Please do as I ask."

The elf raised both eyebrows but did not speak again, instead turning and doing as Portia had bid. When she stepped away from the scale, the side with balls five through eight dipped lower. Portia breathed a sigh of relief. She would have discovered the third of the balls with the heavier one no matter what, but it was reassuring to see the scale actually lower and not have to take it on faith if it was amongst the third of the balls she had not chosen.

"Please put balls five and six on the left side and balls seven and eight on the right," Portia said, speaking more quickly. She knew she could solve the puzzle now.

The elf again did what she was asked, and when the left

side dipped down, she turned for Portia's last instruction. Portia bid that she put ball five in the left and six on the right. When this was completed the side with ball six dipped down. Portia had found the heaviest ball.

Portia felt pride and elation—and relief—that she would be able to return to her world. She stepped forward and held out her hand for the sixth ball. The elf did not move but instead seemed to be waiting for something. Portia squinted at her. Perhaps it was just a formality.

"The heaviest ball is the six ball. Please give it to me," Portia said, looking meaningfully at her hand.

The elf nodded in acknowledgment and placed the ball on Portia's hand. As soon as Portia gripped it, the elf and the fence with the rest of the test items slowly faded out, leaving Portia alone on the path. She held the ball tightly and walked forward onto the path which led again into woods. After several minutes, just when fear started to grip her, she passed by a large tree and found another portal door next to it. It swung open easily for her as she approached it.

On the other side, she reentered the ballroom where the test was being held.

Lady Harper nodded at her reappearance. "Congratulations on passing the first test. We are not surprised." The rest of the elves clapped quietly then stared expectantly at Portia.

Portia felt on edge. She had been so frightened to open the door to even take the test. They could have eased her mind. "Was it then just a test of my bravery?" she said in a low voice, mostly to herself.

But Lady Harper had heard her and responded. "It was

indeed. How perceptive. Perhaps the second test will be more of a challenge." Lady Harper motioned to the second portal door awaiting Portia.

Portia was too irritated to respond calmly to Lady Harper so instead put the six ball on the table in front of the rest of the elves, then immediately walked to the second door and entered.

Once again, Portia stepped into utter silence. The least they could do when creating these worlds would have been to create some birds or some other natural creatures. Absolute quiet was unnerving and unnatural. This world also opened into a path in a woods, but here the woods were snow-covered and cold. Portia rubbed her shoulders and shivered, both from the silence and the frigid air. She considered using her fire magic to warm herself but then decided against it. It would be better to see what she was facing before she expended any energy.

Walking down the path, she encountered a frozen river. There were two male elves dressed in black waiting for her. They looked identical from behind, but when they turned to face her, they looked very different. One had an open face, smiling and confident. The second looked scared and unsure. They could have been twins except for the difference in expression.

The confident one stepped up to Portia and extended his hand in greeting, a broad grin on his face. She gripped his hand, and it felt strong and reassuring. It felt real.

He gave her a small bow and then spoke. "Welcome. Follow me across the river so we may find shelter and warmth.

It is fully frozen. There is no reason for us to linger." He held onto her hand and tried to tug her onto the ice at the river's edge. Portia pulled back hard, freeing her hand from the elf's grasp.

The second elf stepped closer to her, keeping his distance from the first elf. "Wise choice. The river is not frozen, even though it looks so. If you attempt to cross you will surely perish. Stay here where it is safe." He shivered when he spoke. His nose had a tinge of blue to it. He looked cold.

Portia addressed the timid elf. "How long have you been here?" He looked like he would soon freeze to death.

"Too long. But as long as I'm standing on the bank there is still a chance. There is none if I fall in icy waters." He gave the river a dark look and then glanced up at the far bank. There was a portal exit hanging over the far bank. The only way out was to get across the river.

The confident elf laughed at the words of the timid one. "I have not been here long, nor do I plan to be here for much longer. Freezing is for cowards."

If the river truly was frozen, then exiting this world was a simple task of walking across the ice and going out the exit. Portia did not believe it could be that simple. But there had to be a way to pass the test. She felt the tips of her fingers and her nose growing numb in the cold. She tucked her fingers into her armpits and jumped up and down for warmth while she tried to think.

Since she had cryomancy as a power perhaps she could just freeze the river herself. Or use pyromancy to warm herself up to buy some time. Or both. She pulled on her power to freeze the river even more than it was, but instead of her power responding as it always had, she felt a thick cotton sensation in her head. The harder she tried to use her magic, the worse the sensation became. She felt like she couldn't even think.

Worse, she didn't think her magic was working.

Looking at the river, it was impossible to tell if she had done anything. To test her power in a more visible manner, she tried to conjure a ball of fire in her palm. Again, the same cotton sensation filled her head. And there was no fire. Not even a spark. No warmth at all on the palm of her hand. Somehow, her powers were useless in this world. Fear gripped her heart.

She had not realized how much she had come to depend on her magic until it was gone. She could truly die here. Not only would she not return if she didn't pass the tests, but this one had a time limit based on what her body could tolerate. She had to pass it soon or she would freeze to death.

She looked again at the two elves facing her—they represented two options. Perhaps there was a third—to take advice from both of them.

Walking back the way she had come, she looked around in the woods for a fallen branch. She found a thick one, taller than she was and as thick as her wrist. She slammed it against the trunk of a tree to test how solid it was. It reverberated and vibrated in her hands upon impact. It was not so old and rotten as to crumble, which would have been useless to her. Portia returned to the river, ready to take the test.

When she reached the edge of the river, she used the

branch to tap on the ice to test its strength. She used what she hoped was enough force to break the ice if it was too weak to hold her weight.

The concerned elf muttered under his breath and then finally spoke up. "Don't do that. It's not safe."

His teeth chattered even as he spoke, but she did not bother to respond. Staying on the bank was safer at the moment but would still result in death in the long run.

The confident elf laughed loudly and clapped the timid elf on the back. "Don't stay too long. I'm sure someone is waiting for you somewhere."

Portia tried to ignore them both. She faced the far bank and began her journey to it. She focused intently on the ice in front of her, tapping it soundly with her stick so that it bounced up and down on the solid ice. When nothing broke, she shuffled forward to where she had already tested and then hit the ice further out. It was a slow process. Her heart pounded in her chest, but she refused to stop. She was afraid that if she did, she would lose her nerve.

Footsteps came from behind her. The confident elf was following her path. Portia swore under her breath. She didn't know if the ice could hold both of them. She shuffled back as quickly as she could, only making about ten feet before the elf walked past her. Rage filled her at the risk he put her in. Hopefully, he would just go quickly and get off the section of ice she was standing on.

He did pass her and continued on about twenty feet to the center of the river. A crack of breaking ice rang out in the silence, and his next step gave way, dropping him into the water. Before Portia could react, the current pulled at him and drew him under the ice. She gasped in shock. He was completely underwater with no way to the surface. He would never survive.

The dark spot under the ice that was his head raced downstream until it disappeared in the distance. There were no open spots in that direction for as far as she could see.

Portia felt ill and bit back nausea. Now there was just her and the timid elf on the shore. Fear ran through her body, down to her feet, making her legs tingle and the hairs on the back of her neck stand up. She did not want to move another step. The open spot ahead of her showed the raging, fast-moving water that was running under the ice. It burbled and splashed in the open section. It looked dark and angry. The noise the water made was only slightly louder than the pounding of her heart in her ears.

She looked back at the elf on the shore. He looked worse than before. He was moving more slowly, and she thought she could see his face actually turning a shade of blue. He was freezing to death. That was not a solution.

Turning back to the river, she used her stick once again to test the ice. The open hole forced her to take a wide path upstream from the open spot. But now when she hit the ice, it creaked and moved. It was not solid towards the center of the river.

She looked further upstream. The river there narrowed a bit in the distance. Perhaps the ice would be thicker at that spot. She moved in that direction as quickly as she dared, stopping occasionally to rub and blow on her hands. After much testing, she found a section in the middle of the river that was as solid and thick as the edges. That section sent her bouncing stick high into the air with its unyielding solidity. Steeling her courage, she crossed that section as quickly as she dared. Tears came unbidden as she made it to the far bank and safety.

Running back down the shore towards the gate, she looked back across the river at the scared elf, hoping he had seen how she had crossed and would follow. But he had not moved from his spot. Instead, as she watched, he laid down and curled into a ball. She yelled across the river for him to follow her route, but he did not respond. She hoped he was only an element of the test and not a real elf. They could not be so cruel as that, could they, to kill two of their own? But she dared not cross the river again to go get him. There were limits to her courage, so she was forced to leave him there.

When Portia exited the world into the ballroom, she thought she saw at least one of the waiting elves give a surprised start. Some of them really did expect her to fail. Bitterness flooded her mouth. That would not be the case. She would pass, and she would survive.

Lady Harper approached her once again, her face expressionless. "It's good that you know moderation is a virtue above all others."

Portia stared at her, her fear from the last test turning to anger. "Did you just kill two of your own for that test?" She knew she shouldn't glare, but she could barely contain herself. That test was horrific.

"No elves were harmed. I told you we created these worlds." Lady Harper stared at her impassively.

"Well, what about me? You could have *killed* me. And for what, to see if I'm brave?" Portia spit out the words. "You could have just asked me. That hardly seems worth risking my life over." Portia couldn't believe what she was saying, but she was so upset at seeing those two elves die, even if it wasn't real, that she couldn't stop herself. There had to be a better way to do this. Couldn't they just try to teach her the magic? Why were they playing these games with people's lives? It was intolerable.

Lady Harper merely blinked and said nothing. The elves at the table stood and came around Portia and congratulated her on her victory. Portia barely heard them, instead focusing on Lady Harper and trying to decipher her lack of reaction to Portia's words.

Finally, all the congratulations died down as the elves watched Portia and Lady Harper face off. Lady Harper gave a small nod towards Portia. "It is true. We could have asked you. But it is one thing to say something and another entirely to act when lives are at stake. Then it is not so easy. Nor is it so easy to think clearly in such a stressful situation." Lady Harper gave Portia a small smile. "Not only did you act, but you acted thoughtfully and with clarity. The test reveals this."

Portia realized she was trembling. She shoved her hands into her pockets and pressed them in deeply, flexing her arm muscles in an attempt to stifle her shaking. Not trusting herself to speak, she merely nodded at Lady Harper. Portia walked over to an open chair and sat down. She needed to calm down. There was still one more test to take. This day had felt ages long and it still was not over yet.

An elf brought Portia a steaming mug of broth. She took it gratefully, even more thankful that her hands were no longer shaking. Her ears tingled painfully as the warmth returned to them. Her toes tingled as well. Her boots were not so well-constructed as to ward off all cold from the world of the last test. She was dressed for springtime in Coverack.

When she was finally warm, Portia set down the empty mug on the table. Her anger was long gone, and now she only felt tired. She sighed. She could not put this off any longer; it was time to finish the last test. She rose and walked to the third and final door. She took one look back at the expectant faces of the elves behind her and hoped they were not the last faces she saw in her life. Taking a deep breath, she turned and walked through the door.

The world of the last test was not cold and snowy; it was warm like spring. The only thing missing was the sounds of birds, an omission she had almost gotten used to by now.

Recognizing the pattern, she quickly walked down the path to the open clearing she knew was waiting for her. At first, she thought she was just surrounded by trees, but looking more closely, she realized she was surrounded by elves who were standing at the bases of the trees. They were dressed in rich browns and blended into the forest. There had to be thirty or more of them. They stared at her.

A booming sound reverberated through the trees. Another quickly followed. And another. Portia realized it was a drum-beat. Flutes and other instruments she couldn't identify joined in the noise. The odd music drifted through the trees. It was loud enough that she thought she should be able to see the players, but looking around, she found no one except for the elves standing under the trees.

Now the elves under the trees were dancing in rhythm to the music. Portia felt her own legs twitch as well. She relaxed and let her body do what it wanted, which apparently was to dance. She danced her way over to an opening in the surrounding elves. They backed away in either direction, giving her enough room to join the circle.

The line of dancing elves began to move. They peeled away, one after the other, down a path through the woods and away from the clearing.

The rhythm of the music changed slightly, and Portia lost the beat. She stopped for a moment to listen, but when she did, she felt unpleasant pressure on her limbs. Looking down, she saw her hands swelling. Her legs were swelling as well. It was uncomfortable. While she stood looking, her limbs puffed out even further until the pain was nearly unbearable. She looked more closely at her hand—blood oozed out from underneath her cuticle and dripped onto the ground. Her heart began to race.

There was a matching pressure in her face. Her skin was stretched tight. Looking around in panic, she saw the elf behind her dance with exaggerated motions. When Portia didn't react, the elf grabbed Portia's hands and moved them in the rhythm of the dance. Portia felt an instant easing of the pressure in her hands. Her heart leapt. She danced with her whole body, legs, arms, head and torso. The pressure eased instantly. She nodded to the elf behind her while still dancing and turned to follow the group dancing away.

She had taken so long that there was a considerable gap between her and the elf ahead of her. She ran and danced and ran some more to catch up. Each time she stopped dancing and ran, or lost the beat in her dance moves, the pressure returned. She could feel wetness within her clothes. Looking down, she saw blood oozing through her tunic. It made her a little ill. Looking back up resolutely, she focused on the dancers ahead of her and on the music. She had to keep to the rhythm for as long as this test lasted. Hopefully it would not be for much longer.

Ahead, she spied another portal. Each dancing elf made its way to the portal and then danced through. Portia breathed a sigh of relief. There were not more than ten dancers between her and the portal. She only had to maintain her dancing until they were through and she could reach the portal herself.

The music itself seemed to change as each dancer passed through the portal. Portia recognized some rhythms from her own music classes: the lilting rhythms of the coastal cities, the solid marching tones of the lands of the inner kingdom, and finally the long lyrical phrases of The Capital, which was the music named after Coverack itself. She was grateful for her music classes. As much as she had struggled with them, she didn't think she would pass this test without what she had learned from them.

Finally, it was her turn, and she passed through the portal. To her surprise, none of the elves that had passed through ahead of her were present. It was only the elves attending the test and Lady Harper herself. One of the elves brought forth several plush towels for Portia and began patting down her arms and neck and face. When the elf drew back the towel from Portia's face, it was covered in a mixture of blood and sweat. Portia realized with horror that her skin was bleeding everywhere. Nausea pushed at the back of her throat. What a barbaric test. She wanted nothing more than to be back in her own room with a hot bath and clean clothes.

But the elves seemed in no hurry to let her go. They continued to dry her off. One brought a basin of hot water and they washed her skin as gently as they could. Portia was glad her leathers were dark—they hid some stains.

"Congratulations," Lady Harper said, leaning into Portia. "You have passed the tests."

Portia nodded at this as an elf patted at her neck.

Lady Harper did not wait for any further acknowledgment from Portia, instead motioning a guard over from the far door. The guard arrived and looked uneasily at the pile of bloody towels on the floor next to Portia.

"Please alert the royal family their champion has passed," Lady Harper said. When the guard did not look at her, she cleared her throat loudly until the guard reluctantly pulled his eyes away from the stained towels and met her look. "Now, please." Lady Harper's smile belied the steel in her tone. The guard leapt to obey her and ran off.

Queen Lorica and King Consort Aldis returned with the guard and several advisors. It couldn't have been more than a few minutes—they must have been close by. The queen started at the sight of the towels but quickly regained her composure and said nothing of them.

Portia leapt to her feet as the royal couple approached. She gave a small bow, not feeling up to a curtsy and feeling a little silly trying to do one in her mannish clothes.

"Congratulations are in order, I hear," Queen Lorica said, looking at Portia.

Portia nodded in acknowledgment. The queen turned to Lady Harper and tilted her head slightly. "When can you begin teaching Portia?"

"Immediately. We should reach Rocabarra within a week," Lady Harper said and gave a small bow.

"Rocabarra?" Queen Lorica said, surprise in her voice. She frowned.

"I apologize, Your Majesty, but it is only possible for us to teach her the magic in our kingdom."

Portia looked back and forth between Lady Harper and the queen. Several advisors had stepped to the queen's side, clearly wishing to advise her against letting Portia go. Portia knew as the Jack she was valuable to the kingdom. It would be easy to argue the folly of letting her leave it. But Portia really wanted to learn the elf magic. And it sounded important for the future of the kingdom. For the safety of the kingdom.

"Only possible? Or only your desire?" Queen Lorica asked, this time an edge to her voice.

The ballroom was silent at this. No one dared move.

The king consort softly cleared his throat. The queen looked to him and he leaned in, whispering something in her ear. She nodded and turned to face Lady Harper again.

"Since it is clear we are indeed on the same side, perhaps you can share your reasoning for why this magic must be taught in Rocabarra, forcing us to relinquish our champion," Queen Lorica asked, her tone polite but fooling no one as to her true strength. Her mouth was set in a grim line.

Lady Harper's face gave a small twitch before she smoothed her expression. She bowed once again. "Our teacher of the magic of the splinter is in Rocabarra. He is the one that must teach Portia. We do not know the magic ourselves—at least not well enough to teach it. I apologize again, but there is no other way."

The queen quietly considered this statement. "He could not come here?"

Lady Harper tightened her mouth. "No."

Queen Lorica stared at the elf.

Portia couldn't stand the thick tension. She had to say something. "I will come back, Your Majesty. Please, if I need this magic for our kingdom, please let me go and learn it. I will return."

The queen looked to Portia. "It is not your intentions I am questioning." Queen Lorica straightened up, making a decision. "But it is true that we need this magic." The queen smoothed her gown then looked around the room before finally turning to Lady Harper once again. "We will release her to your care for three months. Our guards will accompany you."

Lady Harper nodded. "As you wish, Your Majesty. We will guard her well."

"See that you do," Queen Lorica responded and then turned and walked away briskly. She was followed by her husband and the rest of her entourage.

Portia exhaled, not realizing she had been holding her breath. She was going to another kingdom. To learn magic no human knew. The implications made her head spin. She barely recognized her life from a year ago.

Lady Harper turned to Portia. "Be ready to leave tomorrow afternoon after the festival ends. We will come and collect you at the Academy entrance." With that, Lady Harper and the rest of the elves exited the ballroom, leaving Portia alone with only a few guards at the far door remaining in the room. Portia shook herself a bit then walked unsteadily to the exit herself.

When she got back to her room in the Pyromancy House she gratefully stripped off her filthy clothes and dropped them in the sink to soak. As happy as she was to be there, the quiet of the room unnerved her. Ella and the rest must be at the festival. It was still light outside, and dinner was a few hours away. Portia bathed quickly. There was time to go to the festival to find her friends. If she was going to be gone for several months, this would be her last chance for a while to see them. And the odd events of the afternoon still unnerved her a bit. She wanted to be around people. She wanted things to feel more normal.

The festival was still going, even more raucous than ever. The crowd jostled Portia as she made her way to the magic demonstrations area, thinking it was the most likely place to find her friends. It was the last night, and the city's citizens would stay up late drinking and celebrating and seeing all the unusual things the festival brought to them. Portia struggled through the crowd to see a sign of Ella or Mia or Liam or

Richard. She was especially looking for the twins. Considering how tall they were, they should've been easy to spot.

A hand grabbed at her arm and she whirled, expecting to see one of her classmates. Instead, she jumped back when she saw Mark holding onto her arm.

5

Mark gave Portia a tentative smile as the crowd jostled behind him. She got over her surprise and pulled him close for a big hug.

"Mark, what are you doing here?" she asked as she held him close.

He hugged her back—squeezing tightly then letting go. "I had to talk to you. It's important. If you couldn't make it to see me, then I would make the trip myself." He motioned towards the food stands. "Come, let's get something to eat, and then I can tell you the reason for my visit. As if I need one." The last part was said in a joking grumble.

Portia shook her head. Despite the awful events of their last meeting, she knew he'd been under Deyelna's powers. He never would have hurt her if he had any control over the situation. Deyelna's glam magic had hurt a lot of people. But the former gang leader was gone now and couldn't cause any more trouble between Mark and Portia.

Mark pulled Portia over to a stand that sold fish cakes on a stick. It had been one of Portia's favorite treats back in Valencia, but she rarely had it since it was difficult to make it to the harbor market. That market was not part of the Black Cats' territory, so they only made it there when they were sneaking around and hiding from other orphan gangs.

He bought four sticks of fish cakes, gave Portia half, and motioned over to a nearby bench where they sat and ate. Portia was glad to see Mark. It had been an awful day in some respects, and this was the treat she needed. Mark was like family, his presence a comfort. Just sitting next to him and eating brought back memories of the few times she felt safe in the Black Cats. He was the one she trusted when she felt like she couldn't trust anyone else, especially after John had died.

When they finished eating, Mark put down his sticks on the bench with a sigh. He leaned forward and rubbed his hands, looking around at the crowd. "I did make it back to Valencia—as you know from my note. But there wasn't much to come back to. After Deyelna died, the house was in chaos. She had glammed everyone so completely that when her powers dissipated no one knew what to do." Mark looked at Portia. "The house is gone. It is now a Serpents house. They had taken over all the old Black Cat territory."

Portia looked at Mark in shock. "What about all the members? Are they...?"

Mark shook his head. "No, not dead. At least I don't think so. But they're scattered. I heard rumors that Peter made it back to Valencia and someone saw him at the racetrack. But that was only overheard conversation from two Brown Hares. They stopped talking when they saw me and quickly left."

"What does that mean?"

"I don't know, but they made it clear I wasn't welcome. Perhaps some old Cat members are now part of the Hares and said some nasty things about me. In any case, I wasn't going to push it. There were three of them and just one of me." He sighed, sat back on the bench, and looked around.

"What are you going to do? Are you coming back here to try out for the Magic Academy like I asked you to?" Portia asked, feeling a small bit of hope. She wanted Mark here. It was safer here. As her chosen de facto adopted younger brother, she did not like the thought of him being alone in Valencia. Especially if the Black Cats were gone. Before Deyelna had become the leader, that gang had been their safety in the city. With Deyelna gone, Portia had hoped it would become Mark's safety once again. It looked like that was not to be.

Mark's face turned red. "No matter what you say, I don't think I'd be welcome here—not after what happened. I can't see any reason the Academy guards would ever have for letting me on the grounds again."

"But—"

Mark didn't let her continue. "I've already found another job. There's some wonky religious order that sprung up in Valencia. I think they're a little crazy, but they pay well. They've offered me a job as a page."

"A page? What is that?" She had not heard of such a job.

"Honestly, I have no idea. But they pay in silver every

week. More money than I've ever seen in my life. It has some-thing to do with nobles. I guess I'll find out more next week. They were not ready for me to start right away so I came to see you." Mark looked down at his hands.

Portia wondered if he was hiding something from her. He could have written her a letter instead of making the long journey to see her. "Be careful of any job around nobles. They live by different rules than you and I do."

Mark glanced at Portia sideways. "Are you so sure? These days you are a lot closer to a noble than I am."

This stung. Was Mark accusing her of betraying him? They had always been a team. To hear him talk of her being different from him was more painful than she had ever expected. And she had never expected to hear such words from him. It was unbearable. "I am not. They'll never let me forget that I'm an orphan. We will always be the same." She looked at him intently, willing him to believe her.

Mark snorted and shook his head but did not argue. He stood, looking around at all the richly dressed people at the festival. Portia knew that even in the harbor market of Valen-cia, the well-to-do didn't dress as fine as the average person in Coverack. The royal city of Coverack was wealthy. For some reason, this embarrassed her. He turned and looked at the fine clothes she was wearing. She had on the kirtle and breeches she had bought for her audition for the Academy. She had never worn anything like that while she had lived in Valencia. Her face turned red as he examined her clothing.

Clearing his throat, he finally looked away. "So, what are you studying these days?"

Portia wasn't sure how much she could reveal. She wanted to tell him about her trials with elves, as well as her burden as Jack, but she also did not want to put him in jeopardy. Professor Aelric and Professor Hilda had made it clear that being Jack was serious business, and she was not to tell anyone of her powers. Her need to confide in Mark battled against her desire to protect him.

Protecting him won out. "Just magic stuff—how to be stronger, you know. Your powers are a lot stronger than last time I saw you. Perhaps I should study with you," she said, trying to make a joke.

This got a laugh from Mark. "No, I don't think so. That was desperation."

"So that's the key, hmmm."

This time her joke fell flat. Mark said nothing and continued staring off into the distance.

"I did meet some elves," she said. She thought she could share this much. It caught his attention. He turned to her, his eyes open wide. "There are some here at the festival. We should go see if they're doing more magic demonstrations."

"That would be worth seeing. I thought they were a fairytale," he said, a grin on his face. "It's not like one ever made an appearance in Valencia."

"If you were an elf, would you go to Valencia?" Portia asked, laughing.

"Oh, heck no. I'm not even sure why I'm bothering to go back. Oh yeah, silver," Mark said ruefully.

"They have silver here." Portia reached out to grab Mark's

hand. He let her hold it for a second then pulled away, clearing his throat awkwardly.

"Let's go see those elves then," he said, walking into the crowd.

Portia sighed. Someday perhaps he would consider coming to Coverack to live. She followed him into the crowd.

There were no elves in the magic demonstration, much to their disappointment. Portia tried not to feel that she had personally let Mark down.

The day was coming to an end and the fair winding down. They joined the crowds leaving the fairgrounds. He walked her through the city all the way to the Academy entrance. "I should get going. If I don't leave Coverack tomorrow, then I won't be back in time for the start of my new job," he said.

Portia hated to say goodbye without telling Mark she was leaving Coverack too, but she felt like she couldn't say anything. It was for both of them, and for the kingdom. "Okay. You have a place for tonight?"

"Yeah, don't worry about me. I can take care of myself."

For all of Mark's bluster, he was still her younger brother. But they had both changed a lot in the last year. She no longer felt like she could be so pushy in telling him what to do. She had to trust that he truly could take care of himself.

When Portia got to her room Ella was resting on her bed. She rose and gave Portia a pouty wide-eyed look. "Where were you? I thought you would come find us at the festival."

"I tried. Where were you?" Portia asked, genuinely curious. She had been looking for her friends the entire time she was walking with Mark and had seen none of them.

"Oh, yeah. I guess you didn't know about the eating contest," Ella said. "I should have warned you about that, or left a note. It was sort of last minute."

An eating contest did not surprise Portia. She thought the cafeteria was the favorite part of the school for most of the students. "Let me guess—Richard and Liam."

"And me." Ella looked both proud and embarrassed. Her appetite was well-known throughout the house.

"Of course. And who won?"

Ella didn't answer, instead pulling out a small wooden trophy and holding it up shyly for Portia to see. Portia chuckled. She was going to have to give Richard and Liam a hard time for letting a woman half their size out eat them.

"So, are you skipping dinner tonight?" Portia asked, in mock seriousness.

"Never!" Ella said, her voice rising.

Portia laughed and pulled her bag from underneath her desk. She had just a few minutes to get some packing done before dinner, and could finish the rest before she passed out that evening. Ella raised her eyebrows at Portia's bag but didn't ask about it.

<hr>

THE WORLD RUMBLED AND SHOOK. Somehow, Portia's room no longer had a ceiling but was open to the night sky. Bare tree limbs whipped back and forth in a high wind under the dim light of the night's stars. The moon was nowhere to be seen.

The wind whipped at Portia's covers, giving her a chill. She wanted to grab them and pull them tight to her but her hands wouldn't move. Her whole body was frozen. A cold wind whipped across her face, heavy with the scent of burning leaves and wood.

Above her, a crack appeared between the stars, covering a good portion of the night sky and then spreading wide. She only dimly perceived its presence because of the lack of stars. When she tried to focus on the crack, the black played tricks on her eyes until she could not be sure she saw anything at all.

Two gray scaled hands appeared, one on each side of the crack, impossibly large. They pulled and strained at the crack to make it even wider. Portia's stomach roiled wildly. She felt dizzy—the world was spinning. Still, her hands would not respond even though she wanted to grab the edges of her bed for safety. She felt as if she were going to slide off, perhaps even slide off the edge of the world.

Dimly, she was aware she was in a nightmare. She willed herself to wake but failed. Her heart raced, and she panicked as one of the hands let go of the edge of the crack and came down from the night sky and reached into her bedroom, plucking her up by her nightshirt. The world fell away as the hand pulled her up into the crack, into the darkness, and away from the world.

Portia awoke with a start, her heart racing. The bedding and her nightshirt were soaked with sweat. She had not had one of her nightmares in a while. As if to make up for this, this one was worse than any other she could remember. It was even more horrifying still that she knew part of it was not symbolic. There were real cracks in the sky that led to other worlds. Humans had come through one of them. And there was a name for them—splinters. She wished she did not know that.

The nightmare disturbed her too much for her to attend classes that morning. Instead, she unpacked and repacked her things, positive she had forgotten something. Her nervousness warred against her desire to not be late. Somehow, she felt she would never be ready to go on this trip.

She had left her new dresses in the closet, thinking they would not be practical on the road. Besides, they were too beautiful. She was uncomfortable with such fine clothes. If she was traveling to the uncertainty of a new country, she needed the reassurance of her old clothes more than ever—the breeches and tunics and doublets that gave her freedom of motion, and the confidence of her old life.

She just put the last of her extra knives in her bag when Professor Hilda knocked on the door to her room. Portia waved Hilda in, glad to see her. She had hoped she would get a chance to speak to her before leaving. She had not seen Professor Hilda nor Professor Aelric since her test with the elves and wondered how much they knew about those tests. Did they knowingly let a student place her life on the line?

"Congratulations. I'm sorry I wasn't there when you finished the test yesterday," Hilda said, sitting on Ella's desk chair while Portia moved her bag to the floor. "I'm glad to see you're okay."

Portia squinted at the professor—so she knew. She gave herself a small shake. Hilda had always been on her side, so perhaps there was nothing anyone could have done about it. "I'm glad to see you now," Portia said. "Can you tell me anything about the Elven kingdoms? No one has said anything to me except for what time to be ready to go."

Hilda sighed heavily. "Unfortunately, no. We do not know much about them except for what they choose to share. The one thing I do know is that they do not seem to know the meaning of Jack of Magic. They have not studied our history or else they would know your significance."

"But they know something of a bad event coming?" Portia asked, confused.

"Yes. Perhaps it is an arrogance of theirs to ignore the history of the other kingdoms that share this world. It would not be surprising. The elves have long resented humanity, ever since..." Hilda looked at her hands awkwardly.

"Since... what?"

"Well, since forever. There have been rumors that we stole their lands in the past. I'm not sure as to the truth of that talk. It is a question for the historians. In any case, they do not share their information easily. It is a notable miracle that you are invited to their lands, to learn magic that only they know." She looked intently at Portia. "Do not waste this opportunity."

"I-I won't," Portia said. She suddenly felt very small and anxious about this trip.

"And I just want to remind you, you are still to not share your status of Jack with anyone in Haulstatt. Be careful in the human kingdom—don't let anyone know. Not anyone. There are those who think the existence of a Jack is a blasphemy. They would do you harm. And try to not say too much about it in the elf kingdom either. Reveal only what is necessary to learn."

Portia nodded, swallowing. It was bad enough there was an outside threat. It further ratcheted up her anxiety to think she also had to be wary of all other humans. She had hoped that was a thing of the past.

Hilda rose and hugged Portia. "You'll do fine. Trust yourself."

"Thank you," Portia said under her breath as Hilda exited the room.

She heard Hilda's voice in the hallway, followed by the low-pitched rumble of a man's. Professor Aelric was here. He was her history professor but also the house leader of the Cryomancy house. It was unusual for him to be in this house.

A few seconds later, his face appeared in her doorway. "Greetings, Student Portia. We missed you at class this morning."

"Sorry," Portia said.

He waved away her apology. "It's okay, there are unusual circumstances afoot." He sat down heavily on the chair just abandoned by Professor Hilda. "What you did yesterday was very impressive. And I've never heard of a human being invited to an elf kingdom to learn magic. It is rare enough to be allowed into Rocabarra at all."

"Thanks," Portia said, embarrassed at his praise.

Aelric didn't seem to notice. "I wanted to make sure you got this." He held out a small green book. At Portia's confused look, he spoke. "It's the translation of the book you found, as promised. I'm keeping the original here for safekeeping."

"How did you translate the entire thing so fast?" she asked, taking the little green tome.

He looked pleased with himself. "That was a fun little trick to think up. Even I will admit that. The archivists have book copy spells. We were able to work with one of the spells and my knowledge of the language to have it create a copy while translating at the same time. We practiced by creating another translation copy that now resides in my office, sitting alongside the original." He gave her a serious look. "I didn't want you losing the original out there somewhere on the road. It is a rare book."

The little green book was the same size as the purple one she had left with Aelric, but this one felt different; her fingertips felt the familiar tingle of magic as she held it. She let it fall open to a page. The page was filled with beautiful curling script. Thankfully, Mia had taught her how to read cursive last fall. Her preference would have been printed words, but she wasn't going to breathe a word of complaint to Professor Aelric. He had a rigid sense of propriety, and she guessed that writing in script was a part of that. The important part was that she could read it at all.

"Thank you. Thank you so much," Portia said, truly grateful.

"Of course—stop gushing. It's unbecoming of a champion." Aelric looked uncomfortable. "In any event, I should be getting back to my classroom. I only had a short break." He rose and walked to the door.

"Wait, is there anything I should know about Rocabarra?"

Aelric turned to face Portia.

"Elf kingdom customs and all that. You know more of their history than anyone else I know, I'm guessing. Is there anything I should or should not do? I don't want to offend them and—" Portia did not know how to phrase her question without being offensive. "I can't read Lady Harper. I couldn't tell if she wanted me to pass or not."

"She wants, like the rest of us, to survive. That's all you need to know. Remember that."

Portia looked down at her feet, not much reassured.

Aelric spoke again, this time his voice softened. "You'll be fine. Just get enough rest and remember that your job is to learn and to take care of yourself. You are the only Jack we have."

Portia nodded.

"The guards that will escort you are already waiting at the front of the Academy. Don't keep them standing around for too long." He gave a teasing half smile. "By the way, they didn't get your horse for you. Something about Academy-only access. You have to stop by the stables," Aelric said, and then he was gone.

"Stables?" Portia ran to the window and looked out—the sun was high in the sky. Her heart started racing in a panic and she grabbed her bag and ran out the door. After all that had happened, she was determined to not lose her chance, possibly jeopardizing the human kingdom, by something as silly as being late and getting left behind.

Mia had been planning to teach Portia how to ride some-time that year after she'd expressed an interest, but in the crush of events that school year it had not yet happened.

Portia now severely regretted that lack. She would have gladly given up some of her math knowledge to be able to ride a horse.

Portia ran down to the stables, her bag bouncing on her back. The smell of warm hay and barn wafted up the path towards her. She could hear the animals nickering in the stalls.

Just as she reached the tall double-height doors to the barn, Magisend exited, nearly pushing the door into Portia's face by accident. Magisend was never happy to see Portia. Her face scrunched up into a scowl as Portia skidded to a stop to avoid colliding and sending the noble girl flying back into the barn.

"What are you doing, *commoner*?" Magisend spat out as she reeled back a few steps.

"Sorry, sorry. I don't want to be late," Portia said, biting her lip when she realized she shouldn't have said anything at all.

"Late for what? You don't have a horse here. And I've never seen you ride." Magisend folded her arms across her chest and blocked the entrance to Portia.

"I-I'm going on a trip, you know, to learn how to fit in," Portia said, realizing what a horrible lie it was. She was going to have to come up with a better cover story.

The soft snicker of a horse from just within the barn doors startled Magisend. She turned to see Lady Harper leading out two horses with several other elves and horses behind her. Magisend's mouth dropped into a small oh of surprise at the sight of the elves in the Academy horse barn.

Without a word, Lady Harper walked to Portia and gave her the reins of an older horse. White flecked the horse's muzzle. It nudged Portia in a friendly way. She took the reins and froze in place, allowing the animal to inspect her, not knowing what else to do. Lady Harper walked on leading a much younger stallion, followed by the nine elves with their own horses. They mounted then continued down the path, not turning to see if Portia followed.

Magisend watched the whole thing with amazement then glanced at Portia. Portia swore she saw something resembling respect in Magisend's expression. But Portia didn't have the luxury of figuring that out now—her group was leaving. If she didn't do something, they would disappear over the hill without her.

"Wait," Portia called after them, juggling her bag and the horse's reins. She started to run down the path, dragging the horse along. She could hear Magisend laughing. She stopped, looked at the horse and again at the riders leaving her behind, and resumed running, once again trailing the horse.

"Oh my gosh, stop, you idiot commoner!" Magisend called, barely able to talk she was laughing so hard. Despite her words, she didn't sound as angry as she normally did, so Portia did stop.

"What? They're going to leave me," Portia said, frustration creeping into her voice, threatening to turn her voice into a whine.

"You aren't going to catch them by *running* after them. Get on your horse."

Portia's face turned red. She pursed her lips and looked down.

"You don't know how. This is too much," Magisend said, laughing once again, bending over to get enough breath for deep belly laughs.

"Shut up." Portia knew it was undignified, but she just lost her temper.

"Oh calm down." Magisend trotted to Portia and took her bag and slung it over the horse behind the saddle. She strapped it on with a few loose leather ties hanging there. She then grabbed Portia's left leg and shoved her foot into the stirrup. She pushed Portia up, motioning for her to lift her right leg and get on the horse. Portia did as Magisend indicated and gasped a bit as she sat down in the saddle—she was so much higher than it looked from the ground.

"Now, don't pull too hard on the reins and let this old girl follow the other horses," Magisend said.

Portia nodded at the instructions, a little confused at the girl's kindness. For all her mockery, this was the first time Magisend had ever helped Portia do anything. Portia smiled down at her, but Magisend only laughed again and slapped the rear of the horse, sending it down the path towards the retreating elves. Lady Harper looked back and saw Portia was following and then resumed leading the group away. Portia could still hear Magisend's laughter as they rounded the hill that marked the edge of campus.

6

Portia followed the elves through the narrow streets of Coverack. They passed by the festival grounds where vendors were tearing down their tents and stalls. Portia wondered why they had to wait until the end of the festival to leave. She must remember to ask Lady Harper, if she was ever given the opportunity to ask questions.

Once past the festival grounds, they passed through the more well-to-do areas of the city. The streets opened wider, and the houses were larger and set back on expansive lawns. They were exiting the city through the west gate, a direction Portia had never been before. There was more land here since the buildings were not crushed up against the hard barrier of the sea and the city wall.

Once the horses could ride side by side, Lady Harper motioned for Portia to stay in the middle while she rode on the left and a different elf flanked Portia to the right. Despite nearly being left behind, Portia suddenly had the feeling she was being guarded by the elves. Then she remembered the palace guards that were supposed to escort her. Where were they?

She turned to Lady Harper and drew up her courage. "I thought there were supposed to be palace guards with us. Professor Aelric mentioned they were waiting on the edge of the Academy grounds."

Lady Harper turned to Portia and assessed her with a cool gaze. The horses' hooves thumped on the ground as they continued down the street. Finally, Lady Harper spoke. "Yes, they were. I asked the guards to meet us by the west gate. They were drawing too much attention, and we were not quite ready to leave yet."

This made Portia nervous. She didn't know what authority Lady Harper had to tell palace guards to do anything different. Shouldn't that order come directly from the king or queen? But she would wait until they arrived at the west gate before jumping to any conclusions. There would be people around there, and if she felt the need to get away from the elves, she would not be alone with them. There would be help available. She did not trust the elves, especially after they had endangered her life for silly tests that could have easily been done much more safely. At least more safely for herself. She still didn't know if those were real elves inside the worlds of the tests. The sight of the one elf dying of cold still haunted her.

"Okay," Portia said, glancing unsurely at Lady Harper.

She fiddled with the reins of her horse a bit until the horse tossed its head in irritation and Portia stilled her hands. They were fast approaching the edge of the city, but she still wasn't clear where they were going. She had a rough idea from the maps at school, but the land denoting the elf kingdom had few details drawn on it—it was mostly a beige blotch on the paper. "Where exactly are we going?"

"To the elf kingdom. The capital, to be exact, of Rocabarra. That is where the elf who knows the splintering magic lives. In addition, you need to meet our king and queen for approval of this knowledge. I am only authorized so far and have taken a risk to promise the house of Coverack your teaching. Hopefully, I haven't overextended myself." Lady Harper hesitated for the first time Portia had ever seen then continued on. "But the need is great. Risks must be taken."

It had not occurred to Portia that Lady Harper was taking a risk as well. It did not excuse their risking of her life, but at least she understood it was also serious for them.

To Portia's relief, Lady Harper continued speaking without Portia having to ask questions. "We will be traveling through Holne and then going northwest on the trade road to reach the gate to the Elven kingdom."

Portia nodded. This matched what she could recall from the maps in the Academy. "Will it be much colder there? I mean, if we're going north and all."

"A few months ago, yes, it would have been much colder. But luckily we are past the worst of the season and things are warming up, even in the north. The passes were easy to traverse on the way to the festival. I believe that is part of the timing of the spring festival—one of the few concessions humans have made in an effort to get along with the elves. Or perhaps they just want to celebrate the warmth."

"Are elves always at the spring festival?" Portia asked, suddenly curious. "In Coverack anyway. I don't remember seeing any elves in Valencia."

It couldn't be easy to be an elf in the human kingdom when there were so few. Even now, the stares from the city folk followed them as they wound their horses through the streets towards the gate. The elves were still an oddity here. And that was in this city—one that was much more sophisticated than Valencia.

"So you noticed," Lady Harper said with a small chuckle. "No, it is not easy, nor usual, for an elf to be in the human kingdom. But it is in our best interest to maintain ties, no matter what has happened in the past, for the future can be even more uncertain. Who knows who shall come into this world and wreak havoc." Lady Harper turned to Portia and gave her a small smile, a twinkle in her eye. "Or perhaps the enemy you know is better than the one you don't know."

Portia gave a start. "Are we enemies?"

"It has been so in the past. This was all elf land before the humans arrived. It has taken a long time for those wounds to heal, if they have healed at all."

No, it could not have been easy to lose their land to humans, Portia thought. No wonder this relationship was so tense. That made her feel even more uneasy about the ominous events that no one could quite see in the future. They were bad enough to force elves and humans to work together out of fear of something much worse coming. Could it have something to do with her dreams? She hoped she wasn't seeing what actual splinters looked like, because her dreams were terrifying.

They reached the west gate and found two palace guards waiting for them, playing dice with the regular guards to pass the time. Portia was surprised to see only two. She turned red, realizing she thought there should be at least four more.

One of the guards seemed to read her mind, for he bowed low and said to Portia directly, "My apologies, ma'am, but there have been some disruptions to the south. We do not anticipate any trouble going to the north, so some guards have been pulled to investigate."

Portia bit her lip and nodded. She was uncomfortable that he seemed to know what she was thinking. The more mundane explanation was probably that it showed on her face. Despite her years in the street as an orphan, she had never quite mastered the technique of a game face.

"It is of no concern," Lady Harper said. She gestured to the other eight elves in the entourage. "Surely we have escort enough to make it safely to our kingdom."

Portia thought of the bandits she had encountered on her last trip from Holne to Coverack but said nothing. Surely criminals looking for easy coin would think twice before attacking a dozen travelers, including two guards with the royal crest.

The band exited the west gate. Portia realized with dismay there was only a half-day left of light. They would be hard-pressed to reach Holne before it was black out. Most travelers, it seemed, were more sensible in their traveling plans than they were, for the road was nearly empty. Indeed, in less than an hour they had lost sight of all other travelers on the road as they traveled across the windblown meadows, accompanied only by the sounds of their horses' hooves on the hard-packed dirt. The royal guards split up, one ahead of the elf group and one behind. They looked around constantly.

They approached the woods where a nearby river fed the trees that rose from the dry meadow grasses. Lady Harper motioned for the group to stop for a rest. The horses needed to eat and drink. Portia was grateful at the chance to stretch her legs; her backside was uncomfortable, numb from the unaccustomed riding.

They pulled to the side of the woods, and an elf came to take the reins from Portia. She lifted her leg to get off the horse and realized just how stiff she was. It hurt to straighten her legs. It hurt to stand. It hurt even more to walk. She hissed softly under her breath when she took a few painful steps.

Lady Harper gave her a smile and laughed softly. "It gets easier. I take it this is your first time."

"Oh, so you did notice my inexperience," Portia said, knowing she should not have said anything, but she was still irritated that Lady Harper had almost left her at the Academy.

"Of course I noticed, but child, I saw you take those tests.

You do not need my babying for you to figure out how to ride a horse. Besides, I was curious to see how far you would run. I swear, if you could have carried that horse you would have done so."

Portia had to laugh at that. It was funny. She was usually a quicker thinker. Her horse probably thought she was an idiot. She wondered if it resented carrying such a stupid human.

Lady Harper grabbed a bag off her horse and motioned for Portia to join her underneath one of the trees. The other elves and the palace guard led their horses deeper into the woods to where the stream was running through the trees. Portia could hear the tinkle of the water. She wanted to go get fresh water herself, but Lady Harper held out a canteen to her, and she felt compelled to stay and drink from the canteen instead.

Portia eased her sore bottom onto the hard-packed earth underneath the tree. She gratefully took a cheese sandwich from Lady Harper and ate it quickly, not realizing how ravenous she was until she took the first bite. It was delicious white cheese with mustard and chewy bread. Five of them would not have been enough.

Lady Harper nibbled on a sandwich of her own but did not seem nearly as hungry. She looked around then stiffened, giving the air a sniff. Portia stopped chewing and tried to smell the air herself, but the only scent was the warm yeast from the bread that had been sitting in the saddlebag that afternoon. When Lady Harper did not relax, Portia uneasily lowered her sandwich and looked around. She couldn't see anything unusual.

A *twang* behind Portia's right ear caught her attention. She whirled as an arrow sunk deep into the tree behind her, vibrating with the force of its impact. Lady Harper grabbed her bag and yelled for Portia to follow as she scrambled deeper into the woods.

Portia instinctively flattened to the ground and rolled back towards the tree line, wanting desperately to get behind a tree before squatting to run deeper into the woods. She could hear Lady Harper ahead of her, calling out that there were bandits.

The bright clash of swords rang out through the woods. A horse whinnied and then ran off, its hooves thundering through the undergrowth. Portia pulled one of the knives from the sheath on her calf. She rounded the tree and crouched low while running into the woods—towards the sound of the fighting. She wasn't going to let Lady Harper or the elves fight on their own.

She nearly stumbled on a mass in the leaves. It was one of the royal guards. His burgundy uniform was stained a darker red in the chest where an arrow pierced through the royal insignia. Portia paused just long enough to determine that he wasn't breathing. She looked around but didn't see anything. The sun filtered through the leaves, obscuring the sightline to the west. Even so, the bandits must have moved further in towards the horses and packs.

There was at least one bandit with a bow nearby—the one that had shot at them. Portia would feel better if she knew where that one was. From behind her, she heard footsteps in the leaves. She whirled to look the way she had come. A large bandit dressed all in black strode towards her, an arrow notched in his bow. He looked her directly in the eye and then let an arrow fly. Portia dropped to the ground just in time and heard the feathered arrow pass inches above her head to strike a tree behind her. The oncoming bandit already had another arrow notched in his bow. He hadn't even paused on his advance on her.

Portia scrambled back, getting a tree between her and the oncoming bandit, and then ran as fast as she could, zigzagging left and right to be a more difficult moving target. Arrows flew past her. She had a sick feeling he was herding her towards the rest of the group, but fear gripped her so hard she had a hard time thinking of doing anything else but running.

When she got close to the stream, she saw several elves down and bloodied on the ground. There seemed to be a dozen or more bandits all dressed in black. They looked more like an army than a random band of thieves. The bandit was still chasing her; she could hear his footsteps through the leaves behind her.

Lady Harper jumped out from behind a tree and charged towards Portia's pursuer, wielding an enormous sword. The elf must have grabbed it off a fallen attacker. The pursuer skidded to a startled stop but then let loose an arrow at the charging elf. Lady Harper dodged to the side while still running forward, but her feint wasn't wide enough—the arrow sank into her shoulder. She did not pause, charging the bandit and knocking the bow from his hands with a backhanded swipe of her sword.

The man swore and stumbled back, trying to evade her

wildly swinging weapon. Lady Harper cut him several times until he tripped and stumbled back on the ground. She stepped forward and rammed her sword underneath his leather jacket and deep into his torso. His eyes bulged wide in surprise as a sword tip tickled the back of his throat from the inside.

Portia gagged a bit at the viciousness of the tiny elf. Lady Harper yanked the sword free from the body of the dead man. Red blood stained her white jerkin and coated her sword. Her left arm, her non-sword arm, hung limply. Thankfully, the arrow had not hit her other shoulder.

Harper ran towards Portia and motioned towards the larger battle. Dragging Portia to a vantage point behind a tree, she whispered into Portia's ear, "We need a plan." Portia nodded.

Portia and Lady Harper peered around the tree. The battle was not going well. The second guard went down as Portia watched. Black figures swirled around the elves, surrounding them. They were vastly outnumbered. Could there be two dozen attackers? It seemed like as soon as one went down, another replaced him.

This gave Portia an idea. Duplicates couldn't do real damage, but they could confuse and distract the bandits.

She grabbed Lady Harper's hand. "Give me a second, then we strike." She squeezed the elf's hand. There was no time to explain further—she hoped she would just trust her.

Closing her eyes, she envisioned a dozen more of herself. It was the limit of her abilities, and she knew they would be slightly transparent, but with the setting sun and the confusion of the battle, she hoped it would be enough. Opening her eyes, she saw her duplicates and sent them scurrying into the battle. She watched from around the tree as they ran and circled the bandits, trying to distract them from the elves who were struggling to fight. To her horror, she saw only two elves left standing. She nodded at Lady Harper and they charged but it was too late. Even with the distraction of the duplicates, the remaining elves were struck down.

A scream of rage and fear welled in Portia's throat. She drew on the last of her energy and instinctively created bursts of light in front of the bandits' faces. The men in black recoiled as the bright light stung their eyes. Portia and Lady Harper attacked with their swords. Adrenaline coursed through Portia's arms and she struck as hard as she could, fighting for her survival. She barely registered that she was killing people, having to concentrate on the next person attacking her as soon as the one she was dealing with fell.

Quiet overcame the woods. Portia stood breathing heavily, holding her sword and looking around for the next attacker. But there was none, only fallen bodies. She glanced over and saw Lady Harper doing the same. Lady Harper gave her a grim look and then went to the nearest elf to check for a pulse.

None of the elves or the palace guards survived the battle. Portia counted eleven bandit bodies but thought there had been more of them than that. They must have run away. Hopefully, they had been beaten so severely they would just flee and leave them alone. She didn't like the thought of them waiting in the woods for a second chance to attack.

Tears prickled at her eyes as Portia checked the last body,

hoping for a sign of life, someone, anyone, they could save. But there was no one. Instead, the ground was littered with one broken body after another, some fallen into impossible positions, more blood on the ground than she thought possible, others simply unresponsive, their eyes closed as if sleeping. She looked up and saw Lady Harper give her head a shake—she had not found anyone alive either.

Portia slumped to the ground, her arms suddenly shaking. She could no longer hold her knife and dropped it to the ground beside her. Nausea pushed the back of her throat as the smell of blood reached her. The ground was soaked with it. Her clothes and weapon were covered with it. She had killed, and even the thought that they were trying to kill her first did not make her feel any better.

Lady Harper approached her and patted her on the back before slumping down on the ground next to her. "Are you okay?" she asked Portia, concern in her eyes.

Portia dimly registered this tone was much different from the normal cool attitude of Lady Harper. She could only shake her head. She was not okay. Speech seemed beyond her.

Lady Harper looked at her and squinted her eyes. "I mean, are you physically hurt?"

Checking her limbs and body, Portia realized she wasn't injured. She looked to Lady Harper and saw that more blood had escaped the elf's shoulder wound from the exertions of the battle. The left side of her jerkin was soaked.

"I need you to pull this out," Lady Harper said, indicating the shaft stub of the arrow still stuck in her left shoulder.

Portia nodded and leaned over and grabbed the slick

wood. When she tried to pull it, her fingers slipped off from the blood coating the wood. She wiped her hands on the grass, then tried again, but the arrow was firmly stuck in the elf's flesh. "It won't come out. It will tear you if I pull harder."

"Don't worry about that. If it remains, I will get very ill. The wound needs to be cleaned. This is not something that can wait until we make it to a town." Lady Harper groaned.

"I don't want to hurt you."

"Do you want me to die? Pull it."

Portia got on one knee to get more leverage in the grass and grasped the arrow shaft firmly. She yanked hard and the arrow came loose with the sickening sound of flesh tearing. Portia threw it down and vomited.

Lady Harper hissed, then staggered to her feet. "Stop, child. Now is not the time to be sick." The elf started singing, doing a slow rhythmic dance at the same time. A soft shimmering in the air by the elf's wounded shoulder caught Portia's attention, and she swore she could see the wound healing in time to the elf's singing. She had never seen that sort of healing magic before. The elf's magic was formidable.

Finishing her song, Lady Harper slumped back down to the ground again and laid back in the grass, exhausted. Portia looked around anxiously. There could still be attackers around. Lady Harper turned her head towards Portia while breathing heavily. "Good. Keep an eye out. I'll be recovered enough in a minute for us to leave. You should find our packs and get something to eat. But still keep an eye out." Lady Harper closed her eyes.,

Portia forced herself to get up. Her arms and legs were

still shaky, but there was no help for it. She had to get it together if they were going to get out of there. Looking around, she saw a horse grazing not far into the forest. At least one animal was not completely scared away or stolen. It was close enough that she would be able to go get it and still keep an eye out in the area around Lady Harper. She felt uneasy leaving the elf. She stood still for a minute, trying to sense any other attackers, but heard nothing but the rustle of small animals in the undergrowth and birds chirping overhead.

Walking to the horse, she found a pack on the back that had food. There was jerky and cheese and some hard bread. Gratefully, she chewed some jerky as she led the horse back.

When she returned, Lady Harper was standing over a bandit. She had pushed up his sleeve, revealing a freshly healed brand in the bandit's flesh. It was a small diamond. Lady Harper looked at Portia. "We need to check them all."

Every single fallen bandit had the same brand. "Do you know what this means?" Portia asked, curious. She had never seen anything like this.

"No. I was hoping you did." Lady Harper glanced at the falling sun. The light through the trees was growing dim as the sun neared the horizon. She sighed and stood, looking at the jerky in Portia's hand and the horse she was leading. "Did you see any other horses?"

Portia dug into the bag and handed Lady Harper some dried meat. "No."

"That's too bad. We'll have to walk then. We'll save this horse in case we need to flee another attack. We can't risk exhausting him."

Portia groaned inwardly. This was a sensible plan, but her exhaustion was so intense. She wanted nothing more than to nap on the horse. Or better yet, sleep in the trees until morning. "Do you know how far it is to Holne?"

"Not far, but it will still be dark when we arrive."

Portia grimaced. She did not relish the thought of traveling at night. Turning in the opposite direction of the sun, she saw a full moon rising. At least they would have good light. She thought of Coverack and all the palace and city guards. "Shouldn't we go back to the palace and get reinforcements?"

"No. These bandits came from behind us. From the Coverack area. There will probably be more of them, and it's probably the direction the rest fled back to. It is best for us to keep going. And quickly."

Portia didn't understand how Lady Harper knew where the bandits came from, but she was too tired to ask further questions. They collected all the money purses off the fallen bandits and elves alike.

Standing over one of the fallen guards, Portia looked at the man's peaceful face. It looked like he was sleeping. Somewhere back in the city he probably had a family who would be worrying about him. She reached down and pulled at his scabbard. The royal insignia was embossed on it. More importantly, his name was etched in the leather as well. If they couldn't properly bury them, the least they could do would be to bring back word.

Seeking out the other guard, Portia took his scabbard as well. Using her sharpest knife, she cut out the embossed sections of each—the sheaths were heavy and cumbersome. It would be better to only carry what was needed.

Lady Harper and Portia backtracked to collect their packs from where they had originally been resting underneath the trees. They put their packs on the horse and then struck off towards Holne.

The road evened out as they traveled further from the forest. Portia's nerves were raw trying to hear any noise above the sound of the horse's hooves. Even when leading it on the grass next to the road, the animal made a lot of sound. Truly it was an incredibly noisy beast. Part of her wished she had not found it. The two of them walking without the horse would have been much quieter.

Lady Harper scanned the road in front while leading the horse, leaving Portia to watch out behind them. They had gone for some ways when Portia spotted a dark patch coming up on the road behind them. There were no woods or any other easy hiding spot nearby, so there was little choice but to wait for what was coming.

As it drew closer, the outline of a caravan resolved. It was several wagons long.

"Lady Harper, there are wagons behind us," Portia said.

Turning to look, Lady Harper's face relaxed. "Bandits would not be so bold as to travel in a caravan. Let's see if we can get a ride."

They flagged down the caravan. The lead horse whinnied and shied away from the small elf standing in the road. The driver called out in an irritated tone, "What ye want? Should not be out at night alone."

Portia could only agree with this. She licked her lips nervously. The driver did not seem friendly.

"We were attacked. We ask your assistance in getting to town," Lady Harper said.

"Attacked, eh?" The driver looked around. Luckily, there was no place close by for ruffians to hide. Portia hoped this would reassure the driver. "Well, that's nothing I want to know of. We're running late." He lifted the reins of the horses to move on.

Lady Harper was undeterred. "Wait. I understand your concern." She held out her hand with something in it. "Let me reassure you."

The driver did not flick the reins, instead bringing his attention back to Lady Harper.

The elf walked around the side of the wagon and approached him with her hand held out. Finally, he put his hand out beneath hers. Coins clinked as they fell from Lady Harper's fingers to his palm. He looked down and counted. "Ay, we all have emergencies. Hop in," he said in a much more amenable voice, motioning to the wagon with his head.

Portia tied the horse's reins to the back of the wagon and climbed in with Lady Harper.

A cold breeze passed over Portia and Lady Harper as the day's heat evaporated towards the stars. Portia shivered. She pulled her pack close and tucked her arms in close to her body. She was too cold to sleep, so she looked for more bandits as the wagons rolled along. Lady Harper stared forward intently. The cold didn't seem to bother her. Little seemed to bother the elf. Portia shivered harder and rubbed her arms vigorously.

The moon was nearly overhead by the time they reached the small city. Its perfectly manicured lawns and well cared for houses shone under the strong moonbeams. As they pulled into the central square, Portia wondered if she was always going to enter Holne on the bed of a wagon.

The wagons stopped on one side of the central square of Holne. It looked just like the last time Portia had been there, but she wasn't surprised. It had only been a year or so since she had left Valencia as a homeless orphan. She wondered if the clothing shop she had stopped at was still there. Looking down at her blood-soaked clothes, the thought of new garments was appealing.

They jumped down from the wagon and Portia untied the horse. Lady Harper dug a few silver coins out of her purse and gave one to the wagon driver and then looked for the train boss of the caravan. He was at the lead wagon inspecting the horses. Lady Harper approached him, but he rebuffed her when she held out her hand. A few words were spoken, and he finally relented. Taking the coin, he gave the elf a nod.

"Why did you do that?" Portia asked, curious, when Lady Harper returned. "Didn't you already pay?"

"It never hurts to make more friends. The way things are

going, we need all the assistance we can get. Think of it as paying in advance."

This made sense to Portia, although she'd never had enough coin to make friends that way before.

Walking around, she realized her arms and legs ached. She had gotten stiff sitting in the wagon. Now her body complained painfully just from standing. She stretched her neck then looked around the square. The wagon drivers were leading their horses to the inn she had eaten at a year ago. They were staying there that night. A warm bed and a hot drink sounded good.

Lady Harper seemed to be of the same mind. "Shall we find lodgings?"

Portia nodded. She walked towards the inn, leading their own horse, when Lady Harper grabbed her arm. "The moonlight hid this before, but perhaps we should change. If we walk into that inn covered in blood, it might be difficult to obtain hospitality," the elf said quietly.

Portia stopped walking. She was conscious of the stiffness of her clothing from the blood. As bad as she was, Lady Harper was even worse off—her white jerkin was soaked in blood. And she was an elf. Portia wasn't sure if that was as unusual in Holne as it was in Valencia. She had never seen an elf her entire life in Valencia.

They changed behind a nearby building, taking turns keeping an eye out for any passersby. They were lucky they had not lost their packs. Portia shoved her bloodstained clothes into her bag. She was grateful she had brought a full change.

Once done, they approached the inn. An ostler came to take the horse. Fortunately, the inn was not full, and there was room in the stable as well.

The common room of the inn was just as packed as last time Portia had been there. They wove their way through the crowd to reach the innkeeper behind the bar. Conversation gradually subsided as the patrons noticed the presence of the elf. Lady Harper ignored their stares.

Portia's ears burned red as she tried to ignore them too. She swore she could feel their eyes on her face. As an orphan thief, the last thing she had wanted was to draw any attention to herself. Having everyone stare at her felt dangerous.

The innkeeper was the same balding barman who had helped her when she had passed through before. He had been kind when she didn't have enough money. She breathed a little easier at seeing his face. He smiled back at Portia. She wondered if he remembered her.

They obtained rooms and paid for bathwater to be sent up, as well as their meal in a private parlor. It was an extravagance Portia had never experienced before. She hadn't even known it existed until she heard Lady Harper negotiate for it. She'd only heard rumors that some lived like this. She never imagined she would experience such luxury. But after the long day's events, Portia was grateful they would not have to eat in the common room. It was loud. And there were too many staring faces.

Portia bathed first and then asked for fresh water to wash her clothes. The maid had wanted to take her laundry, but Portia winced at the thought of the servant touching her blood-soaked garments. It was hard enough for her to do it. She did not want to give a reason for gossip within the inn. It also felt uncomfortable to have another work for her that way. Once shoved into cold water, the stiff doublet and pants relaxed and unfolded, releasing the blood and dirt into the water. Portia hoped it would dilute enough to not give away that it was indeed blood.

While she bent to do her laundry, her stomach growled. It had been a long time since her last hasty meal—the one taken in the woods. Unfortunately, she had no other dry clothes than those she had changed into in the alleyway. Gritting her teeth, she told herself there wasn't much dirt or blood on those. By the time she had changed into them in the alleyway, the blood had already dried on her body. Only a few small black flecks were on the garments themselves.

Portia swallowed back nausea, fantasizing about another set of clothing. A clean set. Not ones with flakes of blood from dead strangers. Her skin crawled with loathing as she pulled on the garments.

She washed her hands again, more out of compulsion than anything else. No matter how much she scrubbed, she imagined she could still see the blood on her hands.

Groaning, she stood and exited to find Lady Harper in the private parlor.

Blessedly, dinner came within minutes. It was simple but hot. Portia waited until Lady Harper helped herself and then loaded up her plate. They ate in silence.

"So what shall we do?" Portia asked after finishing the last of the chicken on her platter.

Lady Harper sipped on her wine. She leaned back in her chair, considering the question. "Rest well tonight. But don't forget to lock your door. And your window. It may feel safe here, but those bandits were not normal bandits."

"I'm glad to not know what a normal bandit is like." Lady Harper gave her a small smile that said she was not so lucky. She finished the rest of her wine without another word.

Portia was exhausted. Her head bobbed. She was having a hard time staying awake.

Lady Harper waved Portia towards her room. "Go. Go to bed. And don't forget the locks. I'll see what I can find out about those brands."

Portia did what she was bid. Laying her head on her pillow, she thought briefly that Lady Harper should probably not ask questions alone, but sleep overcame her, worries and all.

———

THE MORNING SUN shone brilliantly through the wooden shutters, falling on Portia's face. She awoke with a start. Throwing open the window coverings, she realized just how late it was. The streets were filled with people. It must have been market day. The noise coming up was oppressive—vendors hawking their wares, children calling back and forth, and the creaking of horses and wagons rolling by.

Rumbling from her stomach told Portia that her body had not forgotten that market day meant eating. It was an association from long ago. The market days were the only days she occasionally got enough to eat. But only occasionally. Even the last year of eating well had not changed her body's reaction.

Dressing quickly, she then gathered her now-dry clothes and folded them and put them into her pack. Hopefully Lady Harper was up as well. If not, she would have to eat breakfast alone. She was too hungry to wait.

She unlocked the door and exited to find the elf. Her room was down the hall from Portia's. A maid looked up in surprise when Portia peered in. It was empty. Portia's stomach tightened in a knot. Surely Lady Harper had not left her there.

Relief flooded her when she found the elf in the private parlor, a sumptuous spread in front of her. She breathed out heavily, chastising herself for having jumped to such a bad conclusion.

"I was wondering when you would rouse," the elf said with a laugh. "I was beginning to think I was going to have to send someone in with a bucket of cold water. But then I remembered your door was bolted, and I had no choice but to wait."

Portia ignored the ribbing. She was too entranced with the impossible spread of food in front of Lady Harper. Throwing down her pack, she sat down across from the elf. She didn't speak a word until she had filled her plate and taken her first bite of pastry. "You didn't wait completely," Portia said, eyeing Lady Harper's plate of crumbs.

Lady Harper laughed heartily at this. "Am I to take it that you would have?" Her eyes twinkled.

There was no fooling her, Portia thought. She shook her head, eyes down, trying to keep from smiling.

Lady Harper drank her coffee and waited patiently while Portia ate. Finally, when she slowed down, the elf cleared her throat. "I have not found any information about those brands."

Dread settled over Portia. She remembered about the diamond shapes burned into the bandit skin—the bandits who had killed the palace guards—and the rest of the elves. Suddenly the food in her mouth tasted bitter and dry. Struggling to swallow it, she sipped some water. Breakfast was no longer appealing. She pushed away her plate.

"I'm sorry about your convoy... and the palace guards," Portia said.

A dark look crossed Lady Harper's face. All mirth was gone. "I'm sorry too." She narrowed her eyes at Portia. "Why are you apologizing to me? Do you know something I don't? Are you somehow responsible?"

Portia shook her head vehemently. "No. At least I don't think so... I'm just sorry they all died."

"Our magic is strong, but we can't revive victims. Once they're dead, they stay that way. Which is too bad." Lady Harper pushed away her cup. "And what do you mean 'you don't think so?'"

Portia's face turned red. "I don't want to sound... I don't know... arrogant, but bad things seem to happen to those close to me. To the people I care about. Or at least those that I'm around." Embarrassment flooded Portia's body. She sounded like a jerk who thought the world revolved around her. But that wasn't it. Too many people around her had been hurt or even killed, and she was starting to be afraid to let anyone close.

Lady Harper waved away Portia's protest. "Bad things happen in this world. Don't take everything so personally." She rose and picked up her bag from its place on the chair by the fireplace. Portia stood up as well, grabbing her own bag. She looked back at the food left on the table. It felt odd to just leave it. That was something she had never done in her life. Food was too precious.

Lady Harper followed her gaze. "I left orders for the remains to be wrapped. We'll come back for it when we get the horse," Lady Harper said. Portia turned to see her understanding expression. She wasn't the only one who didn't waste food.

They exited to the bright morning sunshine.

"Do you know where the guardhouse is?" Lady Harper asked.

She looked around the square, eyeing the crowds of people. The interest was returned. Passersby—peasant and moneyed alike—stared at the small elf. Lady Harper was dressed in shades of blue. It was the same outfit she had been wearing when Portia met her in the palace. The flowing clothes were dramatic, but Portia suspected the interest was mostly in the presence of an elf.

"I do not," Portia said. She scanned for anything that might be a guardhouse. While doing so, she looked across the square to see if the clothier shop was open—the shop she had patronized when she had first passed through Holne. It seemed ridiculous, but somehow she felt that shop had brought her luck. Luck she could use now. But there were too many people in the square for her to see that far away.

"Right. Let me go ask. I'll check on the horse while I'm at it," Lady Harper said, bounding back into the inn. She emerged a few moments later and pointed directly across the square.

Portia's heart raced at that. She was glad they would go in the direction of the clothing shop. She was too embarrassed to ask Lady Harper if they could stop in, but if they just happened to be walking by it later, that might be a different matter.

They made their way through the crowd, their packs making it even more difficult to push through. Lady Harper led the way, not glancing at anyone. Portia hid a smile at the tiny elf making the townsfolk give way.

The guardhouse was not what Portia expected. It was the most rundown building along the entire side of the square. It might even be the most rundown building in the entire town. The roof was faded and stained, the walls scuffed with plaster missing in places. The warped wood frames around the windows and door lacked paint. It did not look like it belonged in this otherwise well-to-do city.

Lady Harper walked directly to the door and firmly knocked. There was no response. Using her fist this time, Lady Harper pounded on the door again. She continued pounding until the door flew open and a surprised guard nearly got a fist to the nose. "What ya want?" he asked, irritably.

"I would like to speak to the captain of the guard," Lady Harper said.

"Oh, would you now?" He leaned against the doorframe, looking down at the small elf. He towered over her. "You make a lot of noise for such a tiny child."

"I'm an *elf*. *Lady* Harper of the Meadows." Lady Harper put her fists on her hips and stared back at him. Portia held her breath as the two glared at each other. The test of wills attracted the attention of those walking by as well. The guard's eyes flickered as he noticed the scene that was forming. People were stopping and staring—their eyes going back and forth between him and the indignant elf. Lady Harper seemed to notice nothing.

Finally, the elf won. The guard's eyes slipped away to the side, and he spoke in a surly tone. "Fine. Wait here." He slammed the door shut.

Lady Harper turned back to Portia and winked.

They waited. The building was not that large. The delay was probably intentional. In the meanwhile, the surrounding citizens grew bored and drifted away.

Even after the last of the citizens had wandered away, Lady Harper did not react to the slight. She stood waiting patiently, so Portia did as well. She'd seen enough chest puffing as an orphan to understand this game.

The door opened. A younger guard appeared—one who had a smile on his face. "Please, come in. I apologize for the delay." This remark caused the original guard, who was now standing behind him, to scowl.

They entered the guardhouse. The inside belied the

outside: it was neat, clean, and well-maintained. There were several desks in the room, as well as a large table in the middle. The younger guard motioned for them to sit at the table. He sat facing them while the older guard leaned against the back wall, his arms crossed.

"What do you want with the Haulstatt guards?" The faintly patronizing tone in his voice made the hair on the back of Portia's neck stand up.

"I am Lady Harper of the Meadows, as I told your compatriot. I am the leader of a convoy to the king and queen of Coverack. Difficulties have arisen on our return journey, so I must claim the prerogative of a guard to the Rocabarra border, per the provisions of the treaty between our two nations." Her tone brooked no argument.

The two guards stared at her. Their mouths were slightly open. Neither seemed inclined to do her bidding.

"It is a matter of some urgency," she added.

The guard cleared his throat then said slowly, "This is not a place for pranks." He stole a look at the elf's ears and hesitated for a moment, then his face settled back down into an immovable visage.

"I assure you, this is no prank." Lady Harper pulled some papers from her bag. She passed them over the table to the guard, who took them slowly from her. He let his eyes drift down and examine the writing. He took a quick inhale.

This got the attention of the guard leaning against the wall. He strode forward and leaned over the shoulder of the second guard to read the paper's contents. Both guards then stared at Portia and Lady Harper, this time much more respectfully.

"Where's the rest of your convoy?" the younger guard asked.

"They're dead," Lady Harper said without emotion.

"All of them?"

"All of them. We were attacked last night between Coverack and Holne. You will find the bodies of eleven bandits in the forest, along with my kin."

Silence met this news. Portia cleared her throat, then awkwardly opened her bag and pulled out the two leather sheath sections: the ones with the palace guard insignia and the guards' names. She pushed those across the table as well. "Our palace escort was also killed."

The older guard swore at this then spoke out, anger and fear in his voice. "How do we know you didn't kill them?"

"Why would we kill them? And if we did, why would we bring the evidence to you?" Lady Harper's voice rose in pitch. She stared at them coldly. "All we are asking for is an escort. As is our right." She sat up ramrod straight, tension along her arms and back. It was the first emotional reaction Portia had seen from her.

The younger guard gave a placating motion to the older guard and turned to Portia and Harper. "My apologies. Of course, it would make no sense for you to do such a thing. I hope you can understand our upset at our fellow guardsmen's deaths."

Lady Harper nodded, the anger in her body dissipating a little. "Regardless, we need an escort."

"I understand, ma'am."

"Lady Harper."

"Lady Harper," the younger guard said. He rose. "Our captain is out on patrol. He will be back shortly with the rest of today's crew. Can I offer you some refreshments? We can wait for their return together."

Lady Harper narrowed her eyes at the young guard but finally nodded acquiescence. He led Lady Harper and Portia to a small side room off the main guard area and left them to find seating in the tiny room, closing the door behind him. Portia and Lady Harper sat on the low couch facing the door. It felt too low to Portia, placing them in a vulnerable position. It took all her willpower to not pace the room while they waited.

The door opened again and men's voices drifted in. The younger guard returned bearing a tray of tea and cookies he laid on the low table in front of them. He did not shut the door behind him when he left again, so voices from the main room drifted in.

One particularly deep voice exclaimed, "Those wretched bandits. We need more help—and we get nothing. Now we're expected to escort two strangers to the border? We are already short-staffed." Mutters of agreement sounded, followed by the thump of a fist slammed on the table. The outer room quieted.

Portia looked at Lady Harper, her eyes wide. Lady Harper sipped her drink and didn't seem concerned at all. "How can you be so calm?" Portia asked.

"Our treaties are very important to both kingdoms. The guardsmen of the city know that, regardless of whatever else is going on here. Something ill is afoot—those bandits are a sign of it—but it is not our concern at the moment. Bandits will be the least of our concerns if we do not focus in dealing with the omens of the future." Lady Harper finished her drink and set the cup on the table.

The skeptic in Portia thought maybe Lady Harper was delusional. The angry tone from the guards just now did not sound like the voices of someone interested in helping them. Perhaps they didn't have a choice. But if it was as Lady Harper said, then the guards must help them, and probably hate them for it while doing so. Dread gnawed at Portia. She did not want to deal with angry guards any more than she wanted to deal with murderous bandits.

Her thoughts were interrupted by Lady Harper. "I have a question for you, Portia. It seems you have a great deal of magic, yet you use so little of it. When we were attacked, could you have done other things?"

Heat rose in Portia's face at the question. She had wondered the same thing, but her magic was not very strong. Perhaps she could have tried to freeze all the attackers, only to give them all a slight chill instead of encasing them in ice. Maybe it would've been better to freeze one than to have diffused her energy into making duplicates. And then there was the warning from Professor Aelric and Professor Hilda to not show too much magic.

She looked down at the ground as she spoke. "I-I... My magic is not that strong. But perhaps I did not make the best choice. I'm sorry. I'm still learning." Daring to make eye contact with the elf, she continued. "I'm not supposed to show my magic to others—at least not too much of it."

"Why is that?" Lady Harper tilted her head in inquiry.

"Because a human who can do so much different magic is known as a Jack. I can't explain it better than the professors did at our meeting. It is an omen of a dire need upcoming. And apparently it makes me a target." Portia put down her half-finished drink. "Attention is not always a good thing."

Lady Harper looked at Portia thoughtfully. "Perhaps that is why those strange bandits were so interested in our group."

Portia hoped not. They were terrifying. And large. She didn't want those sorts of people after her specifically.

Her thoughts were interrupted by the entrance of a larger, older guardsman with an air of authority about him. His hair was white and cut close to his scalp. He entered the small room and grinned, laugh lines wrinkling his face. He sat down informally on the coffee table in front of Portia and Lady Harper after pushing aside the plates there.

"Greetings. I'm the captain here. My lieutenant has briefed me a little on your troubles and shown me your papers. We would be happy to escort you, but we cannot do so today. We're hard-pressed for men at the moment, and as you well know, there is a bandit problem lately." His face grew serious. "I am sorry to hear of your convoy. You have my condolences."

Lady Harper nodded acknowledgment. "Thank you. And my condolences to you as well."

The captain slapped his knee in the ensuing awkward silence. "Well, it's a rough life we choose. It seems to be getting rougher all the time." He rose to leave. "We can go tomorrow."

Lady Harper spoke up quickly. "We need a horse. We lost all but one."

The captain stopped in his tracks and turned to look at her. "I can't give you one—we don't even have enough for ourselves."

"I can give you gold."

He waved away Lady Harper's offer. "Some things are more important than gold, like security. The best I can do is I can rent you a guardsman's horse for the journey. One gold piece."

Portia was shocked at the price. They should be able to buy a horse for that, not merely rent one for the journey.

The guardsman saw the look on Portia's face and answered her before she said a word. "And if you think that's unfair, feel free to buy one in town. I guarantee you'll find none. Just be here tomorrow morning with your gold, ready to go. We leave at dawn." He called out one last instruction while walking out the door. "My lieutenant will return your papers on the way out."

Sunshine was still beating down onto the town square when they exited the guardhouse. Portia saw the clothier shop a few doors down. It was open. "There is a shop I want to visit."

"We have some time to kill. As urgent as our task is, I don't think it's worth risking the journey without a guard. We should buy some supplies at the market while we're at it."

Portia nodded. The market would be open for a few more

hours. She wanted to visit the clothing store first. She pointed the way.

The store's interior looked just as she remembered it last time—dim, and filled with beautiful things. There were a few customers scattered within it, but it was not nearly as crowded as the square outside. The quietness of the shop was soothing to Portia. She didn't like the loud noises outside, nor the constant jostling of walking through the market crowds. Too many hours of her childhood had been spent trying to pick-pocket just such crowded markets.

Alice, the shop owner, came around a shelf of clothing and greeted Lady Harper and Portia. She looked just the same as she had last time Portia had seen her. Her hair was still blonde, and it was still impossible to tell how old she was. The familiarity reassured Portia.

The shopkeeper did not react at all to Lady Harper being an elf. Instead, she nodded calmly, giving a small bow. Portia was gratified when she thought she saw a flicker of recognition in Alice's eyes.

"How can I help you ladies?"

"I was hoping for a new outfit," Portia said, not sure how to begin. "I think the last outfit I bought here brought me luck. I could use more of that." She looked around at the kirtles hanging around the shop and quickly added, "Not another kirtle. I want something I can feel... something that's easy to move in. And..." Her face turned red. She wasn't sure how unusual her next request would be. "Something I can do sword work in. And fight."

Alice's face betrayed no emotion, but her eyes twinkled a

bit. "Of course. I can help you with that." The shopkeeper's calm acceptance was in sharp contrast to the wide eyes of two nearby female customers who had overheard Portia. The customers set down the material they had been holding and scurried out the door.

Alice turned her attention towards Lady Harper. "And for you, my lady?"

Lady Harper gave Alice a small grin. Portia thought, somehow, that Lady Harper liked Alice. She had no idea if she was just imagining it. "I had some fighting leathers that have become irreparably stained. I would like to replace those—if you have something sufficiently small to fit me."

"Of course. I am sure I will be able to do that as well."

As the shopkeeper turned and walked to the back wall shelving, Lady Harper turned to Portia and raised her eyebrows. She had a half smile. Portia hoped that was a good sign.

The shopkeeper called out over her shoulder while looking over her ready-made clothes, "Do you still favor black and red?"

Portia realized she was talking to her. "I was hoping for something different this time."

"Very well. We are off to a good start in that regard since you have not had to visit the well this time."

Portia's face flamed. Lady Harper looked at her again, this time her face starkly curious. Portia turned away and pretended to be looking at a dress hanging over a changing room door. She did not want to explain the fact that she had been so filthy last time she had visited this shop that she had been banished to the backyard to bathe before being allowed to try on any clothing. It was mortifying.

Portia was grateful that Lady Harper did not press the issue. Instead, after a moment, she turned and wandered around looking at the wares while waiting for the shopkeeper to return.

It didn't take long. Alice came back bearing two outfits. One was a cream leather ensemble that resembled Lady Harper's original white fighting leathers. But this outfit was richer, stitched with what looked like gold reinforced thread. It was gorgeous. Lady Harper sighed in appreciation while touching the detailed stitching.

The clothes Alice brought back to Portia were even finer. They were a dark green pant and doublet top, with a fine linen shirt underneath. There was even a jacket that matched. The material felt like heavy canvas—and indeed was thick— but also soft. It was not as stiff as it looked but somehow, she thought, was just as strong as heavy duck cloth.

They tried on the outfits and, miraculously, both fit exceedingly well. The styling of the cream leather was similar enough to Lady Harper's original leathers that Portia suspected it was not made in this shop. How did it get here? How often could there be a need for elf-sized garments?

Portia's outfit hugged her body but still allowed for move-ment. She tested the pants by crouching and was pleased to note there was no binding. She could duck and move and fight in these pants. They were perfect. The same was true of the top, and even of the jacket. She wanted to pull out her longest knife, the one she wielded as a sword, and test it, but was afraid to do so in the tight confines of the shop. Mimicking the motions she would use in such a battle, she found the garments to be perfect.

Portia was happy but not surprised to find the price of these clothes were, again, reasonable. Or maybe unreasonably inexpensive. But Alice did not seem concerned. She had set the prices herself. And the asking price was so low that even Lady Harper did not haggle, instead handing over the coins without a word of protest.

By the time they were done in the shop and had secured some provisions at the last of the vendors open on the market, it was dinnertime. They went back to the inn to pay for rooms for the night.

Portia had been blissfully distracted all day, but as night approached her thoughts turned to their journey starting again tomorrow. The first day of her trip to Rocabarra had been filled with bloodshed and violence. She hoped the remainder of the trip would not be similar. In either case, she had to face it tomorrow.

8

P ortia did not sleep well that night. She kept waking, though thankfully she did not have any nightmares. The third time her eyes opened to the dark room she gave a large sigh and sat up. She might as well rise.

She opened the shutters over the window; there was not a hint of sunrise. It was still the middle of the night and the stars shone brightly over the dark town. It would be hours before Lady Harper rose and they would eat breakfast. Only then would they leave for the guardhouse.

Using a hot ember from the fireplace, she lit a candle. She pulled the translated book from her bag, the one that Aelric had created for her. So many things had happened since he had given it to her that she hadn't been able to look at it until now.

Opening the book under the dim candlelight, she read a middle section at random. It looked like a diary. It was written by someone—she couldn't tell if it was male or female—who described a boat journey they were on. It talked about the cold water and the dark night sky. These were things she understood. But there were other things that were odd to her. The writer was surprised that there was only one moon in the sky. They were also unhappy that the darkness of night had gone on for so long. They went on to describe their relief when the sun finally rose, and even though the light was annoyingly yellow, it was better than the dark and cold of night.

Perplexed, Portia flipped to the front of the book. Maybe she would understand it better if she read it from the beginning. But that was not as much help as she hoped. Indeed, it started in a confusing way. It talked of stepping into the boat from the Holy Gate. Apparently there had been a rush of people coming out of the gate and onto boats that were waiting for them. For some reason, the boats had to be small and narrow, which sounded dangerous on the rough sea described in the book.

Portia had only seen one harbor in any detail—the harbor at Valencia. There was nothing in the Valencia harbor that could be called a 'gate'. People entered their boats from the piers. Nothing about the piers restricted the size of the boat, at least nothing that she knew about.

While there was a harbor in Coverack, since both cities were on the same sea, Portia had never spent any time in it. She had seen it from the seawall that edged the city one day, but she had been distracted by all the goings-on at the festival that day and so had not looked all that closely. It had looked much like Valencia's harbor, just four times as large, if not larger. She would have to ask the guards if they knew of a structure called a gate within a harbor. Or Lady Harper. Portia doubted Lady Harper would know of it since the elves were landlocked, but it was still worth asking about.

Reading on, she realized the writer was a warrior. There was a long section complaining about how difficult it was to keep their weapons dry. They also complained that the land was further than they expected it to be and they were worried about exhaustion overcoming them before they could make their strike. They were the forward guard of some force and were charged with preparing the way for more people to come. Nothing in the book spoke about magic, which Portia thought was odd for a book that had been in the Library of Mages.

She was so distracted by her reading that she jumped when a knock sounded on her door. Looking up, she realized the sky was turning a light pink. It was time to get ready. Putting the book down on the bed, she walked to the door. "Who is it?"

A muffled voice said from the other side, "Lady Harper. I have our breakfast packed. We need to leave in five."

"Okay," Portia said. She rushed to change into her traveling clothes and pack up her belongings.

The hall of the inn was dark when she exited her room. The silence felt odd. She felt her way to the stairs and made it down to the exterior door and exited. Lady Harper was waiting outside holding the reins to their horse. They walked across the empty square as birds chirped in the nearby trees.

The guard escort was waiting outside the guardhouse. The surly guard and the younger one that Portia guessed was the lieutenant were amongst the waiting men. There were six in total. It did not feel like enough to Portia. There had been two Coverack guards and eight other elves that had perished on their journey to Holne. Portia's stomach tightened at the thought of returning to the road with these reduced numbers. She hoped they didn't meet a large bandit group. Perhaps they had killed off the main group.

But at least they could handle an attack by a smaller force.

The surly guard gave a snort as they walked up then glanced at the sun just as it peeked above the horizon. In a low tone he said, "Just in time, eh? Thought we might have to leave you."

Lady Harper looked at him as a small smile played across her face. "Wouldn't that be a little odd if the point was to escort us?"

The younger guard stepped in between the two, heading off the confrontation. "We are also patrolling for bandits. The route has simply been arranged to go in the direction you need to go."

Lady Harper nodded graciously at this and said nothing further.

The younger guard gave Lady Harper and Portia a bow, which elicited a disgusted snort from the surly one. "I never gave you my name before. I am Lieutenant Jassock. Please ask me directly if there's anything you need." He addressed Lady Harper, but his eyes kept looking to his surly guard companion, letting him know the words were for him as well. It was a warning to keep the peace.

Keeping eye contact, he walked over to the surly guard and clapped him on the back and then turned to Lady Harper and Portia. "My pleasant companion here is Zeck." His eyes laughed as he introduced the unhappy guard, who growled under his breath. Portia hoped she would not have to ride near the glowering man. "But enough pleasantries, we must be off."

At his command, his guardsmen moved quickly. Portia took the reins of the horse that were handed to her while Lady Harper and the guards mounted their own rides. The group followed Lieutenant Jassock out of the square to the northeast and towards the road leading to Rocabarra.

Portia enjoyed the morning ride. The town was quiet as most folks were still asleep in their beds. The birds were just beginning to wake and made pleasant songs in the nearby trees. Lady Harper handed her a sandwich of cheese and bread. The bread was chewy but tasted good, the cheese of a good quality. She must've purchased these items the night before, for even the bread smith was not awake yet.

They passed through a wide expansive plain, tall grasses waving in the morning breeze. The air smelled of freshly turned earth. Spring was fast upon the kingdom, and the farmers were making use of the time to prepare for spring planting. In the distance, she spied at least one farmer out with his oxen. Up to the right, she could see the dark mass that was a forest, and beyond that there were smudges on the horizon that Portia thought might be mountains. The plains were reassuring in the lack of cover they provided for any would-be ambushers, even if they provided no cover for the traveling group themselves. Portia wished the grass was just a bit shorter but consoled herself that no horse could be hidden even so. And bandits on foot were much less formidable than any bandits mounted on horseback.

The guards themselves were silent. Portia could not tell if it was through discipline or boredom, or concentration on the surrounding land.

As the day wore on and the sun rose, the rhythmic steps of the horse rocked Portia into a light daze. She was not quite asleep but had difficulty maintaining her alertness. She hoped the guards were more used to this sort of journey and were paying better attention. Portia knew it was the wrong attitude, but no matter how hard she tried, her eyelids kept drooping down. Somehow she managed to stay awake enough to not fall off her horse.

By the time the sun reached noon they were close to the forest on the right side of the road. Anxiety gripped Portia's stomach as she looked towards the dark mass of trees. She hoped they were not stopping there for lunch, not after the events of two days prior when they had been attacked at such a place.

As if reading her mind, Lieutenant Jassock motioned for the group to tighten up and to stay on the far side of the road, away from the forest. They were not taking the risk of stopping there. Portia breathed a small sigh of relief, but she could not stop herself from continually looking to the right to try to see into the trees, to see if there were any men or horses within.

But eventually even the fear of the forest receded as hours wore on. The trees were not as close anymore and were soon left behind. Without the distraction of constantly looking into the woods, Portia's awareness shifted to her growling stomach and the way her back and legs ached. She shifted uncomfortably in her saddle, unused to riding horseback, much less for such a long time. Perhaps they would stop somewhere tonight where she could take a long hot bath.

Lady Harper drew her horse alongside Portia's, offering her a small twig. Portia looked at it curiously but didn't take it. Lady Harper waved the stick towards her, urging her to accept it. "Chew on it. It will make you feel better. Then you'll stop wiggling around and making the guards behind you giggle." Lady Harper's eyes danced as she spoke.

Portia turned around to see three guards suddenly looking away and scanning the horizon from edge to edge. They looked anywhere but at her. Portia quickly turned around again, her back stiff with embarrassment, face flaming all the way to her ears. They had been laughing at her. She grabbed the stick from Lady Harper and bit down on it hard, chewing it as fast as she could.

Lady Harper burst into laughter. "It's not so bad. Every one of us can remember when we first learned to ride."

Portia wanted to believe her, but she was still mortified. She couldn't bring herself to speak.

The screech of metal on metal pulled Portia to alertness immediately. There was something in the grass to their right. Something or someone between them and the forest, which was now behind them and to the right.

Lieutenant Jassock turned his horse quickly and looked around. He scanned the grasses and surrounding area then waved the group to ride down the left side of the road, away from where the noise had come. The land dropped lower there, and they were more protected from whatever was on the far side of the road. Portia hoped there was nothing on the side as well.

"Stay here," Jassock commanded to Lady Harper and Portia. Lady Harper did not look pleased but nodded in assent. He rounded up his men to form a loose semicircle and move them towards the noise in the grass on the far side of the road.

Portia didn't think this was a great idea. The guardsmen were noisy. They couldn't help it with all the gear on their horses. She thought it would be better to sneak up on whoever was there. Who or whatever was in the grass had lost the element of surprise so there was no reason for their group to not claim it back. Not drawing attention to yourself was one of the key rules she had learned as a thief. And Lieutenant Jassock and his men were too loud to do anything but draw attention.

She slid off her horse and handed the reins to Lady Harper who raised her brows. Portia held up one finger to her mouth, hoping Lady Harper would cooperate and be quiet. Lady Harper did one better and slipped from her own horse, indicating she wanted to follow Portia. Portia nodded. Lady Harper took the reins of the two horses and set them under a large rock in the grass at their feet. Portia hoped this would be enough to keep the horses from wandering.

Portia pointed to the far side of the road. The two of them crouched low and ran through the grass to the edge of the road, peering over to the far side. The guardsmen were walking their horses through the tall grasses looking for something, but nothing else was visible. Portia's ears pricked at the sound of metal on metal once again. It was the same sound as before but quieter. It was not from the guardsmen or their horses. It was off to the side of the guardsmen semicircle. They would miss it.

Portia ran across the road, carefully placing her feet so as to not drag them and make noise. Lady Harper followed her so silently that Portia would not have known she was with her if she had not seen the elf running with her own eyes. Portia wished she could be that stealthy. It put any of the thieves she had known to shame.

They made it to the far side and crouched in the tall grass. They were now on the same side of the road as the guardsmen and whoever was hiding in the grasses. Running quickly, Portia pulled out her long knife and headed directly towards the sound. She stopped about twenty feet from where she estimated she had last heard it. She breathed through her mouth, the sound of air through her nostrils sounding far too loud in her ears. She held as still as she could and listened, her ears and hands tingling as she strained to hear any more noises.

There it was again, but softly. Whoever it was couldn't seem to sit still. It sounded like two people shifting on their feet. The metal must have been something on them, some weapon or armor or something similar. Portia turned to Lady Harper and held up two fingers. Lady Harper nodded back, then motioned forward. Portia nodded in agreement with the command to attack, then mouthed the words one, two, three. On three, both she and Lady Harper rushed forward.

What they found were two men—skinny beyond belief—crouched in the grasses. They did indeed have swords but dropped them in fright when Lady Harper and Portia appeared with their weapons drawn. Just to be safe, Portia sent a river of ice towards each man, attaching them to the grasses growing around them. She had been thinking about how to fight off an attack during their journey and had decided fire was a bad idea. It would create too much smoke and could alert possible bandits around them of their presence, something she did not want to do. Especially since the last time they drew the attention of someone it had cost them most of their party. So, for this journey, at least as far as the men would know, her only power was that of ice and cryomancy. She would follow the instructions she was given to not reveal herself as a Jack.

The men squeaked as the ice encased them and came up to their waists. Portia sent a band of ice around their mouths to quiet them, carefully avoiding their nostrils. She didn't want to kill them.

Running around the edges of the small clearing the men were in, she didn't see any other people. There were only bent grasses where the men had walked.

A wave of exhaustion overcame Portia. Running that much magic at once took a lot out of her. She sank to one knee, feeling slightly ill.

Another loud sound came from about fifty feet away.

Lady Harper jumped up to look around but stayed where she was when she saw two guardsmen in the vicinity. Portia was vaguely aware of a struggle in the distance but blackness was encroaching on her vision and she felt weak and about to faint.

Minutes later, Lieutenant Jassock rode into the small clearing with a third skinny man flung across his saddle. His normally laughing eyes were enraged. "What are you doing here? You were told to stay. *Ordered* to stay."

Lady Harper rose to her full height, which barely reached the stirrups of the horse. "And yet here we are, having found our quarry before you did."

"And nearly dying for it," Lieutenant Jassock spit out. He dumped the unconscious man at their feet and then threw down a quiver of arrows and a long bow. "It was a trap. Luckily we kept it from springing shut."

Lady Harper was uncharacteristically quiet at that. Portia sat back. The blackness in her vision was receding, but she was not well enough yet to stand.

Several of the other guardsmen rode up. One of them offered a canteen of water to Portia and she took it and drank deeply, gratefully. The water tasted good. It was cool in her stomach. She held the canteen up to her forehead to allow the coolness to settle on her face.

Zeck rode up leading Lady Harper and Portia's horses. "We're all clear. I rescued these before we ended up carrying these two idiots the whole way to the border."

Normally, Lieutenant Jassock would have said something to curb Zeck's rudeness but this time he merely pursed his lips and nodded. Portia felt bad at that. She did not want to lose their champion. Having an entire escort of hostile guardsmen was not an appealing prospect.

Lieutenant Jassock dismounted and kicked the weapons away from the two men on the ground. Portia realized with shock that what she thought were swords were not nearly so formidable—one was a carved wooden replicate, which would have been useless against a real blade, and the other was a rusty piece of metal so riddled with corrosion and holes it did not look like it could withstand a single blow. These men were in no position to offer battle. What could they be doing there?

Jassock walked up to the men and noticed the ice over their mouths. He turned with a questioning look to Lady Harper and Portia. Lady Harper shrugged and pointed to Portia. Taking a rock, Lieutenant Jassock chipped the ice and pulled it away from the skin, leaving it red and sore around the men's mouths. He held his hand to one man's face, warming it, while another guardsman did the same to the other man. The men were shivering under the weak spring sun. The captured men looked down and refused to meet the eyes of anyone in the party.

The unconscious man groaned and rolled his head a bit on the ground, coming to. Lady Harper went to his side and checked his body. "This one is all right, with perhaps a sprained ankle. It is hard to tell. It's not broken, but it is swelling quickly." Zeck grunted at this. He didn't care how injured the man was.

Lieutenant Jassock sat back on the ground and faced the two men. Portia did not think it was a coincidence he chose to do that instead of standing above them, his weapon at their necks. He was good enough with people to get on their level. "What are you doing here? No good, I am guessing."

The bolder of the two men encased in ice flicked his eyes up to Lieutenant Jassock and spit out in a belligerent tone, "We weren't bothering you. No reason to be attacking us so."

"Did you show such restraint only because there were so many of us?" Lieutenant Jassock asked. "That is hardly the basis for a good relationship. Or were you merely the bait so someone else could attack us?" Jassock nodded at the third man sprawled on the ground.

The belligerent man looked away, his jaw flexing. "You dunno know us. We're good people. It's not our fault."

Portia looked at the men closely. Neither one looked like they'd had a full meal for months; their jaws were sharp lines against their skinny necks. Their clothes hung off them, making them look like scarecrows and not adult men.

"Okay, let's go off that assumption: you're good men. Then what are you doing out here where there are no houses, no farms, no way to live? The only thing you could have been doing was preying on people on the road. Unfortunately for you, this group was too large. Help me understand how you are good people." Lieutenant Jassock pulled a blade of grass and stuck it in his teeth, chewing as he stared at the two men. He waited patiently for their answer. Everyone watched and said nothing.

Silence held for a few minutes, punctuated only by the sound of the wind through the grass and the few noises of insects calling. The belligerent man finally looked up again at

Lieutenant Jassock. He pulled himself up as much as he could while still encased in the ice. It was melting around him, and he would soon be sitting in a puddle. Nevertheless, he tried to show some pride. "I'm a farmer. I had a large farm and a family and helpers. I had twenty-three cattle. Then *them* came along… and destroyed it." He spat to the ground next to him. He lifted his chin defiantly. "Did any of you come to help, eh? No. You fancy guardsmen let my farm be destroyed and my family gone. And whoever is left is starving. You call me a bad man? You all 'tis evil as they are."

Lieutenant Jassock did not say anything to this. He continued to chew the grass, waiting for any further words to come. When none came, he finally spoke again. "That does not sound good. Who destroyed your farm?"

The belligerent man did not look at Lieutenant Jassock. He refused to look at any of the guards. His jaw worked.

"I can't protect you if you don't tell me," Lieutenant Jassock said, leaning in to emphasize his point.

Lady Harper walked and stood in front of the belligerent man so he could see her. His eyes flickered to her face nervously. "Did by chance any of those attackers have a tattoo or a brand of a diamond on their forearms?"

The eyes of both captive men opened wider. The one who had not spoken before whispered, "anti-magickers" as he struggled in a panic against the ice still around his legs.

"Answer the lady," Lieutenant Jassock said firmly.

"Dunno know what you're talking about," the belligerent man said as he glared at the other captive, an edge of hysteria in his voice.

The other man finally managed to free his legs and scrambled to his feet, shakily trying to run. One of the guardsmen grabbed him and easily restrained him. The man's eyes were wide, the white showing as he looked around. His fear was palpable.

Lady Harper turned to address Lieutenant Jassock. "They know of the men that attacked us, but I fear we will get no answers while they are in this state. If these attackers are destroying farms, perhaps that explains the rise in bandits around here. Survival is a powerful motivator."

Lieutenant Jassock nodded thoughtfully at this. He rose, indicating for his men to take the captives. Two of the men had to help the man with the sprained ankle. "We'll ride with these three as guests. When we have some distance from here we can eat and decide what to do next."

At the mention of food, the captives calmed down a little and did not struggle nearly so hard.

To Portia's relief, she was recovered from her efforts with the magic and did not need any assistance getting on her horse.

The captives had no horses of their own so had to share with the guardsmen in the convoy. Portia was glad Jassock didn't make them walk since they looked so thin already. They put an hour's distance between them and the fight location then stopped for a break. Jassock handed each one of the captives a generous hunk of bread and cheese, as well as a piece of fruit. The men tore into the food, wolfing it down. One of them nearly choked on the dry bread, and a guardsman had to come up behind him and clap him on the back, shoving a canteen in his hands to drink from and ease the bread down.

Portia chewed her own lunch, unable to draw her eyes away from the starving men. She felt bad for them. She knew the pain of not having enough to eat and how it would make you do things you never thought you would. These men were desperate. Perhaps they were not bad after all, just hungry and terrified.

After they had all finished their meal, Lady Harper approached the man with the sprained ankle. She touched it gently with a few fingers and he jumped, biting back a yelp of pain. She began quietly singing a tune, thumping her hand on the ground in a complex rhythm. Portia's neck tingled as she felt the magic flowing from Lady Harper to the man. Portia imagined she could see the magic curing his ankle, reducing the swelling before her eyes. The tension in the man's face eased. His brow, before furrowed tightly, relaxed, and his eyes drooped into sleepy exhaustion.

Lady Harper finished her song, eyeing the man's leg critically. The man himself let his eyes close and he drooped forward, seeming to fall asleep in the spot he was sitting.

Zeck whistled under his breath. "Impressive trick there." It was the first nice thing, or the closest thing to a nice thing, Portia had ever heard him say about either one of them.

Lady Harper turned to eye him. "Trick? The man would slow us down the way he was. I fixed that."

"Or just helped him be ready to escape," Lieutenant Jassock said. It was an excellent point, but even so he didn't seem angry. "It's good to not have people in pain. They do stupid things when they're hurting." He looked at Lady Harper closely. "How did you do that by the way? I've not seen that sort of magic before."

"It's elf magic. Not for you humans," Lady Harper said, a touch of haughty disdain in her voice.

Zeck burst out laughing at this. "And there you go, back to being a stuck-up jerk."

"You think I'm saying this just to be rude? Let's see what you can do," Lady Harper said, challenge dripping from her words.

Zeck held up his hands. "Not me. I have no magic to speak of. Why do you think I'm in the guards protecting you? But these others, some of them might." He motioned to the rest of the guards and the captives.

Lady Harper nodded at the challenge. "All right, let us see what we shall see."

The next hour was spent with Lady Harper trying to teach the rhythm and song to those around her. Only Portia was able to follow along closely enough to feel some tingles of magic along her neck. Belatedly, the admonishment to not show her status as Jack came back to her, and she intentionally made an error in her rhythm so her efforts would not be effective. When, in the end, not a single person was able to do the magic that Lady Harper had done, the elf merely laughed it off and said the lesson was over. Portia was not sure if Lady Harper had noticed what she had done.

At the end of lunch, Lieutenant Jassock stood before the three captives. "It's not for me to decide your fates, but I cannot let you stay here to harass travelers along this road.

Come with us to meet with our captain and share what knowledge you have." The men did not meet his gaze. "We can say honestly you did not attack us directly and will vouch for that to the captain. But he needs to know of these events if he is to do anything to help your people. Our people."

At their lack of response, he changed tactics. "And we will feed you as well as we eat ourselves while you're with us. We will also help your families as much as we are able." After a moment, the three men nodded grudgingly at this. Portia was not surprised it was the food that persuaded the men to cooperate. Trust was hard to come by, and the men had already lost so much, but sustenance was a necessity and must be had.

They traveled further north and east on the road for the next several days without additional incident. The grassy plains gave way to the gentle slopes and then the steep rocky hills that marked the edge of a large mountain range. The mountains rose so high their peaks were topped in snow, even in spring. The horses struggled with the incline and the thin air as they climbed the hills towards the mountains ahead. Even Portia felt a little faint as they climbed higher and higher.

Finally they came to a pass between two high mountain peaks. It looked handmade, carved through stone. Portia could not imagine how it had been done. The road upon it was so deep that it was in perpetual shadow with no sunlight ever reaching it directly. The men and horses rode through the dim passage filled with rocks and boulders and small bits of vegetation. Little could survive in the twilight.

When they emerged on the far side of the pass, they

looked down on a land spreading out before them. It was twinkling emerald green and bright under the spring sun. Portia felt like she could breathe again. She hadn't even realized she'd been holding her breath through the mountains.

One of the captive men gasped. Portia's eyes focused more closely on the land down below, and she saw what he was reacting to: a huge structure ran along the base of the mountains between the rocky peaks and the lush land beyond it. It was as green as the land itself, but rose up several stories high, and was just as wide, if not wider, than it was tall. Inside its walls was another similar structure, just as wide, that ran parallel to it. The paired walls ran for miles and miles in each direction, disappearing into the fog of distance. Portia could see no end to it. Spires and peaks ran along both walls, providing places for soldiers and archers to lie in wait. Defensive battlements dotted the walls along their entire lengths. It was a structure of war—or of defense at least.

It was an enormous barrier meant to keep someone out.

Lady Harper drew her horse up alongside Portia's. "The Eternal Wall. We are approaching the passage through it known as the Moss Gate. The wall is thousands of years old. It has fulfilled its function."

Portia looked to Lady Harper, her eyes wide with wonder. She had never seen anything like that in her life. "Why is it called the Moss Gate?"

"Because it is covered with moss, but more so because it is a living embodiment of a race's will. It protects from those who would do them harm."

"It protects humans?" Portia asked. Zeck snorted behind her.

Lady Harper's laugh burst from her chest. "No, you silly girl. It protects elves *from* humans. Elves built that." She stopped laughing and stared at Portia, her large eyes fixed on Portia's. Suddenly, Portia felt ill at ease with her escort. How did Lady Harper really feel about the people around her?

9

They rode down the far side of the mountain pass in silence. The approach to the Eternal Wall took most of the day. Portia noticed with trepidation that the structure was even bigger than it looked the closer they came to it. It was more impressive than the palace in Coverack. The scale was beyond anything she had ever seen before. When they finally reached the bottom of the road leading from the mountain, she felt impossibly small compared to the vast structure laid out ahead of her. What was she doing traveling into the lands of a race that created this? Fear bit the back of her throat, stronger than it had been at any time since she had taken the test of elf magic to get here. She hoped it was not all a mistake. If the elves who had created this were afraid of the future, then what possible horrors could be in store with the coming of The Splintering? Her stomach quailed at the possibilities.

Even the normally jocular guardsmen were silent as they approached the soaring outer wall of the Moss Gate. Four arches marked the opening in the wall, rising several stories above the rest of the wall itself. The entire thing was dripping in moss and vegetation. It looked like a living creature laid low upon the land, waiting for those who would defy it.

Lady Harper rode to the front of the group as they approached the arches of the main gate, her back straight. Portia thought Lady Harper's chin was higher, her bearing more regal, as they approached her homeland.

Four elf guards rode from the gate to meet them. They wore uniforms of green, brown, and black. If not for their horses, it would have been hard to distinguish them from the green wall in the background. It was clever camouflage.

At the sight of the approaching soldiers, Lieutenant Jassock called for the group to halt. Lady Harper turned to him, her face tight with irritation, but she also stopped her horse to wait for the advanced guard. As they waited, Portia could smell the dew on the grass and feel the sunshine on her shoulders. It was a welcome change from the dry air in the mountains and the lack of sun in the deep mountain pass.

When they were within hailing distance, the leader of the elf group wasted no time on niceties. "State your business," he said, his tone brisk. He eyed the humans but addressed his words to Lady Harper. His eyes flicked from human face to human face. Portia thought he was uncomfortable with so many of them in front of him.

Lady Harper held her hand up to Jassock, forestalling any

possible response on his part. "It is royal business. I am Lady Harper of the Meadows. I am surprised to not be recognized." The last part was said in reproach.

The guard's eyes focused on her, recognition coming slowly. He sucked in a breath and then looked around the group again only to return to her. "Where is your convoy? We were expecting nine."

"Things have not gone well. Indeed, I am indebted to these humans for their escort and their adherence to our treaties."

These words surprised Portia. They were true, no doubt, but she did not expect Lady Harper to so easily credit the humans.

They also apparently surprised the elf guards as well. His eyes widened slightly and then he nodded. "Come to the gate then." He raised his arm and waved twice quickly to the guard in the tower behind him. The audible creak of gears and chains and a massive iron gate raising followed quickly.

He led the group, elves and humans alike, towards the gate. Once there, Lady Harper and Portia dismounted. The animals were jumpy. Portia could feel magic emanating off the walls of the structure and the gate itself. She thought perhaps the animals were aware of it as well, even if they did not understand what was making them uneasy. It was difficult to control her horse, and she held on to the reins tightly, hoping it did not decide to bolt.

Lady Harper came to her and took her reins and led both horses to Lieutenant Jassock, who was still on his horse, as were all the other humans. Lady Harper looked up at him, tilting her head. "You aren't coming in?"

Lieutenant Jassock looked around at the vast structure, then back to Lady Harper. "No, I think it's best that we go. I'd not be comfortable going inside those gates, treaty or no." His face turned a little red as his eyes flicked to the elf guards.

Lady Harper stared at him, pursing her lips. Finally she spoke. "Very well. I'll give you our horse, in addition to the negotiated payment for the second one. It would be unkind to keep ours here. It is not used to... this setting." She dug in her bag and handed over the gold coin. "I wish you luck with these bandits. Please let your captain know our king and queen would be very grateful for any information of those with the diamond tattoos. It is of utmost importance."

At the mention of the diamond tattoos, the captives' eyes flared. Between their jumpiness and the panic of the horses beneath them, it looked like they might bolt off at any second. It was only the discipline and control of the guards sharing the horses with the captive men that kept this from happening.

Lieutenant Jassock looked at the horses' reactions and the strain it was putting on his men, and his brows furrowed. He took the coin and the reins from Lady Harper, nodding curtly. "I'll consider the horse advance payment for the information we will provide you."

They rode off without another word, leaving Lady Harper and Portia on the gravel pad in front of the enormous gate. Portia swallowed. She was surrounded by elves, and was in a land she knew nothing about except what little she had learned in history class. And that was not much. At that moment, she wished Mia was there with her lifelong education of the world. Portia realized ignorance was not a comfortable place.

The elves on horseback waited for Portia and Lady Harper to walk in the gate. They passed under the overhang several stories above them. The cool air from the leaves and the structure above them washed over Portia. The air was thick with moisture in the scent of green plants and rich earth. It reassured her. It was so different from the noise and the dirt and the smells of Valencia, where she had spent most of her life. To her surprise, she realized she would rather be here, even with this scare of the unknown and the challenges ahead.

Once inside the gate, they walked into a large courtyard and then crossed to a building nestled on the side of the inner wall, the wall she had seen from above. Elven soldiers walked in and out of the building, conducting normal business. One or two spied Portia and stared at her curiously, but they did not stop on their errands and continued on. Portia looked up at the battlements and saw elf archers staring as well from both walls, inner and outer. They were in a no-man's-land between the two structures. Portia tried to calculate how many soldiers they had if the walls were manned all along their length—it would be an incredible number to do so.

Entering the small building, Lady Harper walked purposely to the back corner where a decorated soldier sat behind a desk, an underling whispering furiously in his ear.

By the number of black and brown bars on his uniform, Portia guessed he was the ranking officer. It surprised her that his desk was in the open area along with all the other soldiers—yet another reminder that elves were not the same as humans. They might do things much differently.

At Lady Harper's approach, the soldier waved away the underling and rose, giving Lady Harper a deep bow. He walked around the desk to her. "Welcome back, Lady Harper. My condolences, and concern, at the lack of your guard."

Lady Harper nodded her head in acknowledgment. "That is appreciated. However, time is of the essence, and I must make my report to the king and queen. We require mounts."

"Understood," the soldier responded. "The ones that your convoy brought have been dispersed for the resupply, but we have two that we can spare for the moment. We were not expecting you for another month yet." Stark curiosity showed on his face.

But Lady Harper was not of a mind to indulge his desire to know exactly what happened. She spoke briskly. "My apologies. Our plans have changed, and it was not within our control to stop. We were both more successful and yet sadly, as you can see, much less successful than anticipated. We have secured the help we need but with conditions."

The soldier looked at Portia, then back at Lady Harper, his eyes narrowing at the possible connection between Portia and conditions set forth by the humans. He inhaled to speak again but thought better of it and exhaled, dropping the pen he had been holding on his desk. "Let it not be said I did not assist you for all possible success." He motioned to the door and led them out.

They walked around the building and along the inner wall to another gate. It was just as tall and wide as the outer gate, but without the complex carvings, overhang, and decorative greenery that made the outer gate so intimidating.

But they did not go through the large gate this time, instead going through a small door set into the wall next to the larger opening. The door was constructed of thick, one-foot-wide wood beams, reinforced on both sides with steel. Elf guards stood by on either side of the wall. At their superior's approach, they opened the door. It took considerable strength, and one soldier had to dig his heels into the earth as he leaned back to pull the door open on its hinges. Just before they went through, Portia looked up and saw a spout high in the wall above her. She knew enough of castle design from history class to know how the spout was used—boiling oil could be poured down it onto any invaders who made it to this part of the wall. This was a functional wall. It was meant to be used for defense.

Once inside the inner wall, Portia looked around and sucked in her breath at the beauty of the land in front of her. It was a deep, lush green. Plants grew with abandon. Even the fields themselves were thick with a variety of growth. It was a sharp contrast to the dry, dusty plains they had passed through on their way to the mountain pass. Herds of deer wandered around grazing on the fields. Portia's eyes could just barely pick out a fence at the far end of the field containing the animals.

The ranking soldier motioned to the inner guard by the door, drawing him close. Portia could not hear what he said to the guard, but the guard soon ran off to the building to their right. He returned moments later leading two deer. The deer had odd saddles attached to them, with long leather sleeves hanging down on either side. Portia's eyes widened. She looked to Lady Harper, who did not react as if anything odd was happening.

"Thank you, Commander. Your generous assistance is most appreciated," Lady Harper said.

She took one of the proffered sets of reins from the soldier and handed him her pack. She mounted the deer quickly, putting her legs into the long leather tubes on either side of the saddle and pulling tight laces that ran up along the back of them. A second soldier approached, taking the pack and strapping it to the back of Lady Harper's deer.

Portia found herself facing a small elf holding the reins to a deer. Horses were bad enough, but these deer were another thing entirely. Beyond the soldier she could see the deer running in the field. And leaping. They could jump their own body height or more. Would they do that with a rider aboard? This was not an animal she wanted to ride.

She looked askance at Lady Harper, but the elf's face was impassive. She motioned in irritation for Portia to mount her steed.

Portia swallowed and looked at the dark brown eyes of the deer. It could be worse. They could ask her to ride something more ferocious. At least the deer didn't want to eat her. She forced herself to breathe in deeply. She handed her pack to the waiting soldier, willing her hands to not shake. He showed her the mounting stirrup on the saddle, while the other elf soldier held on to the bridle of the deer to steady it. Portia was grateful she was not expected to handle the reins while trying to get into the saddle.

With a hop, Portia got one leg over the saddle. She had just settled down into the seat, her legs on either side of the animal, when the deer bucked. It jumped wildly and dumped Portia on the ground then leapt away, breaking free of the elf holding it.

Portia landed with a thump on the dewy grass. It knocked the breath out of her. She lay there staring up at the blue sky and feeling the water seep into her clothes. Dimly, she heard Lady Harper laughing. Portia groaned. She was definitely not a skilled rider.

"My young friend, you must get up," the commander said with a friendly smile as he leaned down and held out his hand. Portia took his hand and got to her feet, brushing grass and water from her backside.

Lady Harper brought her deer around to face Portia. "You will get used to these creatures. They are gentle but a little jumpy," she said, choking down a laugh at the word jumpy.

Oh well, Portia thought, *at least she's not mad*. "Why are we riding deer and not horses?" Portia asked, trying to keep the petulance out of her voice. She did not want to sound like a child but really, it was too much. She had just learned how to ride a horse.

"Because we are going to the capital city. It would take six days by horse. It only takes two by Sika," Lady Harper said.

Two days? These animals could travel three times faster than a horse? Now Portia *really* did not want to get on one. She shouldn't have asked why. Or maybe it was better to have some forewarning? Quickly, she thought about the journey and decided that no, it wasn't better to know about the speed of the deer. She did not want to go three times as fast as a horse.

But Lady Harper was not asking Portia's permission in the matter. They were going to ride the Sika deer. Lady Harper motioned to the leather tubes that her legs were inside of, the tubes that were attached to the saddle. "These braces will keep you mounted. You must get your legs in them quickly when you get in the saddle. The deer are a little feisty." Her mouth curved up into a little smile. "I think they secretly enjoy dumping their riders when they can. As you have found out."

Portia nodded at that. She could not bring herself to return Lady Harper's smile. She felt too silly and embarrassed. She vowed to herself that she would not complain. When the deer was brought back, she steeled herself, then walked forward and grabbed the saddle, put her foot into the stirrup, and mounted. This time, she managed to insert her leg into the leather tube when she got on and pulled the laces on the leather tight. She then put her other leg into the tube on that side of the saddle and pulled on those laces. When that was done, she was able to take her time to tighten the laces on each side and tie the leather into secure double knots. She did not want to be dumped again. It would be much worse if she landed on a rock. Getting dirt in her hair and clothes wasn't so bad by comparison.

Once her pack was securely attached behind her on the deer, she let it walk around a bit, carefully holding the reins back so it wouldn't race off. After a few moments, she nodded to Lady Harper that she was ready to go. They took their leave of the commander and started on the road away from the wall. The deer leapt forward onto the road, their hooves not even seeming to touch the ground. Portia's heart raced at the sudden speed. Her hair swept back as they rode. They were going so fast she had difficulty keeping her eyes open with the strong wind and was forced to squint, making the landscape a watery blur of green. Looking over, she noticed Lady Harper had donned a hat with clear glass lenses over her eyes. She needed to get some of those for herself.

After they had been riding for an hour, Lady Harper pulled up on her deer, grabbing Portia's reins as she did so to stop both of them. The sun was high overhead.

Lady Harper cleared her throat. "There is something you need to know."

Portia looked at her in concern. Now that they were deep in elf country, it did not seem the time to share concerns. Might she not have told Portia whatever it was before they set off on their journey?

"I have agreed to your queen's request because I had to do so. But I am not authorized to speak for my king except for saying he will listen to the request I make. You must prove yourself to our rulers to gain their trust. It is not a given. There is a long history of why that is so." Lady Harper stared at Portia. "Do you understand what I am telling you?"

Portia did not understand, not fully. Had she not proven herself at the trials back in Coverack? She had risked her very life to be here. Would they ask more of her than that? But she did not think any complaints would change the situation, so she had to take another tact. "Yes, my lady. What do you suggest I do?"

Lady Harper nodded with satisfaction. "We shall see how things go. I will give you more instructions when the time comes. The important thing is for you to not take anything for granted. A bad attitude will sink your chances of learning what you need to learn and our chances of a strong alliance to fight off the coming danger."

Portia could think of nothing to say to that. The whole situation was nerve-racking enough, but yet again she would have to prove herself and perhaps be forced to use social skills and court manners to achieve their ends—something she knew little about.

"Let's eat and then resume," Lady Harper said.

After lunch they continued on. At their stop, Lady Harper dug out another hat with goggles from her pack and gave it to Portia. Portia found riding so fast less nerve-racking when she could see.

She was sore and tired when they stopped for the evening and took shelter under a large tree to eat their supper. The deer were easy to care for, only needing water, for they could graze off the land. Lady Harper reassured her it was safe to sleep on the ground in their land, but Portia still slept fitfully that night, rousing from what she thought might have been a nightmare or perhaps just the stone underneath her back.

The next two days passed in a blur of green landscape. Towards the evening of the second day, they crested a hill and looked down on an enormous city that had been previously hidden by the rise. It was impressively large and sprawling. Colored spires and domes reached towards the sky. Curves abounded everywhere. Nothing was like the squares and rectangles of the human cities that Portia had lived in. Homesickness gripped her for just a moment but then passed. This was something new and exciting. She reminded herself to be grateful that she was getting a chance to see this part of the world, something that few humans could say.

"Let us rest here for a moment," Lady Harper said. She reached behind her and pulled out two sticks of jerky, handing one to Portia. "This is Rocabarra. Our capital. I wanted to point out the layout of the city, something you can only see from this vantage. Much like the Eternal Wall design, there are two walls in the construction. The inner wall marks the original city. It had been much smaller then. And wealthier. It was the summer houses of the royals and the nobles. But when the last splintering occurred..." Lady Harper said, pausing to look meaningfully at Portia. "... the nobles were forced to flee and make this city their permanent home. Many others were forced to come here as well, and the city could not contain them all as it was, forcing its expansion. That expansion is marked by the outer walls."

Portia squinted into the distance. She could just make out high red walls delineating the inner portion of the city. It was perhaps just a tenth of the total. The rest of the city sprawled around it, dense with buildings. The chaos of all the elves flooding to this location must have been huge. She swallowed nervously. Was this sort of massive change something humans would have to deal with in the future?

She tried to imagine the entire population of Coverack fleeing but could not do so. Where would they go anyway? The massive wall blocking access to the elf lands meant that direction was not a great option. She tried to remember details of the maps from history class but could not. She knew there were several other human cities, some in kingdoms that didn't border the sea. If they failed in stopping any possible invaders from the Splinter, would the citizens of Haulstatt be forced to flee to those other kingdoms, begging for mercy and admission to their land? And if they did not get it, would they have to plead their case for the elves to let them take shelter with them? She thought about the huge Eternal Wall structure made to keep out humans and thought it not likely they would agree.

"Since the city leaders are in the inner city, that is where we are going. Keep in mind there are few humans here, so there will be many stares as we travel to the inner gates." Lady Harper looked sharply at Portia. "Keep your head about you and don't take offense at anything you might hear. No one will harm you, I assure you."

Portia swallowed at the warning.

They entered the city at the outer wall. Lady Harper's name was enough to gain entry, although Portia tagging along behind her raised a few eyebrows. It was so crowded they had to lead the deer through the packed entryway. Thousands of elves milled around the courtyard just inside the entrance. More passed back and forth through the gate. Portia spotted a few humans in the crowd. It was easy to do, since they towered over the rest. She tried to make eye contact with a few of them, but most looked at the ground and hurried on their way. No one seemed interested in talking to her.

When they got further into the city and away from the gate, they remounted their deer and rode to the inner gate. Portia didn't know where to look, scanning the city from side to side, trying to take it all in. There were shops, just like there were in any city, and many citizens walking on the streets. The city was densely packed with narrow streets. Even the carts of goods were narrow.

Closer to the inner gate, the roads began to widen. There was a wide apron before the inner gate walls all along its border. It reminded Portia of the no-man's-land space in the Eternal Wall. She wondered why everything the elves did seemed in preparation for, or in usefulness for, war. Perhaps they were just cautious. Either way, it made her uneasy.

When they reached the inner city, Lady Harper boldly crossed the apron towards the gate on the red wall. But before she could get there, several large elves ran towards her from the guardhouse. Another ran up to Portia and grabbed the reins of her deer.

"Halt!" one of the elves called out. He spoke with authority.

Lady Harper sputtered, her face tense with rage and surprise. "What is the meaning of this? I am Lady Harper of the Meadows, envoy to the royal house. You have no authority to stop me."

"That is true. However, no humans are allowed in the inner city, no matter who they are with," the leader said, his face stern. "There are *no* exceptions."

Lady Harper was not impressed. "There will be an exception. I have brought this human for an audience with King Magnus—and the audience will happen."

The leader simply stared back, his face impassive. He was not going to budge.

Lady Harper blinked, astonished. Finally, she sighed. "Just so I know, when did this happen?"

"About a week ago," the leader said.

Lady Harper looked at the leader, the gate, and around the city, considering her options. She turned back to the guard, her expression black but her tone civil. "Please tell me where the nearest inn can be found."

The inn he told them about wasn't far. It had the bonus of a stable for the deer. Exhaustion pulled at Portia. It was hard to keep her eyes open. It was just too much change and stimulus for one day. She handed over the reins to the waiting hostler and trudged after Lady Harper into the main reception area. To her surprise, Lady Harper asked for only one room and prepaid for an entire week.

"Are we running out of money?" Portia asked.

"Of course not," Lady Harper responded in a terse voice. She was in a foul mood, and while she had not lost her temper, Portia could tell she was struggling to remain civil. "The room is for you. You need rest, and I need to figure out what's going on and how I'm going to get you to the king. You must be in the inner city, not only to be received but also to gain any instruction in healing The Splintering."

Portia nodded. She took the key from Lady Harper and watched her walk out of the inn. If she hadn't been so weary, she would have felt more fear at being abandoned, for that was what it felt like in the city of elves. Looking around the reception parlor, she didn't see a single human. The elves politely turned away when she looked at them. None were overtly friendly. No one smiled at her. She felt their eyes on her when she wasn't looking.

The clerk pointed in the direction of the rooms and Portia trudged to them, carrying her pack. The room was small but functional. She flopped down on the bed and closed her eyes. She wanted to go to sleep, but the setting sun came through the windows and hit her eyes, reminding her it was supper time. There were only a few bits of jerky and a chunk of stale bread in her bag. If she wanted a real dinner, she would have to get up and go down to the tavern. With a groan, she sat up.

The dining area was just off the main reception parlor. There was no one in it, which made Portia worry that it was closed. But a tiny server saw her standing there and waved for her to come in and sit down. Grateful, Portia found a table and fidgeted until the server came to talk to her. She was glad she was sitting down, so they were at eye level.

"First question, do you have money?" the server asked, glaring at Portia.

Portia was surprised by the question but didn't want to argue. "Yes, of course I do. I think. How much is dinner?"

"Sop and bread is three copper. No meat. If you want meat, you have to pay a silver. Water only. If you want anything else, that's extra too."

Portia opened her money bag and pulled out three coppers, handing them to the server. "Just sop and bread, please."

The server frowned at the coins in her hand. "If you're using human coins, then it'll be five coppers."

Portia didn't understand how the coppers from her own kingdom of Haulstatt could have different values from the elf coins. Maybe the elf coins were larger—but that didn't make any sense. The elves were tiny, so why would they have larger coins? But she was too tired and hungry to argue so she handed over two more coppers.

The elf server nodded and walked away. Portia slumped in her chair in relief. All she had to do was stay awake long enough to eat her dinner and then go to bed. Tomorrow would be a new day and she would have more energy to think then.

While she waited, she listened to the noises of the inn. There were murmuring voices from the front and the slams of doors coming from the back. The tinny echo of pots hitting each other told her the kitchen was close by. The sounds of cooking were a comforting, homey sort of noise. She liked it. She liked being around others. She was used to others being around from growing up in the Black Cat orphan house. It had been packed with orphans. And there were always others in the pyromancy house back at the Academy too. While the noises here were from elves, it was the same thing—she was not alone.

Portia was nearly asleep, lulled by the familiar noises around her, when a crash and a scream woke her up.

10

She sat up, adrenaline coursing through her veins. Whimpers of pain caught her attention. The hairs on her arms and neck stood up. There were no other noises, so she didn't think it was a fight or some other catastrophe, which had been her first thought.

She stood up to investigate. Walking towards where she thought the kitchen was, she turned the corner and found an elf on the ground surrounded by the remains of a pot of stew. The elf was grabbing her ankle, which was close to the pot, and Portia guessed she had dropped it on her foot.

"Are you okay?" Portia asked, bending down to look at the ankle.

"No. I think it's broken. Cook ran off to find a healer," the elf bit out. She was breathing shallowly.

"Is there one close by?"

The elf shook her head. She closed her eyes and grimaced

as she tried to pull her leg up but stopped and exclaimed in pain as soon as she moved her ankle.

Sweat broke out all over Portia. She couldn't stand when anyone was in pain. The memory of Harper's healing magic came back to her. She would try it now. If it didn't work, she could try her own healing, even though she knew it wasn't as good. But maybe it would be enough to stop the elf's pain before the professional healer arrived.

Portia closed her eyes and tried to remember the tune Lady Harper had been singing. She held one hand over the ankle and used the other to tap out the rhythm on the floor. Her voice cracked when she started singing but soon it evened out. The elf opened her eyes in surprise.

Hopefully, it would still work even if it wasn't exactly the same. She should have asked Lady Harper for more information, but at the time there had been too many other soldiers around. Portia cursed herself for wasting time on the trip when she could have been asking Lady Harper questions.

It got easier to fall into the rhythm as she continued singing and tapping. She risked opening her eyes, despite being afraid it would ruin her concentration, to peek at the elf and see if her efforts were having any effect. The elf's face, which had been scrunched in pain, was now relaxed. There was only a slight furl between the tiny elf's brows. Her eyes were closed. Portia quickly shut her eyes again and brought all her concentration back onto the spell. She didn't know how effective it would be if she was stopped too early.

Time seemed to stop. All she knew was her singing and

the rhythm of the song. She concentrated on that. She was so lost in what she was doing that she jumped when someone tapped her on the shoulder. Opening her eyes, she saw two elves staring at her, their mouths hanging open.

The taller of the two, wearing all white, stepped forward after a moment. "I'll take over from here, *human*."

Portia stopped singing and backed away from the injured elf. This must be the professional healer. Portia smiled uncomfortably. She hoped she had not done anything wrong.

The second elf watched with concern as the healer stepped in and felt the wounded ankle with his hands. The healer raised his eyebrows and looked at Portia with newfound respect. "I don't know where you learned this, but you didn't do a bad job."

The second elf turned to Portia, surprised. "That is strong praise coming from one who never says anything good about anyone." She pointed at the healer. "I'm the cook here, and the one you helped is my sister. Thank you." The cook took Portia's hands in her own and pressed them together, her warm hands holding Portia's.

"I'm glad I could help. It's awful to not do anything. I'm glad you're not angry," Portia said.

"Of course I'm not angry," the cook said.

"You might have been, if I had messed it up." Black started to creep around her vision. She suddenly felt a little dizzy and leaned back.

"Child, are you okay?"

"Yes, sorry, just a little tired I think," Portia said weakly.

"And when was the last time you ate? Was that your supper she was bringing out?"

"Probably... sorry," Portia said, embarrassed that it might have been her order that caused this whole ordeal.

"No sorry needed. It's not your fault. Go sit down and your meal will be out soon."

Portia was only seated at a table for a few minutes when a glass of ale, a large bowl of stew, a huge chunk of bread, a bowl of greens, and a giant bowl of cherries and cream were laid out in front of her. She looked up, surprised to see two elves beaming at her. They nodded in unison and said, "Thank you for helping our friend."

Tears welled up in Portia's eyes. "You're welcome, but I can't pay for all this—"

One of the elves winked at her. "We said thank you. And we mean it."

The other elf piped in. "We hear you're staying here for a week. Your dinners are on us."

Portia's jaw dropped. Before she could thank them, the two elves walked away, leaving Portia to face the incredible feast in front of her. The aromatic stew tickled her nose and her stomach growled in response. She grabbed a hunk of bread and stuffed it in her mouth then tried to spoon in stew too, spilling some of it down her chin.

It all tasted so good.

Lady Harper did not return the next day. Portia slept in late. She chewed on the stale bread and last of the jerky while looking out the window and wondering what to do.

The inn was on a quiet street. All she could see out her window was the cobblestone road leading off in either direction flanked by buildings several stories tall. Once in a while an elf would walk by. She even saw a human who scurried along, looking around him as he went. He looked harried.

The remains of her rations were not enough to satisfy her growling stomach. She would have to resupply. Ever since being an orphan and feeling hungry far too often, Portia had made an effort to always have some sort of food in her bags. She never wanted to feel hungry again. So it was time to resupply.

She checked her moneybag. It was still half full. A pang of guilt hit her stomach—some of that money was from the felled elves and soldiers in the woods between Holne and Coverack. But spending that money would not make them any deader than they were.

But first, she wanted breakfast.

Grabbing her moneybag and the translated book, she went downstairs to the tavern. She passed a few unsmiling elves on the way. The tavern itself was packed with elves having lunch. A few turned to look at her, their expressions stern. The unsmiling faces were getting to her when one of the servers spied her standing by the door and came running over, a big grin on her face. It was one of the two from last night—one of the pair that had brought the free supper.

"Welcome. Come, there's a seat over here," the elf said. She led Portia to a quiet table along the back wall. Portia was grateful to be out of sight of most of the patrons. "I'm Jsoth," the elf said, her hand on her chest. "What's your name?"

"Portia."

"Well, Portia, are you hungry?"

"Very." Reflexively, Portia put her arm over her growling stomach.

"Excellent. I'll be back." Jsoth turned without another word, walking to the kitchen.

"Wait, I don't know how much—"

Jsoth called over her shoulder, "Don't worry, you'll get the special." Then she was gone, leaving Portia alone at the table. No one was staring at her at the moment. Portia pulled the book out of her pocket and laid it on the table. She was curious to know more about the warrior who had written it.

Portia had just opened the book when Jsoth was back bearing a tray of food. She put out a plate of meat and cakes, a tall glass of pink juice, and a steaming mug. The food smelled delicious. Jsoth gave Portia a wink and walked off.

Lunch was delicious. She had never seen juice that color, but it was sweet and rich and a bit salty. The meat was crispy. The mug was full of broth, hot and rich. It filled her stomach and warmed her body. Portia felt instantly better when she started eating. She hadn't realized how hungry she had been. The previous day's events and her long sleep had used up all the food she had eaten last night.

The tavern was emptying out as elves left after finishing their lunches. Portia thought it would be okay to sit there for a while and read her book. She didn't want to return to her room. It was small and quiet. Too quiet. She preferred to be here, around others, even if they weren't the friendliest except for the servers and cook staff. Her decision was sealed when Jsoth came back and topped off her mug and took away her empty plates.

She found her place in the book again. The author had just gotten onto the boat along with several other warriors of the advance guard. They were crossing the sea at night, the sounds of more warriors exiting the gate and going onto boats behind them. The author mentioned twenty-one boats. Portia wondered how many were on each boat—perhaps ten or twenty? Or more? In any event, it was several hundred, if not more.

Then, for some reason the author did not describe, no others were allowed to come. They were on their own. The rest of the book was hard for Portia to read, describing in graphic detail many battles and their violence. The author seemed to relish that part and gloried in its descriptions. Portia shut the book quickly when it talked about a pool of blood lapping at the ankles of the attackers. She hoped it was exaggeration. If not, it was the worst thing she'd ever read.

Portia decided to explore the city with the rest of the sunlight. She hoped to find a market where she could buy some food and supplies. And perhaps a needle and thread— her clothing could use some repairs. The Sika saddles had pulled on her pants and were hard on the seams.

She walked about the city, ignoring the unpleasant looks that occasionally came her way. The city was unusually quiet, at least relative to what Portia was used to. She couldn't find a market to buy any further foodstuffs. Hopefully, it was just the wrong day, and perhaps tomorrow vendors would come into the city. If not, she would have to brave walking into one of the shops, but she didn't feel like facing an unwelcoming face just yet.

The next several days passed much the same. By the fourth day, Portia was pacing her small room trying to decide what to do. She had lost her enthusiasm for exploring the city when all she encountered was glare after glare. Once or twice she had spied a human in the distance and ran off to talk to them, but it was as if they had a second sense, and they avoided her by ducking into alleys and side streets and vanishing without a trace. Rocabarra was not a good place to be a human.

Portia also kept reading the book, or at least trying to, but had to stop often and put it down. Even though the actions were done long ago, her heart pounded and ached at the stories of hurt and death it described.

The only highlight of her days were the meals in the tavern. The dinners were free, and lunches were just a few coppers for a splendid spread. She thought she would have to ask Jsoth for a needle and thread if she couldn't find any within the town. Or at least a store that would be willing to sell to her.

A knock sounded at her door one evening. Opening it, she found Lady Harper standing there. A mixture of relief at seeing the elf and some anger at being left alone for so long surged. She tried to remind herself there was probably a good reason.

"Good, I'm glad you're here," Lady Harper said, walking into Portia's tiny room. She sat down on the bed uninvited and looked around. "Small even for an inn."

"It is small," Portia said, thinking how tiny it was when you had to spend all day there. "Where have you been?"

"In the inner city. Things are bad. I have never seen the city like this before. But then again these times are unusual, which is why we had been sent to Coverack to seek an alliance."

"An alliance? I don't understand. You said the elves and humans already had a treaty." Portia asked, confused.

"Yes, a treaty. But we need to work together beyond just a treaty of peace. We need to work together with our armies and our mages and our resources. This is not something that has ever happened before in our history, at least not that I know of." Lady Harper picked at the fabric of her gown. She was back to wearing the flowing robes of different shades of blue. She looked regal, very much a part of the royal house. "Unfortunately, extreme factions in the city are rising up because of the rumors of coming chaos. There has also been some unusual violence. Some are blaming outsiders, specifically humans. But I have managed to talk a senior advisor into coming to meet you. He might have some ideas of how to proceed further."

"A senior advisor?" Portia asked, unsure what that meant.

"Yes, formally they are called Guardians of the City. They are close advisors to the king. This one would like to meet you, enough to venture out from the inner circle." Lady Harper looked closely at Portia.

Portia had washed her clothes and made an effort to look presentable but knew she did not look impressive. Their days of riding horses and stags had taken a toll on her outfit. She still had not found a needle and thread to fix the seams on her pants. Portia's face turned red. She felt shabby compared to the tiny elegant elf.

Lady Harper pursed her lips as she continued her inspection. "The first order of business is to make you look more presentable. Is that your best outfit?"

Portia looked down at the green outfit she had purchased while in Holne. It was her best outfit. She'd left her red kirtle back in Coverack, and she had only her old thieving clothes with her besides what she was wearing now. She nodded at the elf.

"I see. Well, a good pressing will bring a lot of improvement. Change out of those clothes and hand them to me. I'll take them down and see what I can do. I'll also get a private parlor for us while I'm at it."

Her outfit did look much better when there were clean press lines along the sleeves and the pants. Whoever had taken them to press had also fixed the ripped seam on her pants. Portia was grateful. Checking her reflection in the mirror in her room, she decided she was ready to face someone from a royal house. At least she didn't look like a shabby urchin from the street.

The parlor that Lady Harper had rented was small but plush. Three soft chairs were arranged around a fireplace and there was a small table with jugs of mead and wine along with a tray of glasses. Lady Harper and Portia settled into the chairs around the fire and waited for the appearance of the steward. The innkeeper knew where to bring him when he arrived. He had been rather nervous when Lady Harper told him who was coming. It took several coins slipped into his pocket to calm his nerves. She assured him over and over again that his inn would be more than welcoming enough.

A little over an hour later, there was a knock at the door of the parlor. The nervous innkeeper opened the door a crack and peeked in. He was wringing his hands. Sweat dotted his brow. "My Lady Harper, our esteemed guest has arrived."

Lady Harper chuckled, for she could see the advisor peering over the head of the nervous innkeeper, who was blocking the entrance to the room and making rather a mess of himself in front of the high company. She bit back a laugh and drew up a serious face. "Please, kind sir, do let him in."

The innkeeper turned to the hallway and realized his mistake. His face turned a brilliant red. He scurried back out of the way and gently shut the door after the advisor entered.

The royal advisor was tall for an elf. Portia thought he might even be taller than she was herself, and she was not short for a human. He was also thin, as if some giant had taken a normal-sized elf and stretched him head to foot to make him taller. Fluffy hair that ringed his head surrounded a tan bald spot in the middle. A maze of wrinkles covered his face and even his hands. Belying his wizened appearance, he stood up straight. Portia thought it was an odd combination of youth and age.

"Greetings, Lady Harper," he said, with a bow.

"And to you too, Sir Alboka. Allow me to introduce you to Portia, the human I told you about."

Sir Alboka turned to Portia and considered her. Portia felt uncomfortable under his gaze. His twinkling eyes met hers and he gave her a smile. "Greetings, Portia the human. I understand you are key to our proposed alliance with Coverack."

Portia gave him a weak smile and tried to execute a curtsy. She lost her balance, and it ended up being more of a stumble combined with a bow. Nervous butterflies tickled her stomach. Having the hope of the kingdom pinned on her was too much pressure. It didn't seem real. Especially not right now. "Greetings, sir. I'm not so sure—"

Lady Harper waved her to silence. "Let's have some wine, shall we, and then we can talk." Lady Harper poured wine for all three of them and motioned for them to sit in the chairs by the fire. "All right, Sir Alboka, you have met her. Please, if you will, kindly tell us what we must do."

Portia's eyes widened at Lady Harper's casual tone, but Sir Alboka just laughed. He sat back in his chair and sipped the wine, raising his eyebrows at its taste and looking at Lady Harper. She gave him a satisfied smile and raised her own glass. Portia took a sip of her wine out of curiosity and was shocked at the quality. It tasted of flowers and honey. She wondered how much it had cost Lady Harper. It wasn't the sort of thing she expected at such an average inn.

"You never did show proper respect to your elders, Lady Harper, or should I say betters?" he said, a twinkle in his eye.

"Let's just stick with 'elders', shall we? Then there won't be any room for debate." Lady Harper turned her gaze to Portia and said, "I have known this rascal my entire life. And so did my mother. And her mother before her."

"All right, you've made your point. Let's not bore the girl with counting ancestors," Sir Alboka admonished, but there was humor in his tone.

The laughter died away. The three of them sipped their wine thoughtfully in silence.

"In all seriousness, things are not well," Sir Alboka said. "The inner city has been completely shut off·from all newcomers, I am sorry to say, and that includes you, young Portia. They are unwilling to allow the teacher of the Healing of the Splinter outside the inner city walls, nor will they grant permission for him to even teach you without meeting you. I do understand that is why you're here, is it not? You can do magic of all sorts, like an elf?"

Portia didn't know how to answer that. She could do more magic than the average human, but she didn't know if she could do *all* sorts, not the way the elves could. "I was told I was a Jack of Magic. I'm not quite sure what that means. They made me take some dreadful test though to come here—one where I nearly died."

Lady Harper raised one eyebrow at Portia. "Nearly died? I don't remember that part."

"Well, I could have died." It was true, she could have died. She still didn't understand why the test was set up the way it was. Part of her was angry at Lady Harper, and maybe even at Queen Lorica for putting her in that situation. She forced herself to breathe in slowly and calm down. It was not this elf's fault.

"But you did not die since you are here in front of me now," Sir Alboka said, a bit puzzled as to why this was being brought up.

"Yes, that is true. But what I don't understand is, why can't I go in and meet the king and that teacher if I passed the test? Can't the king just decree it?" Portia asked.

"King Magnus and Queen Ceola are indeed interested in meeting you. But they cannot unilaterally allow you into the inner city, not when all outsiders have been forbidden by the council made up by city lords. King Magnus does not have absolute power in the kingdom. The royal house rules with the support of the lords, and as such, he cannot just overrule them. Unfortunately, they are quite worked up at the moment. They have gone so far as to demand the banishment of all outsiders. Applying this to the inner city is just a start for what many want. Many are pressing to go even further and banish all non-elves and other outsiders from the entire city, and perhaps even the entire kingdom. There are rallying cries that the wall is there for a reason and we should not forget it."

Lady Harper tsked at this. "This is a sudden change indeed. There was not a breath of this just last month when I set off on my journey."

"It may seem sudden, but I fear it is based on deep passions. The fear of what has happened *before* is coming back. That is what has terrified so many of the city. It doesn't help that the violence on the streets has seemingly come out of nowhere." His face looked grim. "And it is primarily directed at children."

Lady Harper sucked in her breath at this. Portia felt a little ill herself. It reminded her of the culture in Valencia, with all its orphans on the street and the struggle of the little ones to survive. What was going on?

Sir Alboka continued. "The violence of the last month has put everyone on edge. It seems to come only from outsiders—some claim humans are responsible—and as an outsider yourself, Portia, you are not trusted. You can understand that?"

Portia nodded mutely.

Sir Alboka rose and refilled his glass, bringing the bottle around to refill Lady Harper's and Portia's as well. "But there are rules, even in this time of stress. One of the ironclad rules of the city is that if you are declared a friend of the city, you are not an outsider, not ever. You cannot be barred from any portion of the city that a rightful citizen can go. Obtaining that status would be the easiest way for you to gain access. It would also be politically expedient for the king and queen to say that you are a friend of the city. They could get you in without a direct conflict with the lords." Sir Alboka sat down heavily. "There are those that do not believe in what our mages tell us about the future. King Magnus and Queen Ceola believe them. They want all the resources of the city allied behind them, including the lords. They believe unity is necessary." He drained his second glass of wine and placed it on the table next to him.

"Ah, so there is the path open to us," Lady Harper said.

"Indeed, one. Perhaps the only one." He turned to face

Lady Harper earnestly. "What do you think? Can this young lady make herself a friend of the city?"

Portia looked to Lady Harper as well, curious about her answer. Lady Harper considered her seriously, pursing her lips. "Of course she can."

"How? How do I do that?" Portia asked.

"Help the people of the city. Perform an invaluable service," Sir Alboka said, staring at Portia with half-lidded eyes. "It must be significant—not at the level of collecting trash, but much above that. Much."

Portia swallowed. That seemed like a tall order just to be allowed to learn what she'd come here to learn. But she would try. She knew the people of her kingdom were counting on her. She thought of Mark and the other orphans in Valencia— they were also counting on her, even if they didn't yet know they were in danger. "I can do that."

When the advisor left, Portia and Lady Harper sat in silence in the private parlor. They had another hour or so before the innkeeper would make them leave and make room for the next elite that had rented it. And they had not yet finished the second bottle of wine he had brought for them. Portia wanted to know more about the steward, and the odd relationship Lady Harper seemed to have with him.

Taking a large swallow of wine for courage, Portia spoke. "He looks very old. How old is he?"

"He's six hundred years at least. That is a lot of passages around the sun."

Portia's mouth fell open. She'd never heard of anyone

being that old before. "Is that normal? For elves? How old are you?"

"Not that old, I assure you. No, that advanced age is rare, even for elves. Some have proposed it is part of magic that only he has, or those of his immediate family, for many of them are old too. That is how they became advisors to the royal family. They have seen much. Their wisdom is sound because it is based on our long history and a depth of personal knowledge." Lady Harper rose and put her wineglass down. She brushed off her robes. "And I must tell you, young lady, it is not polite to ask how old people are. At least it is not polite to ask me how old I am. Understood?"

Portia nodded. She had been scolded like that before and didn't understand it. She was looking forward to getting older. Then she could do whatever she wanted. She frowned. If that day ever came.

"I apologize, Lady Harper. I'll try to be a friend of the city. But I am a little confused. How will anyone let me do anything for them if they are suspicious of outsiders? Or more specifically, suspicious of humans?"

"I guess that is part of the challenge," Lady Harper said, ushering Portia out of the room. "I must return and take care of some business. If I think of anything, I will let you know immediately. Meanwhile, do what you can. And stay out of trouble, do you understand me? Getting into any trouble would be the exact opposite of being a friend of the city."

This admonishment did not calm Portia's nerves. Somehow she thought she was more practiced at getting into trouble and skirting the rules than being an exemplary specimen of a rule follower.

She went back to her rooms and dug her knives out of her bags. Once they were strapped to her body once again, she felt more comfortable. She hadn't realized how naked she'd felt without them. What Sir Alboka had told her about the city explained a lot about why there were so few humans on the street. It also explained why the humans who were there were so jumpy. If every elf was thinking a human was trouble, then how could any human be comfortable in public? They were constantly suspected of wrongdoing.

There were a few hours left in the day. Even though she didn't have a concrete plan, it seemed more reasonable to go out to the city to find something she could do rather than sit around the inn and try to come up with a plan. Or maybe that was just an excuse. She wanted to go and walk in the sunshine and stretch her legs.

This time when she explored the city, she did it with more purpose. She made an effort to memorize the streets as she went, looking for possible future escape routes, much as she had done when she was an orphan in Valencia. Perhaps this information would come in handy. In any case, it was better to have it than not.

The sun was getting low as she got back to the inn. There was an elf couple outside arguing with a small boy between them. Portia slowed her pace. She walked close to the wall in order to blend into the background. She wanted to overhear what they were saying. Luckily, they were too engrossed in their fight to take much notice of her.

"I must get these bills collected before the end of business today or my boss will have my head," the female elf said. "I don't understand why you thought I would be free tonight." She paced back and forth, agitated.

The male elf held the hand of the small child. He looked stressed. "I'm sorry. I forgot. But I had no other place to bring him—not with our sitter gone. Uncle Wren will be back soon. He's supposed to meet you both at the south gate at sundown."

"But I can't..."

"I know. I can't either, though. You know my shift starts soon." He tried to stand in front of the female elf, but she paced around him. The child looked down at his feet and kicked the ground.

Portia stepped in front of them. Her heart beat a little faster. Blood rushed to her face at her boldness. "I can help you. I can bring him where he needs to go."

All three elves turned to face Portia, surprise on their faces. The female elf looked incredulous. "Why don't I just hand him over to a kidnapper right now? I would never trust him with a human."

Portia jumped in. "I can understand that. I understand completely. I'm new here, and I know you don't have a reason to believe me, but you can trust me." She thought furiously. How could she get them to believe her? Then it came to her. "I am escorted in the city by Lady Harper of the Meadows. She can speak to my business."

The looks on the elves' faces softened but didn't completely relax. She was going in the right direction.

"A guardian of the city... Sir Alboka... has come to see me at this inn."

At that, the male elf laughed. "Surely you don't expect us to believe that."

"It's true. He came this very day. The innkeeper can vouch for this. He led him in himself," Portia said, hoping the innkeeper would cooperate and tell the truth—if he was even in the inn at the moment. "Please, come in and ask. He'll tell you that. I will take care of your child and bring him where he needs to go." They were almost there. She could see it on their faces. They were considering her words.

But then the female elf's face blanched as she looked Portia up and down. "Even if what you say is true, you hardly look like a substantial bodyguard," she said, skepticism in her voice. She crossed her arms and looked at Portia, all her weight on one hip.

"I know my way around a knife. I can defend myself—and him."

Portia pulled out her longest knife and went through a defensive routine, showing them her skills with the blade and footwork. When she completed the rapid-fire motion, she re-sheathed her knife and gave them all a small bow. *They were impressed*, Portia thought. That much was plain. But they were also a bit afraid of her too, for they had backed up against the far wall.

Portia cursed herself for not thinking things through. How would she get them to trust her now that she had waved a weapon around? "I'm sorry. Perhaps that wasn't the best idea. Please don't run away. Just talk to the innkeeper." She motioned for them to enter the front of the inn with her two hands together in a prayer, begging them to enter. With a slow nod, the female elf turned and walked into the inn, followed by the male elf and the child. The child couldn't take his eyes off Portia and was dragged into the building while staring at her, his eyes round.

To Portia's relief, the innkeeper was at the front desk. Now she just had to say the right thing so he wouldn't get defensive. She rushed to him, around the other elves, and said, "This is the honorable innkeeper who hosted Sir Alboka today. In his private parlor. It was most impressive."

The innkeeper looked up, surprised at Portia's words, then a small smile of pleasure came to his face. He nodded agreeably. "This is true. But then again, I often have royal couriers as guests here. My inn is known for its impeccable hospitality."

Portia piped in, wanting to keep the innkeeper's good mood. "It's true. I was a witness to this very thing since I was in the private parlor with Lady Harper of the Meadows to receive him."

"She was indeed," the innkeeper said. Portia exhaled a small sigh of relief. She got him to admit she was there, part of the group receiving Sir Alboka, without running into any resistance. From her experience with people, she knew their first reaction was usually to say no when asked for a favor, such as vouching for her. But she did not have to ask for such a thing directly, not this way—she had only to get him to talk. "Would you like to see where the Guardian of the City sat?" he continued, soaking up the moment.

The male and female elves looked surprised. They turned to consider Portia once again, as if seeing her for the first time. The little boy elf's eyes could not have gotten any larger than they were already. He backed up and hid behind the male elf's leg and peered at Portia. The female elf approached Portia. "My name is Celaireth, this is my husband, Mawon, and our child, Finrod. It would help us a great deal if you could take Finrod to the south gate to meet his uncle Wren."

"I would be honored. My name is Portia." She gave the elf family a small bow.

The male elf reached into his pocket. "I can give you five coppers—"

Portia interrupted him, waving away his hand. "There is no charge. It's on my way." The innkeeper raised his eyebrows at this but didn't say anything. Portia wanted to get Finrod out of there and to the south gate before his parents changed their minds. She paused though, realizing she did need something from them. "My only request is that you tell any who asks that I did this service for you."

Celaireth nodded at Portia. "Do us this service and we will gladly speak the truth of it."

Portia nodded and then reached forward to take Finrod's hand. He reluctantly put his little hand in hers and she drew him from the inn. She knew she had to get to the south gate by sunset, and it was already close to that time. The sun was hanging close to the horizon. They had to hurry.

Portia walked down the street, determined. She pulled Finrod along to walk faster. Turning back to look at him, she found he was still staring at her with round eyes. It was beginning to make her uncomfortable. He opened his mouth, and a deeper voice than she expected told her in a very grown-up tone, "I should not be guided through the city by a human."

She shook her head in surprise at his pronouncement and nearly let go of his hand. There was nothing she could say to that. Instead, she turned back around and dragged him even faster through the streets towards the south gate of the inner city.

11

They walked quickly through the streets. Portia noticed a few concerned glances at her dragging Finrod. She realized how bad it looked—a human dragging an elf child. If she wasn't careful, someone would think she was kidnapping the boy. She stopped walking and turned to face him, crouching down to be at his level. "I need you to follow me without me dragging you by your hand. People will think I'm doing you harm."

He looked at her, fear warring with an elitist attitude. Finally, he drew up his courage and said to her with just a touch of disdain in his voice, "Of course. As I said, I shouldn't be following a human, much less being dragged by one."

Portia squinted at him. How old was this child? He looked tiny, but he spoke like an adult. It was confusing to her. Perhaps it was an elf thing. "You are correct, of course. But you did hear your parents? It's not safe for you alone. Will you do me—or should I say us—the favor of walking with me. And quickly. We must not be late to meet your uncle Wren, for I have no access to the inner city." She paused for effect and then gave him a devious smile. "Or would you rather spend the night at the inn with me?"

Finrod raised his chin and looked down his nose at Portia. "Never."

"Then walk. And quickly. Without me having to drag you," Portia said, trying to stay calm and not reveal irritation in the tone of her voice. But she was irritated. She thought this elf boy was very spoiled.

"Very well. As long as you stop grabbing my hand."

"As if I want to touch your hand." She felt silly and childish saying such a thing, but really, he was too much.

She stood up and they walked together quickly down the street. Finrod had to do a little half trot every few steps to keep up with her, but thankfully he didn't complain. They made good time. She thought they would arrive just a bit early, which was perfect.

As they turned a corner into the neighborhood just before the inner city, a pack of young children swarmed around them. They seemed to come out of nowhere. Portia guessed they were waiting in the nearby alleyway for any passersby. The children had jostled uncomfortably close as they had passed, touching both Portia and Finrod, which raised Portia's suspicions immediately. She quickly felt around her body for her money bag and her knives. All was still there. She breathed a sigh of relief.

Realizing perhaps a moment too late, she turned to Finrod. "Are you missing anything?"

He looked at her, surprise and confusion on his face. He was still nonplussed from being jostled by the strangers. He clearly did not like being touched by others, especially those who did not ask first.

"What do you mean missing?" he asked.

"Like money. Anything in your pockets," Portia said, impatiently.

Finrod felt around his pockets, a scowl on his face. "My allowance. Those jerks took my allowance." Before Portia could stop him, he bolted down the alleyway where the kids had disappeared. She swore under her breath and tore after him.

"Finrod! Stop!" she called. He moved surprisingly fast for such a little thing. It took her half a block to catch him. She grabbed his arm and stopped him from running further. Luckily, the other children were nowhere in sight. Her greatest fear was that he would get injured fighting with one of them—or worse. But they were gone, and it was only her and Finrod in the alleyway. "You can't do that. It's too dangerous. Didn't you see how many of them there were?"

Finrod once again jutted out his chin. His eyes smoldered. He pulled to run off again, but Portia gripped his arms tightly, refusing to let go.

"They had no right. They took *my* money," he said, spitting in anger.

"They had no *right*, but they did it anyhow. And getting yourself killed or injured by them is not going to make it any better. Do you understand me? They could really hurt you."

She squeezed his arms for emphasis, staring into his eyes and trying to get through to him.

The anger gradually faded from his eyes. His chin came down, and he nodded slowly. He stopped trying to fight her to run after them. Portia tentatively loosened her grip on his arms, finally letting go when it was clear he was going to stay by her side.

"Let's go," she said. "We need to hurry if we are not to be late."

He nodded glumly back at her. They walked out of the alleyway once again. This time, he reached out tentatively and took Portia's hand. She looked down at him in surprise but said nothing. Portia gripped his hand tightly in return. They walked faster.

They rounded the top of the hill and Portia could see the red wall of the inner city boundary. She breathed a sigh of relief. They were nearly there, and the sun was still not yet set.

Just as they started down the hill a man stepped in front of them. His face lit up into a bright smile as he looked at Finrod. "There you are, child," he said. "I've been waiting for you. You're late."

Portia squinted at the man. He was acting as if he knew Finrod, but she was instructed to find his uncle Wren, who surely must also be an elf. She looked down at Finrod. He was scowling at the man. If Finrod knew this person, he didn't like him. That was enough for her.

As she faced the man again, she stepped between him and

Finrod. "I think you have us confused with someone else." She used her most polite tone even though the man made the hairs on the back of her neck stand up. She didn't like him either.

The man just gave a jovial laugh and continued his eye contact with Finrod over her shoulder. He wouldn't even speak to her, continuing to address Finrod instead. "Who is the scrappy one with you? Ah, never mind, it doesn't matter. Little man, it is time to go." He reached out to grab Finrod's hand. But the small elf ducked out of the way, moving to the other side of Portia, keeping her between him and the large imposing man.

"I said you are confused. Leave us alone," Portia said, losing patience. She tried to walk around the man while leading Finrod.

The man shifted his position to prevent them from passing. His laughter stopped abruptly. Finally, he focused his eyes on Portia while an unpleasant look came onto his face. He squinted at her. "Little girl, you can get in a lot of trouble for harassing elves in this place. I suggest you leave my ward alone. We are going to be late."

"He is not your ward," Portia said.

"And you say this based on what?" the man said, crossing his arms.

Portia's heart thumped in her chest. What if she was wrong? What if this was Finrod's guardian? Could the elves have been lying to her before? She looked down at Finrod. "Do you know this man?" Finrod shook his head emphatically. He shuffled behind Portia again. Portia looked back up at the man. "He doesn't know you. That's the end of it. Go away."

"Fine. I'll go away," the man said, acid in his tone.

Before Portia could react, he stepped forward and grabbed both her and Finrod, one with each arm. He had her by her good knife arm. Her other was holding Finrod. But even if he had grabbed her other arm, she still wouldn't want to pull a knife, not if she could help it—Finrod was too close. She had no idea how the elf boy would react. Accidentally hurting Finrod was the last thing she wanted to do. The man pulled them to a nearby alley.

Portia looked around wildly for help. There was no one close by. Closing her eyes, she focused on creating strong light flashes in front of the man's eyes. He exclaimed in pain and loosened his grip on her arm. She stopped the flashes and then looked. Both the man and Finrod were rubbing their eyes. She cursed herself for not having the foresight to warn Finrod. Portia grabbed Finrod by the hand and ran with him a few feet down the alley, away from their attacker.

But there was no obvious place to hide. Portia knew the man's vision would return to him before they could escape at the far end of the alleyway. Nor was there an easy way to hide the sounds of their footsteps as they ran. She pulled Finrod with her to a pile of garbage in the alleyway then crouched down next to it, tucking Finrod under her arm. She held her finger up to her lips for him to be quiet. Once they settled there, she created duplicates of both her and Finrod. Finrod saw the duplicates and his eyes widened once again. He looked at her in shock. She once again motioned for him to be quiet. It was important for him to not make a sound.

Putting the duplicates in the middle of the alleyway, she focused for a second on herself and the real Finrod. She imagined darkness around them—a blackness that would fade into the alley wall. She had heard of the spell while in the Academy. It was not invisibility, not exactly—more of a suggestion to any who might look at the person casting the spell—a suggestion that they were not there. Whoever was looking should only see a patch of blackness. She wished she had spent more time practicing these odd spells she had heard about, but no one was supposed to know about her abilities as a Jack. She had been afraid that if she was caught doing an unusual spell, her secret would be out.

Looking at Finrod, she had a hard time actually seeing him. His face flickered in and out, mostly replaced by a dark shadow. If she hadn't known he was there, she wouldn't have seen him at all. Hopefully they were truly invisible to all others. She did not want the strange man to see them sitting there on the ground, vulnerable in their hiding spots.

A few curses from the man reminded her that he was still there in the alley searching for them. Quickly she directed the duplicates to run away. She focused on making sure they made the sounds of footsteps just in case he wasn't watching the direction they had gone. His yell told her he had spied them running away.

"Horrible children. I'm going to get ten lashes for that for sure. I'll kill them. No one's going to cost me my ale tonight," he said, rage in his voice. He ran after the duplicates, his foot-falls reverberating down the alleyway.

Once quiet returned, Portia felt she could finally breathe again. She willed her heart to slow down. Releasing her grip on Finrod, she saw there were white marks on his forearm where she had held him tight. She gave him a look of apology and rubbed his arm.

"Well, that was exciting. Do you know why that man might have wanted us—or you specifically?" she asked Finrod. She spoke softly, just in case the man returned and was within hearing distance.

"Maybe he was my father's rival. Lots of kids have been disappearing. That's why I'm never allowed to go anywhere alone anymore and I'm stuck here with you," Finrod said, pulling away from her to stand and kick at the ground.

"Hey. That's not very nice. Do you want me to call him back and turn you over to him?"

Finrod looked at Portia, alarm in his face, until he realized she was kidding. He looked down again, abashed. "Sorry."

"No problem. Just be nice to me," Portia said, pulling herself up. She concentrated on keeping the spell of darkness over both her and Finrod as they walked down the alleyway. She did not want to risk being seen again, not by anyone except for the person they were meeting, his uncle Wren.

"Are there really a lot of missing children?" she asked, concerned.

He nodded. "My dad says it's up to twenty now. All higher born."

Portia doubted it was only the higher born children that

were snatched. If the city was anything like Valencia, no one kept track of the lower born. They could all be murdered, and no one would know the difference. But she didn't bother to tell Finrod that. Some things were just too sad, and if he didn't already know it, she wasn't going to be the one to tell him about what happens to poor children.

When they finally reached the open space in front of the south gate Portia relaxed the darkness spell enough so that others could easily see them. There were many elves and humans wandering about in the courtyard in front of the gate, far too many witnesses for someone to try to grab them again. There were also dozens of guards dressed in chain mail and helmets, all armed with narrow swords.

It felt safer there.

Portia looked around the square, realizing she had no idea who she was looking for except that it was an elf named Wren. She looked down at Finrod. "Do see your uncle?"

He pointed to an elf in a fancy uniform. It looked expensive. But it wasn't a military uniform. Instead, it was a rich suit of deep green velvet with long tails in the back of his jacket and a cloth at his neck tied in a fancy complicated knot.

Portia sucked in her breath. "Is he a nobleman?"

Finrod laughed. "I'm going to tell him that. He'll be happy. No, he's a butler. He says his boss is a cranky old goat who will have his neck if he doesn't dress the part. But Wren likes him because he gives him lots of money."

Portia choked back a laugh. She reminded herself to never tell this kid anything personal about herself if she ever saw him again.

They walked towards Wren. The elf's face lit with happiness upon seeing his nephew, but his expression turned to alarm when he saw that his nephew was holding the hand of a human girl.

Portia quickly spoke. "It's okay. His parents will tell you about it. Celaireth and Mawon."

Finrod ran to Wren, who picked him up and swung him around in his arms. Wren gave a curt nod to Portia and then walked into the gate, leaving her standing outside alone. Finrod waved goodbye to Portia over Wren's shoulder as he was carried away.

"You're welcome," Portia muttered to herself. She suddenly felt unclean. Being a human in Rocabarra city was not easy. A little common courtesy would have gone a long way, but apparently she was not worthy of that.

Suddenly she felt angry at the situation she was in—it was impossible. She had risked her life to pass a test to learn elf magic, and according to the seers, the end of the world was coming. Yet here she was, mucking around in some elf city trying to be a friend of the city. If the coming Splintering was such an emergency, then why were they playing around like this? She didn't understand politics. It just seemed ridiculous. They were wasting time.

They were wasting her time.

She glared at all those around her, but no one would make eye contact.

The wave of anger left her just as suddenly as it had come. Railing at the situation would not help. She sighed and kicked at the ground herself. She had learned to be pragmatic a long time ago. Getting things done was how she fed herself and survived on the streets. Getting things done now would help her survive again and learn what she needed to learn to help others.

And one thing she could do here was to investigate the missing children. If there were really twenty children missing, and probably a great deal more, then finding what was going on would be more than enough to make her a friend of the city. Helping one child reach home safely was good, but it was not all that impressive. If she could help twenty, or find out what happened to them, then her help would be undeniable. They would have to admit her to the inner city and let her study the magic of healing the splinter.

She squared her shoulders and walked the way she had come, back to the alley where the man had threatened her and Finrod.

When she finally reached it, the sun had set, and it was fully dark out. Portia wasn't happy about this, but she didn't want to wait until morning to search for clues. If the man had dropped anything or thought to cover up his actions, then waiting until morning would give him too much time to fix things. Besides, she was impatient to get into the inner city and fulfill her task of learning the magic of healing the splinters. She was sick of wasting time. So Portia braved the dark. She figured she could use her magic light in the alleyway to see clues.

But when she got there, she heard rustling around further in the alleyway. There was someone else there. She crept into the opening, keeping herself along one of the walls, to see who it was. At first, her eyes couldn't see anything since the alley was much darker than the street. The walls were so close that little moonlight made it inside. But slowly a figure came into focus. It was much smaller than the man had been.

The figure stopped moving abruptly and then turned slowly to face Portia. It was an elf. A female, serious, if not downright angry, elf. "State your business."

"I... thought I had dropped something," Portia stammered. She didn't know why she made up an excuse. It felt like a habit to not reveal everything. And she had no idea who that person was.

"Something? You do understand that sounds very suspicious, don't you?" the elf said, turning to face Portia fully. "This is not a safe area to be after dark. Not for anyone so young, anyway. Not even a young human."

Portia could not agree more with that. "I know."

"How would you know?" The elf didn't wait for Portia to reply. "I'm going to have to ask you to come onto the street and show me any ID you have. Or traveling papers. You don't strike me as a resident of Rocabarra."

"I'm not," Portia said. She followed the elf to the mouth of the alleyway where the light was better from the moon. Anxiety gripped her heart. She could make a run for it, but she didn't know who the elf was or if she had any accomplices nearby. When they stepped into the main street, the elf's uniform shone under the moonlight. There were metal bars on each shoulder. This was someone with authority in the city. Portia was glad she had not taken off and then been caught. That would have been the end to any possible friend of the city status.

"I'm Sergeant Lyren. I'm in charge of investigating crime in this city. Kidnappings, specifically," the elf said. She opened a tiny leather portfolio and flashed a metal badge at Portia and then shut the portfolio again quickly before Portia could get a good look at it. "It's suspicious of you to be in this alleyway. I'm going to ask you again, what are you doing here? I need to see the traveling papers you have."

Portia swallowed nervously. She didn't know what papers Lyren wanted. And she also wished she had not made up the lie in the beginning about losing something. But she had done so and now had to face up to it. She would not make it worse by continuing to lie. That much at least she'd learned during her time at the Academy. "I... I don't have any papers." At Lyren's irritated look she rushed on. "I was brought here by someone else. The reason I'm in this alley is that I'm looking for clues. I, and a boy named Finrod, were nearly kidnapped earlier this evening. Less than an hour ago. We were here and a human man tried to grab us both when I wouldn't let Finrod go with him."

Lyren crossed her arms and stared at Portia, squinting. "There is so much wrong with that story. First off, why would you be escorting an elf boy? And how did you get away? You're a tiny thing. Or were you in league with the adult human and something went wrong?"

Portia shifted uncomfortably on her feet. She had nothing but her word. Then she remembered Lady Harper. "I'm telling the truth. I was brought to the city by Lady Harper to meet the royal family. It's been delayed by some politics I don't understand. To fix things, I'm supposed to be doing good things for the city, which is how I ended up escorting the young elf."

Sergeant Lyren's eyebrows raised at the name Lady Harper. "I would be very interested in confirming this with Lady Harper herself."

"Sure. But I don't know when she's coming back. She doesn't tell me ahead of time," Portia said. She knew it sounded suspicious.

"I don't mind waiting. Where is it that she comes back to?" Lyren said.

"The inn where I'm staying."

"Then let's go there."

Portia did not want to lose the opportunity to look for clues. "Can we search the alleyway first?"

"For what?"

"I don't know. Some clue as to who our attacker was?" Portia asked.

Sergeant Lyren considered this, looking into the black alleyway. "If there was another officer with me, perhaps. But since it is just you and I, and I don't know who you are just yet, I think we should head back to the inn now." Her tone brooked no argument. Portia shrugged her shoulders and turned towards the inn.

"My name is Portia."

The only response was a grunt from the sergeant as she followed Portia.

Once they reached the inn, it only took a flash of Sergeant

Lyren's badge for the innkeeper to offer the hospitality of the private parlor. He squinted at Portia, who turned red under his scrutiny. She was giving him much fodder for his tales after evening supper.

When the innkeeper returned with a bottle of wine, Sergeant Lyren whispered something to the innkeeper's ear who then went off in a hurry.

Sergeant Lyren poured herself a glass of wine and then sat down heavily in one of the chairs by the fireplace. "I sent word for Lady Harper to join us, and then we shall hear what we shall hear. I hope for your sake you're not lying about knowing her."

"I'm not," Portia said. She bit her lip, wishing she had not said anything at all. She had no reason to feel so defensive. She wanted to find a way to get the sergeant on her side. "The child said that perhaps it was one of his father's rivals. He said others have been kidnapped too."

Sergeant Lyren waved the information away with one hand. "It's common knowledge about the kidnappings. You'd need something more specific to help me. Like the name of the rival."

"I don't know the name of the rival, but his father's name is Mawon and his mother's is Celaireth. His uncle's name is Wren. Apparently he's the butler to some rich person in the inner city. Will this be enough to tell you who the rival is?"

"Perhaps. It's something. And you say the child's name is Finrod?"

Portia nodded.

Lady Harper rushed into the room, surprising Portia. She

must've already been at the inn, or very close to it, for there was no other way she could arrive so quickly. "Evening, Sergeant," Lady Harper said, giving the sergeant a nod.

Sergeant Lyren rose from her seat and nodded back. "My gratitude at your quick appearance."

"Anything for an old friend," Lady Harper said, her voice tense. Portia wondered if there was history between the two of them. She motioned for Sergeant Lyren to sit back down and grabbed her own chair by the fire.

"This human child says you are her guardian in Rocabarra. Is this true?"

Lady Harper turned towards Portia and raised her eyebrows. "Guardian? I would say escort is more appropriate. I brought her here from Coverack. She is a ward of the royal house. Her name is Portia Harris." Lady Harper opened her bag and pulled out the papers she'd been given by the queen and king consort. She handed them over to Sergeant Lyren.

Ward of the royal house? This was news to Portia. She wondered what it meant.

Lyren opened the folded papers and scanned them quickly. Abruptly she folded them again and handed them back to Lady Harper. She nodded curtly. "I see."

"Can I ask what is going on here?" Lady Harper asked.

Portia felt responsible. She hoped they had not greatly inconvenienced Lady Harper. "I was helping someone, and we were nearly kidnapped by—"

"I must ask you to stop speaking at once," Sergeant Lyren said, interrupting Portia's story.

"I don't understand," Portia said. Lady Harper tilted her

head at Sergeant Lyren as well. They both stared at the sergeant.

"This is an active investigation. I must ask you not share any information, Portia Harris, not even with Lady Harper. But it would be most useful if you would assist me with what you know—in confidence."

Portia nodded her understanding.

Lady Harper was even quicker in her thinking. "Of course Portia will help you. And of course I don't need to know any details. But I do ask, I *must* ask you though, that if she provides any material assistance you'll willingly attest that she is a friend of the city."

"Ah, politics. My least favorite. But if she can help me close these cases, then yes, I will testify for your young friend here. But the help must be substantial," Sergeant Lyren said.

"I'll do whatever I can," Portia said before Lady Harper could say anything else.

Sergeant Lyren swallowed the last of her wine and set the glass down on the sideboard. She rose. "Excellent. I will be here tomorrow morning just after breakfast. Be ready to go." She nodded then exited the room.

Lady Harper gave Portia a smile and a thumbs-up. "Excellent work, young lady. Not even half the day and you have already made progress. I'm beginning to see what your kingdom sees in you."

Portia flushed with pride.

Portia rose early the next morning, anxious to get going. She was able to take a bath before breakfast. Luckily, her finest outfit was still clean enough to wear, for she had washed it the previous night instead of falling into bed utterly tired. Unsure what the day was going to bring, she splurged and ordered a full breakfast of meat and eggs and bread. Lady Harper did not eat as much as Portia wanted to, so she thought Sergeant Lyren might also be the same. Nothing was worse than being hungry while trying to get serious work done.

Once breakfast was over, she was too impatient to wait in the dining area. Instead, she went outside and paced up and down the street while waiting for Sergeant Lyren. Finally, the elf appeared, looking exactly as she had the previous night. The metal bars on her shoulder sparkled under the strong morning sun.

"Good morning, young human," Sergeant Lyren said.

"It's Portia." She knew the sergeant was giving her a hard time, but being called young human still irritated her anyway.

"Portia. My apologies, young human," Sergeant Lyren said, a twinkle in her eye.

Portia sighed heavily but gave up. It could be worse.

"Are you ready? We are going to the inner city today, someplace apparently you've never been."

Portia turned to Sergeant Lyren, her eyes round.

"Lucky for you, your information has proven valuable already. I was able to track down the rival to Master Mawon. We are going to his place of business. You'll have to tell me if it is the same person who attacked you and Finrod last night." Sergeant Lyren winked at Portia. "His business is in the inner city."

The inner city. Portia's heart beat faster, but she didn't want the officer to see her excitement so she merely nodded. Sergeant Lyren made her nervous. And she didn't understand what the wink meant—was it a sarcastic wink? Was something bad waiting for her in the inner city? She'd feel better once she understood the law enforcement officer better.

But one thing was clear: Sergeant Lyren was efficient. Or else she did not need much sleep, for she had gotten a lot of work done already. Portia felt uneasily that Sergeant Lyren might have extremely high standards. She hoped she could live up to them.

They made their way through the city towards the inner red wall that marked the boundary to the inner city. There were fewer stares than the previous night when Portia had been dragging Finrod along. Most citizens saw Sergeant

Lyren and moved out of her way, some even bowing respect-fully as she walked by. Portia was amazed at the difference it made to be in the presence of a respected city official.

When they reached the inner gate, Sergeant Lyren pulled out her badge and flashed the guard. The guard tried to step in front of Portia as she followed Lyren, but the sergeant saw his motion and turned on the guard, settling a fierce glare on him. He backed up slowly and nodded again at Sergeant Lyren and allowed Portia to pass. They walked through into the inner city. Portia glanced behind her at the guard who was watching them go with an unhappy look on his face.

Portia followed Sergeant Lyren into the inner city. The streets were immaculate. There didn't even seem to be any dirt or dust on the cobblestones. They shone under the sun. The buildings were in perfect repair, the paint jobs perfect and the plaster flawless. It was as if everything had just been constructed, or it was under some spell to keep it looking new. Even the shrubbery and plants that decorated the buildings were perfect in their symmetry. It felt both comfortable and uncomfortable to Portia. She felt dirty by comparison, even in her new clothes. She hurried to catch up to Sergeant Lyren for she was drawing a few stares from the elves inside the gates. When the watching elves saw her next to the enforce-ment officer, they turned away and went on with their business.

Sergeant Lyren was oblivious to all of it. She walked on swiftly, not bothering to see if Portia was behind her.

They made their way through the city. They passed through an impossibly neat marketplace and into the side streets reserved for large merchants and affluent businesses. Lyren stopped in front of a particularly rich-looking business. Maroon and gold paint decorated the front wall, and the roof was tiled in curving interlocking tiles. It was ostentatious and beautiful, even for this city. Portia wondered if it was real gold.

Two guards stood on either side of the front door. They were dressed as footmen in maroon and gold to match the building, but it was clear they were actually guards. They were burly, even for elves. And they were armed with short decorative swords. But despite all their finery, the swords were real enough—Portia could see the gleam of their sharp edges. She wondered at that. Was there really a need for guards in the inner city? Or was this part of the show of wealth of the owner of the building? None of the other buildings she saw had guards.

Sergeant Lyren flashed her badge at the guards. They bowed as a pair. One of the guards opened the door and ushered the officer in. He would have shut the door behind the sergeant, but she once again used her formidable gaze to make it clear that Portia was to follow. The guard hesitated for only a second and held the door open long enough for Portia to enter as well. Portia felt the door closing upon her heels and wondered if the guard was trying to hit her with it.

Inside, an ornately dressed elf sat behind a secretarial desk. Portia's mouth dropped open a bit. He was dressed as finely as royalty, yet he sat behind a desk and looked for all the world like a secretary. What was this place?

At their entrance, the elf rose and came around the desk

to greet them. He gave Sergeant Lyren a small bow but merely raised an eyebrow at Portia's presence. Apparently a human was not worthy of even a bow.

"We are honored with your visit. What can I do for you, Officer?" he asked.

Sergeant Lyren snorted at that. Portia was shocked at her rudeness. The sergeant didn't have the patience obviously to even play the game of social niceties. "I am here to speak to your master. It's official business, of course," she said, her voice even despite her earlier snort.

"I'm sorry. He is busy today. Perhaps we can schedule another time," the secretary said, then gestured towards the door, clearly wanting Portia and Sergeant Lyren to leave again.

"Oh dear. That is unfortunate. But luckily for you, my friend, I am a patient law enforcement officer. I take my duty very seriously. And in that light, I will stay here as long as needed to see your master. I apologize that I am not able to reschedule," Sergeant Lyren said, a small smile on her face.

"He may not be back today," the secretary said, forcing a smile on his face to match Sergeant Lyren's.

"No worries. I don't mind sleeping on a couch, for I am under strict orders to not return until I have spoken to him. It looks like you and I might have a great deal of time to get to know each other, my dear friend," Sergeant Lyren said then walked to the secretary and put her arm around him, giving him a friendly squeeze. His eyes opened wide at her effrontery. Portia had to choke back a giggle at his shock. Offending the secretary would not help their cause.

"I see," he said, extricating himself from the sergeant's arm. "I understand your time is valuable. Let me go and make some inquiries to see if I can speed things up." He left the room, nearly fleeing. Sergeant Lyren turned to Portia and gave her a huge grin. The elf was enjoying herself vastly.

It was only a few moments later when the secretary returned. "We are in luck. I have received word that the master's schedule has changed. He will be available shortly. Amazing luck, really."

"Amazing indeed. What are the chances of such a convenient schedule change?" Sergeant Lyren asked in a singsong tone. She stopped for a second then stared at the secretary intensely. "We need a private interview room. Just him and I. That is nonnegotiable."

This time the secretary didn't even try to argue. He merely nodded and motioned for them to sit. Portia complied, but Sergeant Lyren paced back and forth in front of the secretary. He pulled some work in front of him and made a pretense of working, but Portia could see his eyes constantly jumping up to watch Sergeant Lyren.

A few moments later, a butler appeared at the door dressed in the same maroon livery as the guards outside. He bowed at all the occupants of the room and said, "The master will see you, Sergeant." Sergeant Lyren motioned for Portia to get up and follow her as she walked towards the butler. "Just the sergeant, please," the butler said with a deep imposing tone.

Lyren waved away his words. "My companion will need to at least see your master for one second, then she will be asked to exit the room," she said, her tone brooking no argument once again. Portia was amazed how effective her manner was, for the butler did not argue but merely nodded his acquiescence. Portia wanted to learn that trick. She wanted to speak with such authority that people would just listen to her.

He led them up stairs that curved around a huge beautiful entryway that was just past the receiving room they had been in. Portia nearly tripped on the stairs due to staring at all the fine paintings on the wall. Each painting sat in its own carved ornate gold frame. Each showed an elf depicted more elaborately dressed than the last. This was a huge, rich family.

They walked down a long hallway to a pair of double doors at the end. The butler opened the doors and ushered both Portia and Sergeant Lyren in. There was an elf standing in front of a large window, his back to them with his hands behind his back. He turned at their entrance.

"The sergeant and companion," the butler said, giving a bow then exiting.

The elf looked at Sergeant Lyren and Portia. He seemed relaxed, but his words were tense. "What is the meaning of bringing a human here?" he asked without preamble.

"My apologies, sir. You are quite right, what was I thinking?" Sergeant Lyren said. She turned to Portia. "Please wait outside. It is important that our audience here is *uninterrupted.*"

Portia understood that meant she was to guard the door. She nodded and quickly exited, shutting the door quietly behind her. She had a good look at the elf, enough to know she had never seen him before. Certainly he was not the attacker from the previous night since he was not human, but there still had been a chance she could have seen him somewhere else. But it was not so. She hoped they weren't wasting their time.

The audience inside the room seemed to take forever. Portia's back began to hurt from standing so long. She leaned against the wall, ignoring the fierce look from an attendant standing down the hallway. He was probably irate she was touching the wall. He himself was standing straight, his arms rigid at his side, only moving his head once in a while to keep an eye on her. Portia wondered why he wasn't coming closer but figured he was probably under strict orders to stand where he was. She was surprised there were no guards by the door to the room with the master but perhaps he valued his privacy in the sanctuary of his business establishment.

After what seemed another half hour, a thump came from within the room, followed by the sound of breaking china. Portia's first instinct was to fling open the door and run inside, but she remembered Sergeant Lyren's instructions. She had been very clear—she wanted uninterrupted time with the master, which meant Portia not going inside. No matter what. She'd seen enough of the Sergeant to have faith that she could take care of herself against the elf that was in there.

But the noise had attracted the attention of the attendant down the hall. He waved to someone Portia couldn't see then came rushing towards Portia. He was followed by three other guardsmen who must have been waiting just inside the room down the hall. Portia swallowed at their charge. They must not be allowed to enter the room.

To make things worse, they all carried short swords. Portia hadn't realized the attendant was armed, for his sword had been hanging on the far side of his body. She herself had her knives, but four was too many for her to take on at once, even if her long knife had almost as much reach as their swords. The only other recourse she had was her magic. Luckily, it had been a while since she had used it and she had some energy reserves.

The first thing she did to slow them down was to ice the floor in front of them. It worked amazingly well, their legs slipping and sliding and one falling outright onto his back. It bought her a few moments.

"She has ice magic," one of the guards yelled, fury in his voice.

Unfortunately, she was so focused on the four coming down the hall she didn't realize there was another guard coming from the opposite direction. He grabbed her arm to yank her away from the door. She gave a small yelp then closed her eyes and focused on making light beams around her and in front of his face. Hopefully they would be strong enough to blind anyone else she had missed coming from the other direction.

"Is there someone else around?" one of the guards yelled in confusion.

"That is not an elf; she should not have more than one magic," someone else yelled.

By this time, several of the guards had managed to cross the ice covering the hallway and reach her. They held their stance in front of her, wary, their swords waving in front of them. A few looked around for others to be the brave one to charge her. One finally found his courage and rushed towards Portia.

They were too close for her to make a full duplicate so Portia in desperation made duplicates of her knife arm and sent them whirling. She looked like an eight armed demon. It would take courage to attack her, even if they knew only one of the knives was real. But the guard persisted in his rush, raising his weapon to Portia. He guessed wrongly and swung wildly as the knife arm he aimed at gave way to nothingness. Portia hit him sharply with the hilt of her knife and knocked him out. He fell to the ground in front of her, forming a partial barrier to any others who would attack her.

This infuriated the remaining guards. As a group they rushed towards her, and Portia inhaled sharply then exhaled and imagined a wave of air emanating from her, pushing all the attackers away. It worked. She managed to blow them back towards the ice, and once on it they slid down the hallway and landed with a crash at the far wall. Portia was shaking with the effort. Darkness came around the edges of her vision, and she feared she would topple over. She put a hand out to the wall, trying to steady herself without making it obvious how weakened she was.

Luckily, just then Sergeant Lyren whipped open the door from the inside and looked out, surprised to see the scene in front of her. She took it all in then grabbed Portia and hopped over the fallen guard at their feet, dragging Portia along behind her. Portia stumbled over the guard but managed to keep her feet as Sergeant Lyren drew her down the stairs.

"Quick," Sergeant Lyren said. Portia needed no encouragement.

They reached the bottom of the stairs. The secretary and butler were standing at the bottom of the stairway, their mouths open in circles of surprise. Portia looked back up the stairs behind them and saw the guards just reaching the head of the landing. With one last burst of energy she froze the stairway all the way to the top, ending with a tall ice barrier that reached from the bottom of the stairs to nearly the ceiling, sealing off the upstairs from the downstairs. Muffled shouts of anger and surprise came through the ice.

Sergeant Lyren nodded her approval then dragged Portia out the door, past the shocked household staff still standing there.

They exited the building quickly. Luckily, no noise from the interior had reached the guards standing outside for they let Sergeant Lyren and Portia pass. The elf and human walked several blocks quickly, putting some distance between the maroon and gold building and themselves.

"Well, he's not responsible for the kidnappings. I'm sure of that," Sergeant Lyren said.

Portia looked at her sideways. She was curious to know how Lyren was so sure, but judging by the noise from the inside was a little afraid to ask what interrogation techniques the sergeant had used. She scared Portia a little.

"Okay, talk, young human. I counted at least three types of magic back there. The light beams were so bright they lit the room from under the door. Humans are not supposed to do that. What gives? Who are you exactly, Portia Harris?"

Portia glanced over but Sergeant Lyren wasn't even looking at her. Instead, she looked steadily forward and walked quickly. It was weird to hear the sergeant use her name. And it impressed Portia that Sergeant Lyren had taken in so much information in such a short time. But that also left Portia in the uncomfortable position of having to explain herself. She swallowed. Her professors had not explicitly warned her about hiding her skills in the Elven kingdom, only to other humans. At least that was what she thought. Besides, her skills were the reason she was here. It was because she *was* different from other humans. "I'm a Jack."

Sergeant Lyren gave her a glance at that. "I've not heard of such a thing. What is it, exactly, to be a Jack?"

Portia could answer this one honestly. "I'm not exactly sure. I'm just learning myself. But I can do more magic than the average human can. At least more types of magic. I'm not all that strong. Speaking of which..." Portia said, and she stopped walking. The black was returning to her vision, and she felt faint. Rest was needed, and soon.

Sergeant Lyren saw immediately that Portia was weak. She ushered her to sit down at the table of an outside café they were passing by. Her fierce look silenced the glare of the elf waiter standing outside.

"Bring us some mead and some bread and cheese," Sergeant Lyren said to the waiter. When he didn't move, she yelled in his direction, "Now!"

He scurried off to do as she bid.

Portia was grateful to sit down and rest. When the mead arrived, she drank half the glass in a few long swallows. She ate the bread and cheese gratefully. Her strength slowly returned to her. Sergeant Lyren did not ask her any further questions, instead letting her eat and recover. Portia felt her stare and knew the sergeant was evaluating her, but she was too tired to care.

When Portia was recovered, they rose from the table. Sergeant Lyren dropped a coin on the table as they left, not bothering to ask how much the bill was. Portia doubted the waiter or the establishment would challenge the officer, no matter how much she had left. But she was grateful to see it was a silver coin and knew the place had not been unfairly paid. Oddly, it gave Portia more trust in the sergeant. She'd been ripped off herself too many times in the past to want to deal with someone who was not honest.

After they exited the inner city, Sergeant Lyren turned towards Portia as they walked. "Okay, we are away from listening ears. I want to learn more about what this Jack status means and how you came about it."

"I... don't know. I think I was born this way," Portia said.

Any further explanation she might have had was interrupted by the man from the previous night stepping in their path. It was the same man who had tried to kidnap her and Finrod. His face was screwed up in fury. He had a black eye, which made him look even meaner. Portia wondered if he had been waiting there all day to try to ambush her again. Luckily, Finrod was nowhere in sight, and instead she was in the companionship of the sergeant, a fact the man seemed to have missed. Or else he foolishly did not care or understand what he was getting himself into.

"You foolish girl. You'll not get away from me again. And I'll make you pay for the night I had last night," he said, his eyes boring into Portia. She could feel hatred emanating off his body. It was fully focused on her.

Sergeant Lyren almost looked excited as she stared at the man. She pulled her own weapon, a knife similar to the one Portia carried, and widened her stance to a fighting one.

"Hello, young man. Are you here to play with us?" Sergeant Lyren asked.

The man dragged his eyes away from Portia and looked at the elf sergeant, seeing her for perhaps the first time. Some fury left his face to be replaced with apprehension. But he didn't run.

"If you call it play to lose your life," he said, bravado in his voice.

"That is not something I've experienced nor plan to anytime soon. You'll have to tell me. Oh wait, you'll be dead," Sergeant Lyren said, not missing a beat.

Portia drew her own knife. She didn't feel strong enough to do any more magic, but knife work was reflexive to her. It didn't require as much energy. Besides, there were two of them to one of him, even if he towered over them both.

The man lunged towards Sergeant Lyren but then veered towards Portia and jabbed at her with his blade, ducking out of the elf's counterattack at the same time. Despite his size, he was quick on his feet. Portia was quicker. She used her knife to block his and then swept along his clothing with it. The quickest way to see if he had any tattoos was to take his shirt off for him.

And it worked. He backed away from Portia's counterattack and looked down in amazement as his shirt fell in tatters to the ground. There, upon his right forearm, just the same as the bandits in the road, was the diamond tattoo. Portia sucked in her breath. He was one of the cult members. Here, in Rocabarra. In the Elven kingdom. The capital city of the Elven kingdom. Dread settled into her stomach. This was not a lone attacker. More than likely, he had other accomplices nearby.

Luckily for Portia and Sergeant Lyren, none of his other friends were close enough for him to rely on them. He looked at the elf and girl with their blades out, then to the remains of his shirt on the ground, and made the decision to flee. He ran down the road away from them.

Sergeant Lyren ran after him, yelling for others to stop him. But no bystanders stepped in front of the huge man running down the street. Portia could hear Sergeant Lyren cursing under her breath as she ran after him. She would have joined the elf in her pursuit, but she felt too weak herself to do so. Portia needed to reserve some energy in case anyone else came to attack her.

Sergeant Lyren returned empty-handed, a black look on her face. "I take it that man was your attacker last night. Why did you take off his shirt instead of just stabbing him outright?"

Portia was shocked at the question. "I'm a guest here. I didn't want to attack a stranger."

"Self-defense is another thing entirely. You see that man, and I'm with you, then you stab him, do you understand me?

At least enough to keep him from fleeing. Get his leg or something."

Portia nodded at that. She did not relish the thought of hurting anybody but wasn't going to argue with the sergeant. Hopefully it would not come up again. "Can you do magic?" she asked Sergeant Lyren.

"Not much. Not enough to stop that man. Why didn't you do any? Still too weak?"

Portia nodded. Perhaps she should have tried harder. But she was too afraid of passing out in public, alone. If the sergeant had been running off after that man, there would be no one to defend her. Portia did not feel safe enough in Rocabarra to leave herself vulnerable like that.

"So, the shirt. There must have been a reason. You don't strike me as the type to torture people with no reason. Why did you take his shirt off?" the sergeant asked.

"To see if he had any tattoos. And he did. I think that tattoo is a symbol of a cult. One that's causing problems in the human kingdom. A lot of problems. The guards are struggling with them. Its members are terrorizing common folk so badly that it's hard to get anyone to talk about it." Portia tried to explain, not feeling fully confident in what little knowledge she had.

"Perhaps that explains our crime wave here. Things have changed here quickly. And not for the better. But then again, you understand that since now you have to become a Friend of the City to even be in the inner city." Sergeant Lyren motioned for Portia to join her walking back towards the inn. There was nothing else to be done here for the moment. Portia was grateful to be going back. She was exhausted.

When they returned to the inn, Sergeant Lyren insisted on buying Portia a meal. Portia knew she got free dinners but wasn't sure about lunch, so she didn't argue. Indeed, she was too tired to argue. The sergeant wanted to know more about the cult, but Portia had little knowledge to share. Sergeant Lyren promised to return again to talk to Lady Harper about this issue. Perhaps the royal envoy would know more.

The sergeant left before Portia had finished her meal. There was no one else in the dining room except Jsoth, who was folding napkins around silverware. Portia was not looking forward to going back to her tiny room, so she asked Jsoth to not clear her setting and then she went to her room to retrieve her book. She might as well sit in the dining room and sip tea and read her book while she waited for Lady Harper to return. There was nothing she could do now except perhaps take a nap, and she wasn't ready to do that yet.

But the book was not reassuring reading. The author was not a kind person, at least not judging by anything written in the tome. He spoke of the base camp they set up on an island and more rejoicing in the bloody raids they had inflicted on the city they were attacking. The description was specific enough that Portia gasped out loud when she realized the author was speaking of Coverack. The bloodbath being described happened in the capital city of the kingdom of Haulstatt—if it was the kingdom of Haulstatt back then. But of the city described being the city of Coverack, there was no doubt. It described the location in minute detail, right down to the purple stone of the royal castle, a stone that Portia had seen nowhere else in her limited travels. She was sure there was no other city that had such a purple castle settled just so upon the city wall facing the sea.

Another gasp followed when she realized the dead and dying described in the book were elves. The author had a different name for them, something she didn't recognize, but the author made it clear they were not the same as the invaders. The author felt little remorse in cutting them down and killing them because they were so different and little and small. And they wanted the land the elves had. They were going to take it no matter what the cost. Portia put down the book in shock. No wonder the elves had constructed such a huge wall to keep out humans, if indeed this book was written by a human. She could now understand the massive scale of the Eternal Wall that ringed the elf kingdom.

"Fun reading?" a concerned voice asked.

Portia looked up to see Lady Harper standing in front of her. Her face turned red. She felt guilty by association and horrified at what she had just read. Somehow she felt personally responsible for what happened to the elves. Looking up at an elf who had been kind to her made her feel worse.

"Not fun reading, no," Portia said. Lady Harper looked concerned, tilting her head in question. "It's about a battle. I think it's when... the invasion of Coverack happened. When it was held by elves."

Lady Harper looked surprised. "No, that would not be fun. It was a horrible time for our people. How did you come to have such a volume?" Lady Harper picked up the book and opened it. She scanned a few lines and Portia could tell she was able to read it. "We know our own history, that much is true, but we have nothing so specific as this volume. Where did you get it?"

Portia swallowed. She didn't think it was a secret but still felt strange telling the elf what she asked. "It came from a special library on the Academy grounds. The Library of Mages, although it doesn't have much about magic in it. The librarian herself... I think she was a little surprised too. This is a translation though. Few people could have read the original."

Lady Harper nodded and sat down opposite Portia. "That is probably how the original survived. How did you get this translation?"

"It was given to me by one of my professors. He has the original. For safekeeping."

Lady Harper pursed her lips. It looked like she wanted to ask more but did not. Instead, she waved over the server and ordered a glass of wine. "Well I have some good news for us. You're going to meet the king in the morning."

"But how? I haven't actually done anything yet," Portia asked.

"Sergeant Lyren seems to think otherwise. She has already put in a good word for you. It's enough that we've been granted access for you to the inner city. The king would like to meet you before he makes a decision about whether you are allowed to learn the magic. It is one step at a time. You must do your best to convince him tomorrow. We need an alliance—human and Elven—to prevent another such occurrence as detailed in this book."

Fear gripped Portia. It was one thing to read about the massacre of the city, it was another to have to face such a thing in person. They had to succeed in stopping another invasion.

13

Portia awoke nervous about her meeting with the king and queen. She wished she had brought along the locket she had gotten from Elyas. Somehow holding it made her feel better. But she sighed, knowing she made the right decision to leave it back in her room in the pyromancy house in Haulstatt. She would have been sad if she had lost it on the road. And that was more than possible, considering they'd been attacked once while traveling, and then again as part of the kidnapping attempt she had thwarted in the city.

Lady Harper and Portia made their way to the castle. A special letter of invitation granted Portia passage into the inner city. It also earned her a few interested looks from the guards.

The castle was sprawling and intricately constructed, in a style completely unlike any of the buildings in Haulstatt. The roof flowed in curves. It rose over each narrow window and then down again. Nowhere was it straight. But even with its curves, it was still fitted with ramparts for archers. Additionally, an entire outer wall encircled the structure, itself dotted with narrow windows and spouts for hot oil. All of it was constructed of a deep ruby red stone. The stone glowed. The castle was both a beautiful place to live and a well-constructed defense for its inhabitants. It was more impressive than the one in Coverack, something Portia would have not thought possible until she saw it with her own eyes.

They were led through the castle by a steward. He walked extremely fast for such a small elf. Portia regretted their pace, for she longed to stop and stare at all the beautiful objects displayed along the way. As in the Coverack castle, there was also a portrait room filled with portraits of royalty, this time all elves.

When they were introduced and ushered into the throne room Portia sucked in a gasp of surprise. It was packed with noble elves. These must be the royal court. They were dressed in incredible finery—silks, velvets, and even some material she didn't recognize, one that had fine strands that stood up in the air and waved like dandelion seeds in the breeze. But there was no breeze in the throne room, so the material itself gave the illusion of a living creature wrapped around the elf wearing it, breathing and watching Portia, along with its owner.

King Magnus sat on the throne that was only a few steps higher than the surrounding crowds. The throne was carved of dark wood that ran in swirls and hollows. Queen Ceola sat on a similar wood throne, one that was slightly smaller than the king's. There was an opening in the stone floor around both thrones and it appeared the thrones were growing from the ground beneath and into the room. Portia sensed that the thrones were much larger than the portion visible in the room, and that they ran down below the room they were in, if not further. She could feel magic from their direction and wondered if it was from the king and queen, or perhaps from the thrones. Or both.

Guards kept everyone at a respectful distance. The elf king and queen were surprisingly young. Most of the surrounding attendants and noblemen and women appeared older. One particularly obnoxious advisor stood close to the king—almost over him. Portia instinctively wanted to push him away from King Magnus. The intensity of her loathing for the standing elf took her by surprise. She struggled to push it down as she performed an awkward curtsy to the king and queen and once again chided herself for not practicing this basic skill more. It seemed she was always asked to use it, and she did it so poorly.

King Magnus waved his fingers at the advisor next to him who then stepped forward and cleared his throat and spoke. "This human child is brought before the court, named in a petition to be Friend of the Elves." He did not hide the skepticism in his voice. The king scowled at that but did not correct his advisor's manner.

Unhappy grumbles from the noblemen greeted this pronouncement. The king let the grumbling continue. He looked over the crowd. Portia thought he might be looking for the reactions of specific elves, but she wasn't sure. He was calm in the face of the apparent opposition. For the first time in her life, Portia was grateful to not be a king or queen. Orphans had more freedom, and less disapprobation.

Finally King Magnus raised his hand. Silence came over the throne room. "Bring in the witnesses," the king said in a quiet voice.

A side door was opened by two footmen. A troop of six guards escorted in the merchant Sergeant Lyren and Portia had visited yesterday, as well as Finrod, Sergeant Lyren, and the sullen human assailant who had attacked Portia twice. The assailant had been given another shirt, one that ill fit him and was too short in the sleeves. It revealed the diamond tattoo on his forearm.

Portia sucked in her breath in surprise. Somehow, overnight, Sergeant Lyren had found their assailant and brought him in—for Portia had no doubt this was Sergeant Lyren's work. Again she was impressed with the capabilities of the elf. Murmurs filled the throne room as the noblemen jostled for position to see who was being brought in.

Portia looked at the merchant nervously. She was surprised to see him there. She had no reason to think he would say anything good about her.

Sergeant Lyren gave her a wink, as if to calm her, but as it had done before, her wink gave Portia nothing but confusion.

Finrod gave Portia a warm smile. He too winked at Portia and then looked at Sergeant Lyren, who gave him an approving nod. At least there was one person, no, two—if indeed she could count on Sergeant Lyren—who were fully on her side besides Lady Harper.

"We will hear from the merchant first," the king said.

The merchant stepped forward and gave the king and queen a bow. He turned to face Portia and then all those in attendance in the throne room. "I have been called here to bear witness on the character of this human. Some would say I am a fool to speak words on behalf of a human girl, but I have seen her work firsthand. She aided the law enforcement officer here while taking care to do no permanent harm to any of my staff, despite overwhelming odds against her. She met her obligations yet harmed no elf, despite severe provocation." He looked around the room, serious, then added with a wry smile on his face, "My only complaint is the water stains in my hallway rug, but I have been assured that those will be taken care of in the name of the kingdom." His chuckle was the only sound in the room.

This was not at all what Portia expected him to say. For she had prevented his workers from doing their jobs and protecting him. But it was true that she had made pains to hurt no one.

Portia was not the only one surprised. Angry murmurs arose from the noble elves. At least one cried out 'traitor'. Portia flushed with anger and embarrassment. Was it so hard to believe a human could do something worthy?

King Magnus motioned for silence, which slowly came to the room. "Is there anything you would like to add?" he said to the merchant.

"Only that I would trust her to guard my child," the merchant said.

His testimony confused Portia. Did Sergeant Lyren really interrogate him, or was it more of a test for her? Portia looked to Sergeant Lyren, who refused to meet her eyes and instead looked around the room and tapped her feet as if she was not paying attention to the testimony. Portia was not fooled. The sergeant was too perceptive for that.

Finrod also had good things to say, although he did mention it was humiliating to be led around by a human, even a good human. But his haughty remarks, delivered in the piping voice of a child, brought laughter into the room and eased the tension.

"Sergeant Lyren, please speak your piece," the king said.

Sergeant Lyren stepped forward to address the room. "Portia Harris has provided an invaluable service to our force. As we all know," she said, looking around the room for confirmation, "there has been a rise in violence and kidnapping directed at our young elves." Angry mutters met this. "I fear there are many more that we don't even know about yet. But thanks to this young lady, we have word of a cult that is more than likely responsible. You see in front of you one of the members of the cult. This is our true enemy. Portia Harris has helped reveal them. Lady Harper of the Meadows can fill us all in on further details. I fear we have much work to do, but at least we know now where to focus it."

Lady Harper nodded agreement.

The volume of chatter in the room rose to a fever pitch. Angry elves looked at the attacker who glared back at them sullenly. He was unrepentant, his jaw set in a firm line. He hated all in the room but fixed his glare most especially on Portia—he loathed her most of all. Portia stepped closer to Lady Harper.

The king waved to his advisor.

"Silence!" the advisor said.

"You are allowed to speak to these charges. What say you?" King Magnus asked the man.

The man flexed his jaw and stared forward resolutely, neither speaking nor acknowledging the king. One of the guards stepped forward, his staff raised to strike at the back of the man's knees, but the king's hand stopped him.

"You will answer me," the king said.

Again the man said nothing.

King Magnus sighed and then stood up. He sang in a soft musical tone, a melody Portia could barely hear, even standing so close. But despite its quietness, she could feel the power emanating from the king. Magic flowed from him, directed to the man. Portia felt its strength in the back of her neck and arms.

The man widened his stance but it was no use. A force pulled him down to his knees. He hit the floor hard with his knees and nearly fell completely over but pushed himself back up. He was unable to raise a leg to stand so was stuck kneeling in front of the king. The man finally no longer towered over the crowd. They drew close to see him despite the warning looks from the king's advisors.

The king stopped singing, but unlike other times when Portia had witnessed elf magic, the tingle of the casting continued even when the melody stopped. The throne behind the king hummed, resonating with the tune the king had been singing. The hollows in its carved wood held the notes much longer than would have naturally been possible.

The king walked up to the man, facing him from mere inches away. He said softly, "Answer my question. What say you about this young lady?"

The man's mouth opened, and he gagged. Words were coming from him despite his trying to swallow them back. He glared at the king, fury in his eyes. Finally, he could prevent himself from speaking no longer and the words gushed out. "I don't know that *girl*. But I suspect she is a Jack. She endangers us all, just as this kingdom does with its failure to recognize the glory of the coming of the others."

One of the guards could take this no longer and struck the man in the back of the head with his staff. The king held up his hand to prevent further blows.

"Tell us of this glory," the king said.

"The golden age is coming. You, and all here, are fools. You would stop it. The golden age must not be stopped and must be welcome. All those who oppose it must be deposed." Spittle ran down the side of the man's face. He was shaking, but from fighting the magic or from the depth of his hatred, Portia could not tell.

"You speak of treason," King Magnus said softly.

The room was quiet. All onlookers held their breath, waiting for the man's response.

The man looked around wildly, as if for the first time, the whites of his eyes showing. He struggled to shut his mouth, but it flew open again. He put his hands over his mouth, trying to keep from speaking, but with one motion from the king his hands were magically forced down. His words came once again against his will. "It is treason to resist the golden age. It is treason to allow a Jack to live. I am not the one committing treason—you are. You will all perish soon. This kingdom will crumble, as it should."

The king turned from the man and walked back to his throne. With one motion from his hand the sound coming from his throne stopped as he sat down. He eyed the shaking man from his vantage point. Finally he turned to the guards around the witnesses. "Take this man to the dungeons. We will tease the rest of this out later." But he held up one finger to stop the guards. "There is perhaps one question that must be answered now. Are you a member of the cult Sergeant Lyren speaks of?"

"It is the order of the righteous. It is no cult. We are the rightful heirs of the golden age." The man thrust out his chin defiantly.

King Magnus nodded and waved for the prisoner to be taken away.

It took four guards to control him. They roughly hauled the man to his feet and dragged him from the room. He struggled the entire way. The watching elves drew back from the struggling man and watched him until the door was shut behind.

Portia realized she was shaking. The king's power was formidable, no matter how young he looked.

As soon as the doors shut behind the prisoner the elves in the room began speaking. Nobles were yelling for the man to be executed and for all humans to be removed from the kingdom. Portia's stomach tightened at the anger and loathing she heard when the word human was used by those around her.

She looked to Sergeant Lyren to see if she should be concerned, but the sergeant was unperturbed.

Lady Harper calmly gazed out at the crowd.

Portia concentrated on her breathing. If those two were not concerned, then perhaps all would be well.

The king let the muttering go on. Once again he seemed to be looking through the crowd and looking for individual reactions. Nothing seemed to bother him. The queen was checking the reactions of those around her as well. She stopped looking, contented, before the king did and stared ahead. She waited patiently for him to speak.

Finally, the king held up one hand and the muttering ceased. "You have heard the evidence regarding our young friend here, Portia Harris. Based on the evidence, I am ruling that she is a Friend of the Elves. She has the right to all the rights of a Friend of the Elves, and she will be given the honor and respect as such."

A few angry yells greeted this pronouncement. One nobleman went so far as to step forward and call in the king's direction. "She should be banished, as should all humans, based on what we just heard. We have no way of knowing if she is any different from that man. All humans are the same."

King Magnus fixed his gaze on the noble, who stopped speaking. The elves cleared around him and he was on his own in front of the king. His face turned red and he stepped back, trying to bow and get out of the circle of attention, but it was useless, for when he backed up the crowd retreated as well, and he was still standing alone.

"Your concerns are heard, Lord Wellesley," the king said.

The elf swallowed at the mention of his name. He bowed his head and said nothing further.

"However, the clock will strike soon. We do not have the liberty to debate forever. If this girl can help in our fight, we owe it to ourselves to make use of the opportunity presented to us," the king said. "Does anyone else wish to speak against Portia Harris with a specific complaint? Do any know her well enough to speak against her?" The king looked around for others with objections, but no one dared step forward. The silence held in the room for several breaths.

Finally, the king waved his hand. "Very well. You are dismissed. Leave."

The room emptied from the back, the noble elves and advisors filing out the two sets of double doors there. Portia moved to leave with them, but Lady Harper held her back with one hand. She also held back Sergeant Lyren, who turned in surprise at Lady Harper's hand.

"Your exemplary service might be needed in the future, so you should see this," Lady Harper said to Sergeant Lyren, whose eyes flickered to the king. "By royal request."

Sergeant Lyren nodded at this, a pleased smile flicking on her face and quickly disappearing again.

The only others remaining were Queen Ceola and several guards. All others had left, including the senior advisors. Portia had never seen the human queen and king consort in Coverack without their advisors nearby.

When the last of the nobles exited the room and the doors were shut behind them, King Magnus turned to Portia. "What

I've heard here publicly, and privately as well, about you is impressive. Welcome to our kingdom, young Jack Portia."

Portia stammered and blushed. She didn't think she would ever get used to being addressed by royalty. "Thank you." Curiosity burned in her stomach, and she forced herself to be brave and speak. "You Highness, what clock are you talking about?"

Her face burned red, knowing she should not have volunteered the question, but she hoped she would be forgiven as a human who didn't know proper protocol. Lady Harper sighed at her brazenness.

But the king merely stood and motioned for the others to follow him. He led them deep into the castle, past the rooms of plaster and lathe and paint. They went into passages that were carved of rock, with the limbs of trees and tree trunks growing through them. The outside of the castle looked like any other building, but the inside connected into underground passages seamlessly; there was no sharp boundary between building and cave. She wondered if the castle was just the tip of the massive structure extending far below.

Finally, they reached the end of a long dark hallway. It was lit with torches. The smoke from the torches wafted up to the ceiling and, looking up, she could see small pinpricks of light where shafts had been placed to provide fresh air. Two of the guards with them went to the door ahead and opened it. Just inside, there was another set of doors. This time, only the king approached. He pulled a key from his belt and placed it on the lock holding the two doors shut. It didn't look like a normal key but rather something magical, for he placed it on the lock after which a loud click sounded within the doors. The king stepped back, and the doors swung open on their own.

Inside was a huge cavern as large as the throne room. The walls sparkled and shone in the dim light. At first, Portia thought it was water flowing down the curved walls, but a closer look revealed gems and gold flakes embedded within the stone walls themselves. The walls curved up to the ceiling where the roots of a gigantic tree raced across the ceiling in all directions. Directly below the tree above them, in the center of the cavern, sat a gigantic hourglass. It was twice as tall as Portia and half again as wide. The glass containing the sand was warped and wavy and not completely clear. Instead, it shimmered in a subtle rose color. The hourglass looked like a gigantic flower nestled in the middle of the room.

Portia stepped closer. The sand was not flowing evenly: sometimes it stopped, the sand held motionless in the air, and other times it flowed backwards, racing back up through the narrow center of the hourglass to rejoin the sand at the top. She turned back to the group. Lady Harper was not surprised, nor was Sergeant Lyren. Everyone knew what the hourglass was except her.

King Magnus stepped forward towards the glass. "This clock tells us the time until the next splintering."

Portia's mouth fell open as she looked back at the gigantic structure. "Then you know when it will happen."

"Vaguely. We can read it to within a year. At least that is the best guess of our mages, for it has only been tested by the last splintering, when it was constructed in desperation."

Portia knew the last splintering was when humans had arrived. She swallowed at the reminder of the bitter history between humans and elves.

"It tells us that the splintering is close," the king said. "That is why Lady Harper was sent to Coverack. I admit surprise that she returned with you, but if we are to have an alliance with the humans, that means we must trust in their techniques. You are one of their strongest techniques from what I have been told." He glanced at Lady Harper. He must have great trust in the royal envoy indeed. Portia vowed to herself to make it well placed. She had to protect all their lives.

"Can I... Can I touch it?" Portia asked. The clock pulled at her. She wanted to get closer. She wanted to touch the wooden frame and the glass containing the sand.

The king nodded permission.

Portia stepped closer to the clock. She could feel the magic emanating off it. It too was a tool designed to prevent future catastrophe, just as she had been. She felt an affinity for the clock, stuck in a dark cavern and the depths of the castle. With her hand on the glass, she felt vibrations, deeply rhythmic ones. It pulsed as if it were breathing, as if it were alive. She sucked in her breath, surprised.

The king's voice brought her back to the group. "But it is running out of time, as are we. If we are to avail ourselves of your help, then you must begin your training immediately. It is not easy. The magic to heal splinters is a specific type of healing magic." The King stopped speaking, looking around at his guards. He thought for a second then continued on. "Of all the elves so skilled in our kingdom, our best is old. Very old. And he is, of course, an elf."

Portia turned at the last statement. She didn't understand the significance. Of course he was an elf. "Could you not bring him to the splinter with your army as a guard?"

King Magnus stared at her. Finally, Lady Harper replied. "Jack, knowing what you know of humans, what do you think would happen if the elves brought an army into Haulstatt Kingdom?"

Portia did not know how to answer that. She didn't think it would go well. There were few elves in the human kingdom, and even in the capital city of Coverack, the elves were not all that well received. How then would a gigantic force, all armed, be received? At the very least, it would cause panic amongst the humans, if not outright fighting. It would be a distraction against the real danger—the unknown that might come through another splintering. From what she had read of her book, the humans and the elves had been evenly balanced. Neither one was able to overpower the other completely. What if the invaders were not like that? What if they were so powerful that all fell before them?

No, having a war between humans and elves would be a disaster. They needed to focus on the real danger. The danger of who would come through the gate of the splinter.

14

They stood in the cavern in silence for a moment watching the sand continue its path through the gigantic hourglass.

King Magnus nodded at Portia's sober expression. "A guard would not be well received by the humans, nor would an army. We could negotiate for these things to come to pass, but that would take a great deal of time, and trust that might not ever exist. Even so, we are working on it. Unfortunately, events might not wait for the slow path of diplomacy, nor account for all obstinacy." He sighed heavily. "But it is good you are a quick one and understand the problem we are facing. You will be staying here in the castle. Quarters are being arranged. Your lessons start tomorrow."

He walked away, followed by the queen. Once he was gone, it was only Portia, Sergeant Lyren, and Lady Harper along with a few guards left in the hourglass room.

Lady Harper smiled at Portia and took her hands in her

own—an unusually warm gesture for the elf. "You did it. Well done."

"I feel like I haven't done anything yet," Portia said.

"Oh you will. After a few days of lessons, you'll feel differently," Sergeant Lyren said, ruefully.

Portia looked at her quizzically.

Sergeant Lyren laughed. "This teacher has taught many of us. I will not spoil it by sharing more, except to say rest well tonight, young human."

LADY HARPER and Portia stayed in the hourglass room a bit longer while Sergeant Lyren left to tend to her duties. Portia placed both hands on the hourglass and felt the humming of the gigantic structure. She thought she could pick out a pattern to it, but every time she was close to deciphering the rhythm, the beat changed. The resonance flowing through the wood and glass was so deep that it felt like it was a rumbling coming from deep within the earth. She wondered if the hourglass was somehow connected to the ground below it.

A servant came to the door and cleared his throat. "Quarters are ready for the Friend of the Elves," he said with a bow when they turned to face him.

He led them through the castle, down long hallways, back into the portion of the castle that was made of glowing red stone instead of the carved walls within the ground. They crossed a large courtyard filled with manicured shrubs and beautiful flowers towards a far tower. Portia looked around.

The tower was as far from the castle as it could be and still be on the grounds. Friend of the Elves or not, she was being kept at some distance.

Lady Harper noticed her gaze. "Yes, this is intentional. But there are advantages to being so far from the main compound. You will also be far from the lords."

"Are the lords going to cause me trouble?" Portia asked.

Lady Harper hesitated, looked around, then spoke quietly. "Our goal is to avoid that. Some might try to interfere, but most are simply not used to you yet. You don't have the time to woo them to your side, so the best thing is to avoid them. You need to concentrate on why you're here, which is to learn the magic of the healing."

Just as quietly, Portia responded, "Very well." She was glad to be far from the lords. She knew she was not the most diplomatic, and she didn't wish to expend the energy to try to get them on her side. It cost her too much energy just to do magic.

They climbed the tower. Portia's room was at the very top. It was a large circular room that encompassed the whole top of the tower, reached by the circular metal staircase that wound up from below through the floor. She was glad she had some experience with climbing buildings, but even so, the open circular staircase made her stomach jump. It was a long way down. She had to find some rope and keep it on her at all times. There was some wisdom in always having a second escape route available, even in the castle of a king. Or especially so.

A bed, a desk, and few chairs furnished the room. Portia's

bag hung on a hook on the back of the door. Pulling it close to check its contents, its lightness told her without even looking that it was empty. Portia's heart beat quickly until she walked to the nearby wardrobe and opened it: all her clothes were inside. The translated book sat on the desk, and her money bag was inside the top drawer. She'd check its contents later, out of sight of the watching servant. The money bag being there surprised her. And worried her too, for she had thought it well hidden within her room at the inn. It was her backup in case the one she carried with her was stolen.

Lady Harper looked around the room in approval, and then dismissed the servant who had escorted them there. She walked across the room and picked up the book and opened it to the bookmark that Portia had left in it.

Portia turned her back to Lady Harper to hang her bag up again, straightening and smoothing it unnecessarily. The last time she'd read that book, it told of attacking the elves in the invasion of Coverack itself. "I think that section is about an invasion of Coverack. But the author spoke of the residents being elves," she said, the last coming out in a rush.

Lady Harper sighed. "Yes. We built that city. The Elven kingdom bordered the seas for a long time." She shut the book and held it for a second before setting it down again and facing Portia. "But we are not as entirely innocent as you might think. It's true we built Coverack. But it was built on the ashes of the city that had been there before, one whose name I do not know. One built by dwarves." Sitting heavily into a chair. "As angry as we are at the humans, the most truthful amongst us must admit our own guilt. We have done just the same. We pushed others out of their home."

This was news to Portia. Turning slowing away from her bag, she gapped at Lady Harper. She wanted to ask more, but all her questions were a jumble in her mind.

Lady Harper waved away her gaze. "I'm sure some historian will be thrilled to bore you with the history, young friend. Truly, I don't have many details to share with you. It's not much spoken of here," Lady Harper said.

Portia nodded. She would try to be patient. Her stomach growled. Even with her large breakfast, she was hungry again.

Lady Harper heard the noise and snorted. "Your stomach is as regular as that hourglass. I think it is lunchtime. What say you?" She shook her head. "Why am I asking? You're always ready to eat, I've noticed."

Portia could not disagree with her. It was embarrassing that Lady Harper had noticed, but not nearly enough to shame Portia from wanting more food.

"I'll see what the arrangements are for lunch," Lady Harper said. "Stay here."

When Lady Harper exited, Portia picked up the book again. She wanted to see if it said anything about dwarves. She didn't think it likely since she barely recognized the description of elves, but it was worth trying. Skimming the book quickly, she saw nothing but more descriptions of bloodshed in the city streets, but one section did catch her eye. It was describing elves performing magic. The human narrator had never seen such a thing before. He was fascinated. It had been amazingly effective at rebuffing the human advances into the city, until the invaders began to plan for it. Nowhere did it speak of a human performing magic. If that was so, then when did humans learn to do magic?

But even with the best planning on the invaders part, the Elven magic had been effective enough to chase the humans back to the island they had come from—the island beneath the gate. When the invaders were pushed back, their retreat was complicated by the presence of other humans. Humans from a different tribe. They were not friendly, and the author spoke of despair of ever surviving since they now had to fight on two fronts: the new human invaders, and the enraged and put-upon elves defending their lands. Portia chewed her lip reading this. Humans sounded awful. War sounded awful.

Lady Harper knocked on the door. "Ready to see the dining hall?"

Portia's stomach responded with a loud rumble. She ducked her head in embarrassment and quickly put the book down.

Lady Harper led her back down the tower and towards the main castle. To Portia's surprise, when they entered the cavernous dining hall, she saw the king and queen, as well as nobles seated on long tables, along with household staff and others.

She turned to Lady Harper. "The king eats here? With everyone else?" It didn't look right. Only his finer clothes marked him apart, although she did notice that most of the nobles sat together and away from the king, occasionally sending him sharp looks. They sent their sharp looks towards many others in the room as well.

"Yes, he does. The new way of eating was one of the changes King Magnus instituted when he became king. He wants to know more about the workings of the castle, as well as the concerns of the staff. It infuriates the nobles." Lady Harper sniffed. "You should hear their ire when the king goes on the streets to talk to his citizens. One or two of them might just die of stress and upset. Silly creatures."

While Portia watched, a commoner approached the king, giving him a bow and then taking the seat the king indicated near him. The nobles at the nearby table glared at the commoner who studiously kept his gaze away from them. The nobles were trying to intimidate the poor man, but neither he nor the king paid them any attention. Portia stifled a laugh. She liked this king.

Lady Harper and Portia sat at the far end of the long table the nobles were seated at. Portia wished they could have sat anywhere else, but there were no open spots. Where they sat was not a popular place. A few of the nobles glared down the table at them, but Portia ignored them.

A server quickly brought them boards filled with food and glasses of ale. Portia ate quickly. She was gratified when the server brought her a second serving after she finished her first. At least she would not go hungry here.

"Where can I learn more here about Coverack when it was Elvin? It might be helpful to know that history," Portia asked Lady Harper. If the elves were the root of magic, perhaps this was somehow important.

But one of the noblemen must have been listening to the conversation for he piped in after her comment before Lady

Harper could respond. "You know nothing of this? And yet you are Friend of the Elves? This is a bad omen. You are too ignorant."

Portia knew she shouldn't respond, but his arrogant tone and disregard was just too much. "I'm still in school. I'm still learning."

"You'll not learn anything of value in that human kingdom," the nobleman replied with disdain.

"That is terrible to hear. Please tell me where I can learn. Is the knowledge in your library?" Portia asked, putting an innocent tone into her voice.

"Of course it's in our library. You should read it," he said.

"Then I will. By your invitation," Portia said, smiling at him sweetly. Lady Harper chuckled as she sipped her ale. "Who do I owe this great debt to?" Portia looked at him from under her eyelashes.

The nobleman sputtered at her reply.

Lady Harper leaned towards Portia and whispered in a voice meant for the nobleman to hear. "It is Lord Conwood."

Portia nodded her thanks to Lady Harper and then turned to Lord Conwood. "Thank you, Lord Conwood. I'll convey your respects to the librarian."

The nobleman looked at Lady Harper and then back at Portia, a frown growing on his face as he realized he'd been tricked. Somehow he had offered the use of their library to Portia. He couldn't take it back now without looking like a fool. He scowled and looked away, finishing the rest of his meal quickly.

Portia was drinking the last of her ale when King Magnus

rose. All the diners scrambled to their feet. On his way out the door, he walked past Lady Harper and Portia where he paused and addressed Lady Harper. "See that our young friend makes it to the library this afternoon. Lord Conwood is a generous man."

"Yes, Your Highness," Lady Harper said.

Lord Conwood's face turned red, and his fist clenched as he heard the exchange.

Portia looked down at her food. The king must have heard her exchange with the nobleman. She hoped she hadn't offended him. But he had offered the use of the library, so perhaps all was well.

The king left. Portia turned to the noblemen and saw them as one staring at her, their glares fierce, but none as daunting as Lord Conwood's angry countenance. A few had their mouths hanging open. At her gaze, they quickly looked away, some muttering in anger. The last to turn was Lord Conwood. Her heart sank. This was not good. She had made enemies. Powerful ones. And she had done so in less than half a day.

But Lady Harper did not seem concerned.

The library was a part of the castle itself. It was also made of the ruby red stones. It was as large as the main library on the campus of the Academy grounds. It must have taken a significant part of the castle, and it looked like it had been expanded from its original size, for in some areas parts of the red stone looked cut away, as if two separate rooms had been joined.

"I'll come and collect you later," Lady Harper said. "I

have official business to attend to. The librarian will help you. She's been here for as long as I can remember. She knows everything there is to know about these tomes." Lady Harper pointed to a small elf seated in the corner of the library.

The librarian was hard to see at first since she had white hair and white clothing and was sitting by a set of glowing white candles. She was reading a book beneath their light. The elf looked ancient—like Sir Alboka, but in miniature.

The elf flashed Portia a huge smile when she approached. She had so many wrinkles on her face that it was hard to see her gray eyes. But her voice was clear and melodic, belying her age. "You look for something, yes, my young friend?" The elf spoke in common but with a heavy accent. Portia could barely understand what she said.

"Yes. I want to learn more about the city now called Coverack, in Haulstatt," Portia said.

"We have little current information about Coverack." Her smile drooped a bit.

"I mean, I guess I want to know more about it when it was an Elven city. I don't know what it was called back then."

The elf leapt to her feet, surprisingly fast for being so old. "That is a different matter. There is no common word for the name of the city, it is only known in Elven." She sang a short melodic phrase. Portia didn't understand why. "That was the name of the city," the elf explained. Portia knew she would never be able to remember that. Was the entire Elven language also sung?

The librarian led her to a wall of books. "These books are

about the old land, before the Eternal Wall was built. They should have the information you seek."

She pulled one of the books from the wall and gave it to Portia, who opened it to read. The script was nothing she had ever seen before. It curved and rolled more complexly than even the cursive of the common tongue. Sweat broke out on her brow. She couldn't understand it.

The librarian noticed her consternation. "Can you not read Elven?"

Portia shook her head. Tears pricked her eyes. The magnitude of the challenge ahead of her became clearer. What if the spells she was to learn were also written in the Elven tongue and no one would explain them to her? How would she ever learn them? It would be possible to learn Elven, of course, but would take a great deal of time. The image of the huge hourglass flashed in front of her. Time was not something she had a great deal of.

"Enough of that," said the librarian, scolding. She patted Portia on the hand and then took the book from her. She flicked her fingers at Portia and sang a sharp tune rising in pitch so high that Portia's ears first hurt then couldn't hear anything. She looked at the elf directly and could see her mouthing words, but not a single tone reached her ears. The elf stopped singing, then beamed at Portia with a smug look on her face. "Okay dear, you're set."

Portia did not understand what she meant.

The librarian gave the book back to Portia. "Read it, dear."

Portia opened the book. It looked just the same as before. She looked at the librarian, confused.

"Try to unsee the letters."

"Unsee? What does that mean?" Portia asked.

"Look down at them, but don't look at them directly. Unfocus your eyes. Relax. Breathe in deeply and just stare ahead, sort of in their direction." The librarian smiled at her reassuringly.

Portia look down at the book again. She tried to relax her gaze and not look at any word in particular. Nothing happened. She glanced up, but the librarian waved for her to look down at the book again. Portia tried again. She gazed down in the general direction of the book but didn't look at any particular line or word. She concentrated her breathing in and out. Out of the corner of an eye a word flickered in the air above the book. She tried to look at the word directly and it disappeared. She gave a heavy sigh and then concentrated on her breathing again, and on unfocusing her eyes. Suddenly, the entire page, written in common, floated above the original page of the book. It was a translation that floated in space above the original text of the book. She gasped in surprise. When she tried to focus directly on the translation it disappeared again. Portia stifled the frustration she felt. She didn't want to appear ungrateful to the elf. She would just have to practice, for the technique did not come naturally to her.

"That is amazing," Portia said. "Thank you."

"Oh, it's just a little spell I know. You're set now," the librarian said, patting Portia's hand.

"How long does this last for?"

"A few decades, give or take. Long enough I suppose. They came up with it 'bout a thousand years ago," the elf said as she walked away. "That book in your hands will tell you what you want to know."

Portia watched her go, amazed. Lady Harper had told her the Eternal Wall was about a thousand years old. That spell must have been needed for the elves to communicate with the humans, and perhaps the dwarves as well.

Sitting down at a nearby table with the book, Portia opened it to the beginning. It had an introduction telling what the book was about. It promised a tale of the elf warriors recovering some prisoners from the humans who had taken them. The elves had also healed the splinter, what Portia thought was the same thing the humans called a gate, to the other world. Old elf magic healed the splinter. This must be the magic she was sent here to learn.

She sighed heavily and put the book down for a moment. It was a lot to take in. But she needed to know what the book said, so she picked it up and pushed on.

Lady Harper found her there several hours later. Even with the translation, the book was difficult to read, and Portia was tired. She looked up at Lady Harper standing over her. Lady Harper had dark circles under her eyes. Her face was drawn. She looked as exhausted as Portia felt.

Lady Harper leaned against the table. "You'll meet your teacher today, even though your lessons don't begin until tomorrow. The king will introduce you, for it is his great uncle who will teach you."

"The teacher is royalty?" Portia said.

"The teacher would have been king, but he thought preserving the knowledge of healing a splinter was a higher duty to his people. Few can do it. Legends have it that many of his close advisors were irate, saying that the last splinter was healed forever and there was no more threat. But he would not listen, no matter how much they yelled." Lady Harper rubbed her eyes. "Luckily for us, he had great foresight. His name is Lord Fife, but he prefers no title. You'll see soon enough."

Portia rose. She clutched the book close to her to take it with her, but Lady Harper put a hand on the tome and shook her head.

"All books in the library must remain here," Lady Harper said. "You'll be allowed to return."

Portia reluctantly put the book back on the shelf. But before walking away she pulled it back out again, just a bit, so it stuck out a half inch more than the other books. She wanted to be able to find the book again.

They met King Magnus and a single guard by the entryway to the castle. Portia was surprised to see him standing there waiting. She never thought she would ever see royalty wait for her. She ducked her head down in embarrassment. He was dressed much more casually, and if she had not known he was the king, she would have thought he was a merchant from the city—and a modest merchant at that. She still was amazed at the wealth she had seen in the merchant district of the inner city. Portia wondered at the change in the king's appearance.

There was a carriage waiting for them in front of the castle. It too was much more modest than she expected. Portia sat next to Lady Harper, and King Magnus sat opposite them.

His guard rode standing on the back. The carriage took a path through a quiet part of the city. It looked like a forest, but Portia knew they were still within the city grounds. The woods went on for quite a while. If it was a park, it was an enormous one. At the far end of it, buildings made with blue stone appeared. They looked like the buildings at the Academy in Coverack. Did the elves create the Academy in Coverack as well as the buildings here? Were all magical buildings blue?

A bell sounded while they exited the carriage, and masses of Elven students poured down the steps of a nearby building. Portia felt a little homesick seeing them. She walked down the path with the others and thought of her friends back in Coverack. She wondered what Liam, Richard, Mia, and Ella were doing. Did they miss her? Magisend was probably relishing how far behind Portia would be when she got back. Portia stopped walking in surprise. It was shocking to realize she even missed Magisend Lucy Gwynn of House Riddlepit. Shaking her head at that, Portia caught up with the others. She must truly be feeling ill to miss Magisend, her archenemy at the school.

They came upon a smaller building set aside from all the rest. It was in the midst of a beautiful yard of wildflowers, surrounded by a low white fence. It looked more like a private cottage than a school building. The king opened the fence gate personally and waved Lady Harper and Portia to enter. He shut it behind him, preventing the guard from following. The guard nodded. He turned and stood at attention in front of the gate.

The king knocked on the door, and an elderly female elf answered. She wore a black dress and white cap.

The elderly elf led them past two dark front rooms in the cottage. They looked little used. They continued until they stepped into a huge sunlit kitchen with yellow painted walls. All the light in the cottage seemed to be concentrated in the kitchen and nowhere else.

King Magnus paused just inside the entrance to the kitchen and made a bow. An elderly elf sat in a high-backed wheelchair by the fire. He was covered in warm blankets despite the heat in the room. Lady Harper gave a curtsey. Portia quickly performed a curtsey as well. The elf in the chair raised a wizened hand at them and acknowledged their entrance.

The female elf ushered them to a long table that faced the wheelchair. They all sat facing the man while the female elf made them all tea. It was a homey setting. Portia would have enjoyed it more, but she was uncomfortable knowing that she was sitting in this intimate setting with the king of the elves, as well as someone so revered that the king of the elves bowed to *him*.

The elf in the chair did not have long flowing robes of the scholar, as the professors did in Coverack. Nor did he have any riches upon him like Sir Alboka had. He was dressed in plain brown homespun. He stared at Portia and then finally spoke in a weak voice. "I see the Jack has come."

Portia swallowed and nodded. She didn't know what to say.

"I am Fife, as they have probably told you." He said

nothing else as the maid served them all tea and then exited the kitchen. Portia longed to pick up her cup but didn't dare until King Magnus or Lord Fife drank theirs first. Her throat was dry and scratchy.

"I am happy to have you here for many reasons," he said, ignoring the cup on the table next to him.

"Me?" Portia said, horrified that her voice came out in a squeak.

"You. We needed a successor."

Portia's eyes widened. She waited for more, but Fife closed his eyes. He snored gently. She looked at Lady Harper and King Magnus, confused.

The king sighed and said to Portia, his eyes serious, "We have not told you all. Part of the reason we have agreed to teach you is that healing the splinter between worlds is not something all elves can do." He held up a hand to hold off Portia's questions. "Yes, most elves can do most magic, but for some reason the mending spell to heal the splinters is differ-ent. Some elves can do it incompletely, but most cannot do it at all. The closest we have had in several generations is Lord Fife. And he is growing very old."

Portia swallowed and looked at the elf snoring in the chair. If the elves could not even do this magic, then what chance did she have as a human girl? No wonder they had not shared this information with the human kingdom. It was too much of a weakness. But why were they sharing it with her?

Lady Harper stared at Portia. "Knowing this was how I knew the king would at least hear the request from Haulstatt." She looked abashed for a moment. "It is also why I was so skeptical of your ability to do it." Lady Harper's look turned serious. "But be warned, even the lords do not know how dire this situation is. If they did, they would impose on Lord Fife to teach nonstop until he found his successor. He has been trying for seventy-five years, but they would push him even harder—into his grave."

"Which I will not allow," King Magnus said. Portia suddenly understood why he was the one making the introduction. "You are not to share this information with anyone."

Her desire to know more overcame her sense. "But why are you telling me?"

The king sighed. "My new ways are not always welcome in the kingdom. They say I am too forthcoming to the common ones. This is one of those ways unwelcome to the lords: I believe that individuals do their best when they are trusted—and they know the stakes. The kingdoms of our world hinge on the healing of future splinters to prevent disaster." He stared at Portia intently.

Portia lowered her head, hiding her nervousness. "I will do my best."

"Of course you will," Lady Harper said sharply. Portia pushed back the irritation she felt at that rebuke. When had she not worked hard for Lady Harper?

King Magnus turned to Lord Fife. "Fife, what time should Portia be here tomorrow?"

Fife did not respond except to snore even louder.

The king sighed and stood. "At least introductions have been made. We'll leave word with Marit on our way out."

They filed out of the kitchen. Portia was the last to leave.

She turned to take one last look at her new teacher and gasped when he winked at her. As she turned to say something to the king, she heard an even louder snore from behind her. Turning to Lord Fife again, he looked firmly asleep. Had she imagined his wink?

15

Portia's head ached. The drum sounded in her skull, and the vibrations passed over her skin, enveloping her. But still, she couldn't tease out the rhythm that was behind it. And she needed to understand the rhythm, for it was critical to the healing spell for the splinter.

Fife was drumming on a hand drum that he had propped on the chair in front of him. His stick strokes on the stretched leather head were surprisingly strong for such an old elf. He sat in front of the fire in his kitchen, the only location they had ever met at.

She stared at the torn parchment in front of her in frustration. It was today's surrogate for the splinter—the tear between worlds that allowed others to pass through. But the parchment remained stubbornly torn. Further down the kitchen table, a charred spot marked where she had set another piece of parchment on fire by starting to heal it and then faltered halfway through. The spell was dangerous if not completed. The sudden flames that had enveloped the parchment in seconds made that clear. The fire had scared her, and she had stopped singing completely when the flames broke out. She shuddered to think what would happen if she failed while healing something much larger, such as a real splinter. Would those standing nearby burst into flames if she failed? Or worse yet, what if they were trying to pass through while she did so? A shiver ran down her back. But it probably would be no worse than what would happen to them if she succeeded in healing it while they were passing through. An image of a human split in half came unbidden to her mind. Her breakfast curdled in her stomach.

In previous days, they had practiced on fruit and cloth. Nearly anything that could be damaged was a good surrogate, for the splinter spell most of all was a mending spell. She had to get the spell down on simple objects before she could do a repair of space, a much more ephemeral thing than an object she could hold in her hands. She knew she had some healing skills, for she had been able to heal her own bruises, but she was not nearly as good as the healer had been in the Academy. That healer had been able to heal Portia's wound without a single scar. She wondered why that human wasn't chosen for this task. But that was a different sort of healing—one not dependent on music and rhythm—and Fife had been adamant that the splinters could only be healed with a spell rooted in music. The elves had thousands of years more experience in magic than humans, so Portia thought it was reasonable to take their word. His word.

"Enough," he said and stopped beating the drum. "You're

exhausted. We'll accomplish nothing more today but to frustrate you."

Portia felt gratitude that Fife showed no impatience. It would have been hard enough without adding the disapproval of her only teacher in the elf kingdom. For King Magnus and Lady Harper had decided it was safest if Portia was isolated from all other students. Luckily, Fife did not teach many others, so it was easy to see him every day.

Portia had been allowed to go back and visit the chamber of the hourglass. She wanted to see how much time she had left before the splinter occurred. Every time she went, she was nervous there would be no sand at the top. But every time she entered the cavern, there had been at least a little. Some days it even seemed there was more at the top than there had been the previous day. On those days she breathed more easily. But it would have been less stressful had her lessons been going better. She felt she was getting worse, not better. That charred wood on the table was a testament to one of her many recent failures.

"I'm sorry, I'll do better," Portia said, tears pricking her eyes.

"Yes, yes, I'm sure you will." Fife put the drum on the table and rolled his chair over to the bell pull for Marit. "But you need rest. And practice without the pressure of my staring at you. I think you have the rhythm inside of you now. You have heard it enough times. But the stress of trying in front of me, I think, has made it too difficult to work the spell. Go somewhere else and practice. Play with it."

He stopped speaking to concentrate on breathing. It came

in and out of his mouth with a wheeze. This difficulty was a sharp contrast to the strength he showed when drumming. Portia wondered if he drew some strength from magic while the spell was being created.

He caught his breath then continued. "There is a practice area on the separate patch of Academy grounds where no one will question you. It is expected of all students to do work without their teachers. And despite the recent ban, there have been human students in the past. There are perhaps one or two still here." He paused again. Portia ached seeing him struggling to breathe, but she didn't dare interrupt him. "No one in the school now will question your being there to practice."

Portia nodded. She gathered up the torn paper and other bits they had been using and shoved them in her bag. The morning was only half over, and she had some time before lunch. She did not want to return to the castle having failed yet again. Hopefully, she would have success before the lunch bell sounded. She didn't want to ask another question but didn't want to risk being where she shouldn't be.

"Can you tell me exactly which yard it is?"

Fife was still having trouble breathing. Explaining where the practice yard was located would take effort. So instead, she quickly created a map of the city in fire in front of him. She had been exploring the city and the elf school grounds every morning for a half hour before meeting him for lessons. It had not taken long to memorize every building and garden on the campus. It helped that the boundaries of campus were clear, since all the buildings belonging to it were constructed of the blue stone.

Fife looked up at the map and nodded in approval. He pointed to a small garden in the separate grounds. The separate grounds were halfway between the castle and the Academy. The second morning of her studies she had glanced out the carriage window just as they passed the low wall of blue brick marking the property. It was odd to have it in the middle of the city and not close to the other school buildings. After her lesson that day, she had walked back to the castle and explored the area on her way. She had looked over the fence into the grounds. A single elf student threw fireballs into the air and created images of animals in the fire at the apex of the toss. The song of his spell was as mesmerizing as its effects on the fire.

Portia marked the location in her mind and then wiped the map from the air just as Marit entered. The maid was Fife's constant companion. She looked nearly as old as he did. Portia wondered once again how long they had been living together in that little cottage.

Portia ate some dried fruit and nuts as she walked down the street of the elf city. She liked to keep extra food with her, but that was especially useful here where she didn't feel welcome in any of the shops within the inner city. Her current snack had come from the breakfast table that morning. There were always bowls of toppings for the gruel they served everyone. Fruits, nuts, honey, and yogurts were laid out in dishes on the main tables. That morning Portia had ignored the dirty looks sent her way when she dumped half the bowl of fruit and nuts on her table into a bag to take for later. Everyone there knew she was under the king's protection, so despite any anger they might have towards her, no one dared say anything to stop her.

But even with the king's favor, the lords' harassment had continued. In the dining hall, they stood in her way in order to force her to walk around them, a trick repeated in the castle halls and grounds if they happened to see her there. But the lords' satisfaction was reduced when she had simply found her way around them without so much as a comment, not even pausing to return their foul looks. The harassment tapered off with her lack of concern, even if some persistent lords would not give up the effort. Now she didn't even notice their glares as she took extra food. It was a small price to pay for having enough to eat. She had made it a point to whistle in contentment as she walked by them that morning.

But her contentment had did not lasted long that day. Portia scowled as her fingers brushed the torn parchment stuffed in her bag while grabbing another handful of food. Why was she having such trouble with the healing spell? She could normally figure out how to cast a spell, even if her version was not as powerful as those cast by others. But this one was different. Somehow it came out sideways when she tried it. It often destroyed rather than healed.

The garden Fife pointed to in the second grounds was empty when she reached it. She breathed a sigh of relief. Despite the immunity granted by the king, it was still draining to have to deal with other elves. It was better to be alone to work on her magic. She wanted to give it her full concentration.

She sat cross-legged on the grass in the middle of the garden. Pulling out the torn piece of parchment, she set it on the ground in front of her. Since she didn't have the drum with her, she closed her eyes and remembered the beat that Fife had been beating out that morning. Much to her surprise, it came back to her. She still couldn't quite predict the rhythm on her own but somehow her mind remembered what she had heard. She relaxed.

Perhaps she was trying too hard. Maybe it was like the translation spell from the library—if she focused on the rhythm, she would never understand it. She had to focus on something else and let her hearing resolve it without her conscious control, just as the translation of the book had resolved in her mind as soon as she stopped forcing her eyes to focus on the words.

Portia closed her eyes and remembered that morning's lesson, but this time she concentrated on remembering the feeling she had from the music and didn't focus on the beats of the music itself. Then she added focus on her breathing while also remembering the feeling. A flash of magic burst along her neck and back. She opened her eyes and saw that the tear in the parchment was halfway healed. As soon as she had opened her eyes to look, the healing stopped. But it had been successful. Releasing the spell, she picked up the parchment to examine it. The heal showed as a dark yellow line where the two pieces of parchment had rejoined. The spell had left a dark scar on the object. To fully succeed, she had to be able to not only heal it but heal it cleanly without a single mark left of where it had once been rendered into two pieces.

But she had partially succeeded. Despite how far she had to go, elation lifted her heart.

She lifted the parchment up to the sun to see if it revealed any further flaws in her efforts. While raising the paper, she spied motion in the corner of the garden. Her heart pounded. Someone was coming towards her quickly. The back of her neck prickled—there was something odd going on.

She scrambled to her feet. A young elf dressed in a bright green that matched the shrubbery surrounding the garden ran towards her. If she had not been looking in just the right direction, she would not have seen him until he had been upon her. As it was, she had only a second's warning. She was too tired and flustered from casting the elf magic spell to cast another one so quickly, even one she was so comfortable with as Mark's light magic. Instead, she pulled out her long knife and got into a defensive stance just in time, for the charging elf had a knife out in front of him. It too was bright green. Only his dark eyes did not blend into the background.

Portia swore as he made contact, the momentum of his rush knocking her aside. Blessedly, her training kept her on her feet. She pivoted to face him as he charged her again.

He pulled a second longer knife from a sheath strapped to his back. Its reach exceeded that of Portia's long knife. It was comically large on him. He jabbed at her with it. And he was fast. Portia had to dance back to avoid his reach.

She maintained her side to side defensive swings to block the elf's awkward jabs. Looking around, she didn't see any other attackers. But there were also no other students. She was on her own.

There was a large tree nearby, its trunk several times the width of her body. She eased towards it while blocking the elf, wanting a safe spot for her back. He was so fast that she was constantly turning and pivoting to keep him in front of her. It didn't help that she had spent the morning working magic. She was slower than she would have been normally, for the magic drained her strength.

She reached the tree and got her back to it. The elf realized what she was doing too late and had been unable to stop her. Rather than give up, he redoubled his efforts. He jabbed at her with the long blade and then swung in for a counterattack with his other hand, hoping she was too slow to get back into a defensive stance after blocking his initial attack. She was quick enough, at least for the first dozen or so attacks. But her breath soon came in ragged gasps. Her arm was burning with the effort it took to keep swinging. The attacker just kept coming. He was untiring.

Finally, she was too slow recovering after one attack, and he managed to knock her long knife from her right arm and then nick her shoulder with his shorter blade. He cut through the fabric of her tunic and left a thin red line across the top of her shoulder. It oozed blood but was not deep. Regardless of the superficiality of the wound, a look of triumph crossed his face.

His look enraged her. Drawing on renewed strength, she lifted her right leg and kicked him in the chest. He was surprisingly light, and her kick threw him back ten feet. He landed on his rear and then his back. Portia rushed towards him and grabbed his arm holding the longer knife by the wrist. She bashed his arm on the ground, aiming for a rock she saw. His arm made a sickening sound as it hit the rock, and he released the blade. Portia grabbed the long knife.

But while she was getting his knife the elf managed to wiggle free from underneath her. He scrambled back then got to his feet. He held the little knife he still had in his hand as a defense. Portia, still enraged, rushed at him with his own weapon. She cut through his defensive block like it was nothing and slashed him on the hip. He howled in rage and then turned and ran.

Portia breathed heavily. She wanted to chase him, but her side was burning, and her breath ragged. Watching his back recede from her, she summoned an ice spell. She could at least freeze him to the ground until help came.

But little magic came. What should have been a stream of ice racing towards the elf was only a trickle of water that soon tapered off to nothing. There was no ice. Even worse, as soon as Portia used her magic she felt her energy draining away in a torrent. Darkness rushed up towards her. She hit the ground with a thud. The last thing her eyes saw before they shut was the elf scrambling through the bushes and over the blue wall.

PORTIA DRIFTED in and out of consciousness. She dreamed of being trapped in a cave below ground. She was lying on her back on the cold ground, her arms and legs unable to move.

The ceiling was so close it tickled her nose. She panicked and tried to scream, but no sound came. In those dreams she hyperventilated until she passed out, a strange pressure on her chest.

One time she revived enough to know she was in a soft bed. Cool sheets covered her body. She wanted to touch one, but her arms were so weak she could barely move. It was night, and the room was lit only by one small candle. There was someone in the dim room with her. She focused her eyes and saw Fife in his chair. He gave her a smile. She tried to smile back, but the darkness overcame her again. She closed her eyes.

Sometime later, she woke again. It was morning this time. Fife was gone, if indeed he was really there and it wasn't just a hallucination. Instead, a young page sat in a wooden chair by the window. He was staring at her with wide eyes. Portia got the sense he had been staring at her nonstop while she slept.

She blinked at him. He leapt to his feet. Before she could speak, he ran out the door. His footfalls echoed down the corridor. She was not in her tower. This room must be part of the main castle.

A few minutes later, a nurse came into the room, a large white apron covering her dress. She clucked at Portia and came over and put a hand on her forehead. Whatever information her hand told her, the nurse was satisfied. She left the room without a word to Portia and returned in a few moments with a tray holding a cup of tea and a bowl of broth. She set them down on the bedside table next to Portia.

The broth smelled delicious, but Portia didn't have the

energy to sit up. When she didn't move, the nurse clucked her tongue and pulled Portia upwards, propping pillows behind her.

"You okay love?"

Portia nodded, the effort of such a small movement exhausting.

The nurse pulled the chair vacated by the page close to the bed and sat on it, then spooned the broth into Portia's mouth. Portia was too hungry to be humiliated by being fed like a child. She drank the broth. It was warm and soothed her throat as she swallowed.

When the broth was done, the nurse laid Portia back down and left again. Portia quickly fell back to sleep.

The next time Portia woke, she was startled to see not only Lady Harper but also King Magnus. They sat in chairs next to the bedside and faced her, their concerned looks scaring her more than her illness. This time she was gratified to realize she had the strength to sit up on her own and she did so, facing both the king and Lady Harper.

"Have you been here long?" Portia asked.

"I have come and gone several times over the week," Lady Harper said. "The master healer thought you would recover more fully today after eating yesterday. That is why the king is here now."

Portia feared she might have done something wrong, but they didn't look angry. "I don't understand why I'm so sick," she said, finally. She didn't want to sound like a petulant child.

"You've been poisoned," King Magnus said quietly. "You tried to do magic, didn't you?"

"Yes, but what does that have to do with poison?"

"There is a special kind of poison, prohibited for centuries now, that only goes into effect if it's victim tries to use magic. The longer the poison has been circulating in the victim's blood, the stronger it gets. You are lucky in that you only had a small dose and used your magic soon after being exposed."

Poisoned? "How?"

Lady Harper leaned in and touched Portia's bandaged shoulder. "From the knife wound. It was confirmed by testing the blade on the ground next to you. Luckily, I knew all the weapons you had with you so I could testify to the lords that it was not your blade. Do you remember anything about who attacked you?"

Portia shook her head.

King Magnus cleared his throat. "We guessed you had disarmed the attacker and taken his own blade. Is this true? And if so, were you lucky enough to hit him with it?"

Portia nodded. "I got him much better than he got me. But he was able to escape, and I collapsed to the ground. I don't understand how that could be."

"Because he didn't use magic," Lady Harper said.

Fear gripped Portia's heart. She couldn't collapse or be sick if she used magic. It was too important, especially now. She wasn't even proficient at the healing spell she needed to learn. "Is this permanent?" she asked, panic in her voice.

"No, not permanent," the king said, "but you will be disabled for a while. The timing could not be worse. This was intentional. Someone knows what you're learning and wants to stop you. Stop us."

"How long will this last?" Portia asked. She sat up in the bed. She could feel panic pulling at her.

Lady Harper looked away. That did not reassure Portia. The king looked at her and clenched his jaw. Finally, he spoke softly. "We don't know. Most incidences we know of where this poison was used, the victim did not survive. Our healers have little experience in treating it. And any who might have experience with this banned drug will not come forward to share their information with us, for it is a capital offense to own it, much less use it."

The king rose from his seat and paced the room. He stared out the window. Portia picked at the blanket in front of her. She did not want to interrupt his thinking. She realized there were no other attendants. This too must be a secret from many others.

He finally turned to face her again. His face was set. "Rest well, young Jack. Fife is waiting for you to return to your training. As we all are."

With that, he nodded at Lady Harper and left the room. The noise of guards rising, their armor jostling, drifted down the hallway into Portia's open door. The king's guard must have been waiting down the hall. Portia had never seen so many armored guards within the halls of the palace before. They must be on high alert now.

Lady Harper brought over a small sketch for Portia and laid it on her lap. "This is from Fife. He wanted to give it to you personally but could not stay until you awoke again. He apologizes for what happened to you. He feels responsible. But I... You will talk to him soon enough, I am sure."

It was a sketch of Portia and Fife. Merit had drawn it the last time Portia had stayed there for lunch. Portia had mentioned she was missing her locket of Elyas and Fife offered her a replacement. Portia held the sketch up. She didn't even recognize herself—she looked like an adult in it.

16

Several days passed, Portia's strength returning slowly. She woke each morning, opening her eyes to see the sketch of her and Fife propped on her nightstand. It was a welcome way to begin the day. The rest of the time passed in boredom. It took some convincing to even let them allow her out of bed. She was specifically told to not practice her magic until she was given permission by the physician.

But Lady Harper did bring her the translated book. Portia finished it and then picked at her bedcovers and stared out the window, considering what life had been like during the last invasion. She felt helpless without her magic. When no one was looking, she got out of bed and did push-ups and sit-ups and stretches. She could at least strengthen her physical body.

The physician came in on the seventh day, a glum old elf with always mismatched clothes. Today was orange polka dot pants and a red-striped shirt. Her perennial frown was a sharp contrast to the lively attitude of her outfit. "Good morning, young thing. Shall we try your magic today and see if you explode?"

From anyone else, Portia would have thought this was a joke, but the physician's face was serious. "I hope I don't explode."

"Me too. I'm planning on an early nap, and cleaning up would take too much time."

Portia scrunched her forehead. This was not reassuring.

The physician held out a thimbleful of water. "Turn this to ice. Only this thimbleful."

Portia focused on the tiny metal thimble holding a few drops of water. The water crystallized and expanded, rising to the top of the thimble. It was a clear blue, solid piece of ice.

"Excellent. Now how do you feel?" the physician asked.

Portia felt nothing, or rather she felt just the same as she had before she had used her magic. There was no drain of her energy. She didn't feel weak. She smiled in satisfaction.

"Excellent. I see you feel good. Now we know it takes a week. Had no idea. I don't lose patients too often, so it's good to not start with the king's pet. Course there was that one time with the court jester, but that king liked me enough to over-look one dead jester." The physician prattled on, her volume lowered to a mumble, and she packed up her bag and walked out the door without even a wave to Portia on her way out.

King's pet? Portia shook her head to get the image out of her mind. She was no one's pet. Surely the king did not think so.

The next morning, Portia was summoned to the throne room. She had been allowed to go back to her tower the previous night. Her clothes had all been cleaned and pressed, but nothing else had been disturbed. She dressed in her finest green outfit and went to meet the king.

When she got there, it was filled with nobles, as it had been the first time, as well as a large contingent of guards. Sergeant Lyren stood close to the throne. The noise was immense. The sounds overwhelmed Portia after a week in the quiet healer's area.

After Portia was announced, King Magnus motioned for her to step forward. "We have had the records searched. The poison that was used in the attack on you was from a single source—one that should have been destroyed a century ago. Sergeant Lyren has taken my charge to verify its destruction and to rid us of any that might be left." The king paused for a second, his eyes dark, then continued on. "The lords believe you should go as well, since only you can identify your attacker. They believe it is your duty as Friend of the Elves to do whatever you can to protect us."

Portia nodded acceptance. Out of the corner of her eye, she saw Lord Wellesley and Lord Conwood smirking in her direction. Of course they wanted her to go—they probably hoped she would never return. She wondered if they had a direct connection with the elf who had attacked her. "My pleasure, Your Majesty. That is a most wonderful idea. I applaud Lord Wellesley and Lord Conwood for their quick thinking."

Lord Conwood scowled but didn't deny it. Nor did Lord Wellesley. Portia smiled at them both sweetly. She had guessed correctly.

"I do have a boon to ask in return as a Friend of the Elves. May I make such a request, Your Majesty?"

King Magnus tilted his head. "You may."

"It is only this. If indeed this poison was not destroyed, and we are successful at destroying it now as well as identifying those who used it, I ask that the friendship that has been extended to me be extended to the other humans, so that in a time of crisis, if in the dire situation that they need to flee their lands..." Portia said, bowing her head low, then added more softly, "I ask that they be allowed refuge in Rocabarra." She did not dare look up.

The room exploded in angry conversations. She could feel the upset radiating from the lords. They did not want any humans in the inner city, much less letting humans being allowed to flood into Rocabarra.

"That is a lot to ask for such a little one," the king said, his face expressionless.

"It is, Your Majesty. But please hear my reasons. If this poison is not destroyed, it could be used at the critical moment we need magic the most, the moment we must heal a splinter. If that happens, then all is lost—for humans, elves, or any other who inhabit this world. Can you name a price for preventing such a catastrophe?"

King Magnus rubbed the arm of his throne, thinking. He was not yet won over.

"And if we succeed in this, it will be less likely that any such help will be needed," Portia said.

"This is true." The king considered Portia, then the lords glaring at him. He closed his eyes, then opened them and nodded. "Very well—"

Angry shouts interrupted the king. He motioned to his guards, who pounded the butts of their spears down on the floor, creating a loud banging that reverberated in the hall. Silence fell in the throne room.

"I am still king here," he said, anger flashing in his eyes. "You have asked the Friend of the Elves to prove herself, and she has agreed. She has asked a boon in return for risking her life, which is her right, and I have granted it. There will be no more said about this." He glared around the room. Several lords fisted their hands in anger, but none dared defy him.

Sergeant Lyren cleared her throat. King Magnus acknowledged her with a wave of his fingers. She stepped forward towards the throne. "If I may be so bold, if Portia is to come with us, I ask that her weapons be upgraded. It puts us all at risk if she is vulnerable and must be protected more than would be needed if she was properly outfitted."

"Your point is well taken, Sergeant Lyren. Please take her to the royal armory before leaving. I would have this quest started today. It has been left too long."

Two guards escorted Sergeant Lyren and Portia to the royal armory several floors beneath the throne room. One stayed to keep a record of what was taken, but Sergeant Lyren knew she had access to all that was there, and the glint in her eyes showed her excitement.

She first pulled Portia over to the sets of full armor. Luckily, Portia was still small enough that many of the suits designed for elves would have fit her, but Portia shook her head at the heavy metal plate, and instead pointed towards the piles of leather reinforced doublets with leather pieces for the arms and legs. It would be much easier to move and fight in such trim gear. Portia did not envy the guards their metal armor.

While she was trying on the dark green leather she selected, Portia's eye caught a sword hanging on the wall. It was the narrower blade the elves used, which would be lighter and perfect for her. The blade itself shone a brilliant copper color, one she'd never seen on a weapon before. Emeralds dotted the hilt, and the scabbard below it was wrapped in green leather. It felt familiar to her. Without thinking, Portia went to it and pulled it off the wall. The guard reacted abruptly, but Sergeant Lyren held a hand out to stop him. Portia didn't notice.

She gave the blade a few trial swings. It balanced perfectly in her hand. Portia's experience with swords was limited to the practice with Professor Aelric—that story to Mia and Ella had not been completely made up—but while she was still more proficient with knives, she felt there was more potential with this sword. It felt a part of her. She was loath to put it down.

"You have exceptional taste, young human," Sergeant Lyren said. "Do you want that blade?"

"Yes, very much... But I think it's best that I don't take it, for I am more comfortable with knives right now." Portia sighed. "I should prepare for this immediate quest. I don't feel ready yet with the sword." She reluctantly put the blade back on the wall. The guard relaxed.

"That shows a great deal of wisdom, young human. Most impressive. So, if that is not your chosen weapon, let us examine the knives that are here."

"I'm comfortable with the knives I have," Portia said.

"Are you sure? It is not often that a king offers you access to his armory," Sergeant Lyren said, prompting Portia to look at the knives. "At the very least, yours should be sharpened."

The knives laid out on the table were varied, often in pairs. Portia saw a set of curved daggers with ebony handles. She picked one up and felt its balance. It was finely made.

"Remember, you will not be able to use any magic. You must be comfortable with the weapons you choose, for they'll be all that's between you and your enemies."

Portia stilled. For as long as she could remember, she'd had access to her magic when she needed it. This quest would be dangerous indeed.

Sergeant Lyren leaned in and picked up the matching knife to the one in Portia's hand and handed it to her. "The king would be happy for you to use these. Please take them."

Portia accepted them and put them on her belt.

Sergeant Lyren and Portia met up with the rest of the soldiers for the journey outside the castle. The soldiers had stags waiting for them. Portia was proud of herself for being able to mount her stag on the first attempt, lacing the leathers around her legs on both sides before the deer could get any ideas about throwing her off. She smiled in delight at her accomplishment. Sergeant Lyren laughed.

No one spoke as they traveled through the inner city, the outer city, and then finally entered a forest nearby. The stags rode through the densely packed trees at full speed, ducking around trunks and under branches. They seemed to have an innate sense for how tall the riders were and never ran towards a branch that would strike one off their backs. Portia was grateful for this, since the animals went so fast it could hardly be said that she was guiding hers. It was more accurate to say she was hanging on tightly in order to not be thrown off into the wind. She was also grateful for the hat and goggles that Sergeant Lyren had handed to her before they started off.

Several hours later, they reached a lake, its blue waters shimmering in the sunlight. It was visible for some time before they reached the edge of the forest, shining brightly through the trees. Sergeant Lyren motioned for the group to pull up before they lost the cover of the forest.

A scout dismounted his stag and crept ahead to the edge of the tree line. He looked over the lake for several minutes and returned just as quietly. "There is activity by the lake. The tower appears intact."

Sergeant Lyren scowled. "The records stated this tower was destroyed. It was a holding place for the poison, and the headquarters for those outlaws who created it. Did no one verify it was actually destroyed?"

"Perhaps they did, or they didn't. Or perhaps the record keeper was bribed," Portia said. She knew from personal experience how many weak spots there could be in a story, especially one that was over a century old.

"This is true. Whatever the record says, the tower is here and intact." Sergeant Lyren motioned to the two scouts of the party. "Go find out what activity there is. We will wait here."

The soldiers went to their duties. Some tended to the stags, bringing them water and allowing them to graze, while others sat in groups and pulled food from their packs to eat. Sergeant Lyren and Portia sat together. Portia chewed a cheese sandwich. She was not hungry but knew she should eat.

"Remember, we are not to use magic. If this is the source of the poison, then we can count on any weapons we encounter having it," Sergeant Lyren said around a mouthful of grapes.

Magic was so instinctive to Portia that she was afraid she would forget and use it without thinking. She breathed in deeply to calm herself. "What about magic we use before we are exposed to the poison?"

Sergeant Lyren tilted her head. "What do you mean?"

"What if we lay traps? Or enscroll our weapons with magic? We wouldn't be invoking the magic in that moment—it would've already been done. Would that not be useful?" Portia asked.

"Most likely. My understanding is that the danger is from the moment of using magic after exposure. If magic has already been placed... Honestly, young human, I'm not sure."

Portia nodded at that. Not enough was known about this poison. But she thought her logic was sound—sound enough to take the risk for an advantage in battle. "I'm going to enchant my blades."

Sergeant Lyren stopped eating and stared at Portia. "That could turn out poorly."

"I'm wagering not," Portia said, rising. "I think it's worth the risk. I can stop using the knives if I feel any ill effects." She pulled her blades from her belt. Sitting back down, she placed the blades in front of her and considered what would be the best magic. Her strongest were fire and ice. Duplicate blades could be useful as well, but they might also confuse her and not just her enemies in the heat of battle. She didn't want to risk that. She looked at the two blades and a plan came to her. She placed the magic on them. Bless the mages, she still felt well after setting the magic. There were no side effects from her earlier poisoning. She had not dared use any magic until now, not since the test required by the physician. Despite being declared cured by the physician, Portia still felt a little skittish about using magic.

Sergeant Lyren watched her work while finishing the rest of her lunch. Several soldiers also came over to watch. They looked on curiously.

"I'm enchanting my blades. Would you like me to do the same for yours?" Portia asked the soldiers.

The soldiers looked to Sergeant Lyren for her command. Sergeant Lyren shook her head reluctantly. "You may be correct, young human, and this may be a good plan, but I'll not risk the entire quest on this gamble. My soldiers will not use magic, not even previously placed."

Portia nodded at this. She couldn't argue with the reasoning. It was possible she could end up dead from what she was doing now. She didn't want to be responsible for anyone else falling.

The scouts returned from the lake. One stepped forward to report to Sergeant Lyren. "We were not able to get very close. The ground has been cleared around the tower, and there are lookouts posted around the hill it is upon. We estimate there are fifty humans and elves there. It seems to be evenly mixed. One elf passed by close enough while carrying firewood that we could see a diamond tattoo on his forearm. They may be all cult members, if that is what the diamond tattoo means."

Portia sucked in her breath at this. She knew this was the likely situation, but it was a different thing to find it true in fact. Fifty cult members. Here. In the elf kingdom. And this was in addition to the roving bands that she knew were in Haulstatt, the kingdom she had come from. Where had this cult come from, and how had it spread so quickly? Or had it always been there and she simply had not noticed since she had been so focused on simply surviving?

It was surprising the cult was not limited to humans either. A shiver went down Portia's back. She shuddered at her lack of understanding of what was really in the world.

Sergeant Lyren rose. She sighed heavily. "This was worse than I feared. But if we are lucky, they will not all be professionally trained as soldiers and we will have some advantage. We also have the advantage of surprise. We'll stick with our plan. The first goal is to secure and destroy the poison cache. The second is to capture as many of these members as possible. But do not hold back, we must get this poison at all costs. Meet all force with greater force."

Portia's stomach roiled, remembering the skills of the party that had attacked the convoy on its way to Rocabarra. There might be more of them professionally trained than the sergeant expected.

Since there was no cover near the tower, Sergeant Lyren decided to wait until dusk. The sun would be coming from behind them from over the treetops. It would shine in the eyes of the cult members as the soldiers charged. It was not much cover, but it was some.

When the sun was a little over the trees, Sergeant Lyren gave the command and the group charged. The elves ran silently across the grass towards the tower by the lake. The attackers split into two groups to surround the building and then fanned out into a wide line. The grasses were tall enough to provide some cover, and the group made it halfway to its target before the alarm was sounded by a man getting water down by the lake.

Cult members dropped what they were doing. Some ran towards the attackers, while others ran away. Most of them were dirty and dressed in rags There was one or two who wore finery and seemed more disciplined—and were armed. One of the cult members, a better dressed one, pulled a knife from his belt and ran at the leading soldier. He was skilled with his knife work and managed to nick the soldier on his arm despite the superior reach the soldier had with his sword. Once the cult member did that, he turned and ran. Sergeant Lyren swore when she saw that. She knew it meant the blade was poisoned, for otherwise the cult member would've fought harder to do more damage. But instead, he thought the nick was enough and that the soldier would die on his own if he tried to use magic. Luckily, the soldiers understood their danger. No magic was used.

The battle raged on. Understanding that the soldiers were not going to use magic came to the cult members as well. No soldiers fell from using it. Looks of fear increasingly crossed the faces of the defenders. A yell of retreat came from one cult member, one more finely dressed—and perhaps the leader—and they all fled to the tower. Sergeant Lyren and their soldiers had the field, but what they really wanted was the tower. And now it was filled with cult members. It was also an easily defended location: the walkway near the top of the tower was filled with men and elves, and smoke poured out from the fires at the top that Portia guessed were heating oil. For all their rags, they were organized like an army.

Sergeant Lyren called for the second part of their plan. Soldiers ran back to the woods and returned with bunches of dead sticks and branches. Leather straps were produced from one soldier's pack and small catapults were constructed. Two soldiers put on strangely shimmering gloves and pulled out a bucket constructed of the same material. The gloved soldiers pulled a sticky black substance from a leather carrier and placed it in the bucket, which was then hung over a small fire. Once hot, the substance was poured onto bundles of dead sticks, lit on fire, and shot towards the tower in the makeshift catapults. Looking closer, Portia saw even the catapult straps were lined with the shimmering substance.

The bundles landed around the tower, sometimes hitting it and sticking and burning in place. Others landed around the base. Smoke poured around the building. Several bundles were aimed for the top of the tower. At least one made it through an open window.

One of the cult members grabbed a bundle to throw it back off the tower. The fiery tar stuck to his hands. He couldn't get it off nor put out the fire. His screams seared Portia's ears.

After an hour of this assault, smoke poured out the windows of the tower. Cult members staggered out the door, coughing. A few lay down on the ground and did not get up again.

When the soldiers had exhausted their supply of tar, Sergeant Lyren held them back for just a little longer. It was only when the smoke coming from the buildings died down that she motioned for the second attack. This time there was much less resistance, so many of the cult members having since succumbed to the smoke. A few, those who had hidden around the base of the tower and not been inside, proved the strongest resistance. There were some seasoned swordsmen in the lot.

One of the king's soldiers was cut down in front of Portia. She swore under her breath and leapt forward to engage the attacker. Each stroke of her knives alternated fire and ice. She was close enough to see horror cross the face of the cult member. He desperately tried to get closer to her, to touch her with his blades, blades she knew were contaminated with that deadly poison, but she managed to fend him off, finally leaving him frozen in a pile connected to the base of the tower.

The other soldiers were doing well. She knew one or two had been nicked by the cult members' blades, but no one had forgotten their commands and used magic. They suffered no other casualties. The cult members couldn't say the same. Nausea tugged at Portia's throat when they were done, and she saw the bodies lying across the ground and on the stairs of the tower. She knew the stakes were high in this battle. They were not fighting only for this tower.

When all cult members were either down or surrendered, Sergeant Lyren called for a halt. She scowled as she walked the grounds. There were many fallen cult members. Several surviving members were led away to be tied up under the watchful eyes of the king's soldiers. They glared at Lyren, but she didn't waste time with them. They could be interrogated later when it would be safe to use magic to get the truth out of them.

"There are so many. So much of this poison exists. I counted at least seventy treated weapons here. This is supposed to be a rare, rare poison." She shook her head. Motioning to a small group of soldiers nearby, she pointed to the tower. "Search it for survivors. Be careful of traps. The record stated any poison would be in the lower rooms, in the building treasury. Search them and report back. If you run into any troubles return for assistance."

The soldiers ran to do her bidding. Sergeant Lyren continued to pace the field. She checked her wounded, as well as the fallen cult members. They would have to stay the night by the tower. It was dusk already, and the sun was nearly below the horizon.

Several soldiers returned from the tower and ran to Sergeant Lyren. Portia rose from where she was sitting at the tension in their faces, joining the sergeant to hear what they had to say. "There are several holdouts in the basement, Sergeant. I don't know how they survived the smoke, but they did. It's tight quarters. They will not escape, but it will be difficult for us to gain access to the basement and secure it."

Sergeant Lyren considered this information. "They might have run in after the fire. Is there more tar available?" The soldier in charge of the supply shook his head. "Very well, we will have to do this the hard way. Keep five behind to guard our prisoners. The rest of us will have to take care of this. I don't want them sitting down there when darkness comes. They could cause too much mischief." She motioned to two other soldiers. "Gather some wood for torches and follow us as soon as possible."

Portia fell in line behind the sergeant and the remaining soldiers. She expected a command to stay back, but none came. They were all tired. She guessed Sergeant Lyren was not going to refuse any help.

When they reached the top of the stairs, a scrambling noise came from below. Standing in the doorway, they cut off the low dusk light coming in, and it was impossible to see the bottom of the stairs. Sergeant Lyren silently motioned for the soldiers to get into a line starting down the stairs. She placed two with slingshots on the edge of the stairs to cover them. Portia wondered how effective their cover would be since it was so difficult to see into the inky blackness. Did elves have better vision than humans? Portia could see nothing.

At Sergeant Lyren's signal, the slingshots sent payloads of loose rocks down the stairs for diversion. While the stones clattered down the stairs and onto the stones below, the rest of the soldiers rushed silently down, only the occasional clinking of their armor betraying their motion. A bloodcurdling yell from the first soldier chilled Portia as he met the blade of a defending cult member from below. Portia rushed forward, holding out her escrolled blades; they would give some light when they struck another object and the magic was activated.

They pushed forward. They needed to get off the narrow stairway and onto the floor below so they could properly swing their weapons. Portia reached the ground and engaged with a cult member. Her blades glowed alternately red and blue as the fire and ice magic was activated with each stroke. Cult members fell back, alternately burned and frozen. Portia tried to not see the damage she was doing. She concentrated on clearing a path around her. The king's soldiers also worked in the dim light until two soldiers came pounding down the stairs with torches held high. A dozen or so cult members sprawled on the ground, while several others held their hands up at the raised swords of the oncoming soldiers. There were so many fallen that Portia thought some must have died earlier from the smoke from the tar the soldiers had thrown into the tower.

Sergeant Lyren called a halt, giving the non-fallen cult members a reprieve.

Portia breathed heavily. She tried to not look at any of

those lying around her. She would never get used to doing violence.

"Watch the stairs," Sergeant Lyren said. She was breathing heavily but didn't stop moving. "We must find the cache and destroy it."

Portia looked around the room. A metal door was inset into the far wall, partially blocked by fallen cult members. They must have been trying to get in and couldn't. Portia ran to the door. It was locked, as she expected. Portia pulled the small pick she always kept with her and put it inside the keyhole. The lock resisted—the metal must have warped from the heat—but she managed to turn the tumblers and open it. She pushed on the door slowly. A soldier with a torch came closer to shine light in the room. There was no one inside, but there were large wood and leather trunks scattered on the ground. One was open, with clay jars scattered around it. More jars were inside.

Sergeant Lyren ran into the room and peered into the open trunk. Using the tip of her blade, she lifted the lid of one of the clay jars. It was full of a dark, oily substance. "Poison." She looked around the room at all the trunks. Going to another one, she lifted the lid. It, too, was full of clay jars. "So much. I didn't even think it was possible for there to be this much poison."

There was one open dusty spot where another trunk had been. It was missing. If it had contained jars of poison, then it was a considerable amount gone. Sergeant Lyren kicked at the spot in the floor and swore.

There was enough poison in just one trunk to fell an army. Portia's stomach roiled at the thought.

Sergeant Lyren turned to Portia. "Have you been struck by any poison?"

Portia looked down at her arms and legs. She had several scratches from her engagement with the cult members, but none seem to have penetrated her armor or reached her skin. But she couldn't say for sure. "I don't know." Sergeant Lyren nodded. "But I have been able to use my blades with no ill effect. Perhaps I can destroy the poison with them?" Portia held up one of the ebony handled knives.

"We must try," she said. She nudged a soldier and pointed to the surrendered cult members. "Get *these* out of here then get some firewood. And hurry."

The soldiers scrambled to follow her orders, shoving the cult members up the stairs with their blades pointed at their backs in case they decided to try anything.

Portia and Sergeant Lyren opened all the leather cases. They carefully flipped the lids off the clay pots using the tips of their knives. All their weapons would have to be thoroughly cleaned when they returned. Once all the poison was exposed to the air, Portia sent fire over it using her blades. She did not invoke the magic directly, instead striking at the wood and leather cases holding the pots with her escrolled blades. The wood smoldered as fire slowly caught hold on the trunks. It was not hot enough to destroy the poison. But soon soldiers scrambled down the stairs carrying more dry wood. They placed it carefully on the smoldering leather and wood trunks until a roaring blaze flashed up, sucking all the air in the room towards it. Portia and the rest scrambled out of the room and towards the stairs. They had just minutes before they would not be able to breathe and would meet the same fiery end as the poison itself.

A soldier from the top of the stairs called down a warning. "More cult at the top of the hill. Hurry!"

17

They raced to the top of the stairs and looked to the hill. A large number of cult members were highlighted against the fading sky along the hill to one side, while shadowy figures walked in the tree line in the other direction. Portia wondered if all the king's soldiers were out of the forest. It was possible. There were many of them around the tower, including several guarding some cult prisoners.

The light was fading fast. It would be difficult to defend their position, especially since they could not retreat inside the tower. The fire blazed from behind them. They were open on three sides, only protected on the side facing the lake. They were greatly outnumbered by the reinforcements that had come for the cult members. How many of them were there? Were even more coming?

Portia gritted her teeth and made her decision. She would have to try her magic. If they relied on swords and knives alone, they would be too outnumbered. They would not be able to defend themselves during the night. Closing her eyes and whispering a thought to the mages, she pulled on her magic to create a node of light. She made the smallest node she could control to see what the effects were. She had no wish to need the healer's help again. Tentatively testing her limbs, she found no weakness. There had been no large drain of energy from her core. She breathed a sigh of relief. She must have escaped exposure to the poison, despite all the contaminated weapons around them.

Portia slid past soldiers until she was next to Sergeant Lyren. "Cover me. I'm going to lay some protective nodes of magic spells. Stay off them for now." Sergeant Lyren gave her a surprised look and opened her mouth to speak, but Portia didn't wait. Instead, she ran to the edge of the yard in front of the tower and began laying nodes of magic. She knew the elves could see the nodes, but there were enough humans amongst the cult members to trip the nodes despite that. Portia had never known of a human who could see a node. Instead, the human cult members would barrel over them and activate them. Portia doubted the cult members would advance slowly enough for the elves to guide the humans.

Sergeant Lyren whispered orders to the soldiers behind her. They rustled into place. The heat from the tower itself was increasing. The stones themselves were hot to the touch, and Sergeant Lyren and the soldiers had to step away. Luckily, there were embankments of dirt thick with grass and moss that they could partially hide behind. They ducked down low to keep the fire from highlighting their position and revealing them.

The embankments were the only protection they had. They were lucky the cult members didn't have catapults.

One of the cult members on the hill had a scroll. Portia glanced up one time while she was working and saw him trying to read it in the dim light. He glanced down the hill at her and their eyes met. She quickly looked away and continued to work, hoping that one of the king's soldiers was giving her cover. She had to concentrate on the magic she was laying down. But the cult member's gaze stuck with her. He seemed to have recognized her, although she had never seen him before. Seconds later, she heard him yell, "That's our target. That's the Jack. We must get her!"

Portia groaned and ran back to the tower where Sergeant Lyren and the soldiers waited. How did the cult members know who she was? She berated herself for having given away the secret of her magic skills to anyone in the elf kingdom. She should have kept her abilities a secret, at least as much as possible.

Portia nodded at Sergeant Lyren. She had laid down nodes all around the building. She felt exhaustion from the effort, but it was the normal exhaustion she always felt from doing magic, not the life-threatening energy drain that pulled her into the darkness she succumbed to after having been poisoned. Hopefully, the nodes would be enough to help them defend their position until morning. There was no chance of escaping during the night, not while they were surrounded. The best they could hope for would be to make it to daylight and then push through the line surrounding them.

They huddled around the tower, drawing closer to it as the fire inside died out and the stones cooled. Several times during the night, a group of cult members rushed the tower. In the darkness, the attackers would charge the tower and, on their approach, run over nodes of magic. Pillars of fire and ice raced up into the sky, and other times flashes of light exploded in their eyes. It was enough to break the forward momentum so that Sergeant Lyren and the soldiers could pick off the remaining attackers and prevent them from drawing closer. After the fourth such attack, the cult members gave up and the night was quiet. But Portia didn't trust the peace enough to sleep. She knew Sergeant Lyren had set a watch, but Portia stayed awake as well and watched on her own.

When the dawn came, Portia saw that most of the nodes remained set and untriggered. She could tell because the ground was undisturbed in those areas—there was no melting ice nor scorch marks from fire. The only thing that would not have left a trace were the nodes for light magic, and she knew she had used those sparingly and only interspersed with other magic.

Sergeant Lyren outlined the plan for breaking through the lines while they ate the remains of their bread and cheese from the day before. They had not brought provisions for a second day, so there was little to eat. Hopefully their stags were still tethered off in the forest so they could make a quick escape once they broke through.

The king's soldiers walked from the tower through an

open section in the nodes that snaked around like a maze. The elves led the way since they could easily see the nodes. To their surprise, the cult members charged down the hill from the surrounding area. They had been waiting for the group to leave the tower. But again, the humans led the cult charge, and they ran over the magic nodes and set off the contained magic all at once. In the darkness, the cult had not realized the magic was seeded into the ground. They must have thought Portia and the others were using the magic on them in real time. It was a fortunate stroke of luck for Sergeant Lyren and their group.

When the magic exploded in their faces, the forward members of the charge tried to stop but couldn't fight the momentum of their charge, for the ones behind them relentlessly pushed them forward even further into the field strewn with magic. The cult members alternately hit fire and ice nodes, first freezing and then burning in flames. Screams filled the air. The king's Elven soldiers could see the nodes and ran around them, cornering the cult members who had escaped hitting the magic nodes themselves.

After a short, frenetic battle, the screams died down as the cult members stilled. A few had surrendered. Portia looked for the one who had held the scroll last night amongst the survivors but did not see him. Across the field, Sergeant Lyren rolled a body with her foot then leaned over and pulled the scroll from the fallen person. It must be the same cult member.

Portia jogged over to Sergeant Lyren, who was reading the scroll. Portia leaned over her shoulder to look. Sergeant

Lyren's body stiffened and she rolled the scroll back up and handed it to Portia. "Read it. It's in common."

Portia's hands shook as she unrolled the scroll. It was in rough, shaky handwriting, but still legible. It had orders for her death as well as Sergeant Lyren's and the king of the elves. It described Portia physically, right down to the green outfit she normally wore. Portia's hands shook even more upon reading that. They must have been spying on her somehow.

Sergeant Lyren called to her soldiers. "We must leave now. This is an order for the killing of the king. Who knows who else this has been sent to or who else is part of this cult." The soldiers rushed to prepare for transit. All arms were taken from the surviving cult members. Two soldiers were charged with bringing them back to the city, while everyone else was to ride back on the stags.

They raced back to the city. The stags flew through the woods even faster than on their outward trip. Portia was grateful she had tightened the leather around her legs as much as she could. Falling at that speed could be fatal.

Midmorning, they emerged from the woods just outside the city limits. Motion caught Portia's eye just past the city gates where there was a small road going north towards the countryside. There were several people walking the road, but what caught her attention was a small elf struggling in the grip of a man. She squinted. It was Finrod. What would he be doing out here? Who was holding him?

Portia yelled to Sergeant Lyren, who turned to her with a scowl. They had to get back to the city as quickly as possible, for the king might be in danger. "Sergeant Lyren, that's

Finrod over there. He would not be out here. He lives in the inner city."

Sergeant Lyren looked in the direction Portia pointed and squinted. She hesitated for a moment then motioned for the guard to come to her. She handed the scroll to the guard. "Take this to your captain." She motioned for a few of the soldiers to come with her, and the rest to go with the soldier holding the scroll. "Hurry!"

Sergeant Lyren, Portia, and their soldiers raced towards the group by the northern road. It was quick work to disarm the men holding the children captive. Pushing the sleeve of one of them up revealed the diamond tattoo of the cult. Sergeant Lyren swore.

Portia leapt down from her stag and landed in front of Finrod. "What are you doing here?"

Finrod's frightened look was replaced with happiness when he recognized Portia. "Human."

"Be nice," Portia warned. Despite her words, she smiled at the young elf.

"Nice human," he said, smirking back at her.

She hugged him, and he pushed back at her, pretending he didn't want the embrace. "Seriously, Finrod. What is going on?"

"You weren't around, and I was snatched on a trip to see a tailor. My parents need to get better escorts."

Portia could not agree more, but she was not going to confess that to Finrod. He didn't need further ammunition for his acerbic remarks.

There were several other children. They must have all

been grabbed by the cult members. It would all have to be sorted out within the city. But in the meantime, they had to get back. They needed to see the king.

They left the children with the guards at the gate with strict orders to keep them there until Sergeant Lyren returned, and then they raced into the city. Once they reached the palace, they ran through it to the throne room. The captain of the guard had made it to the palace before them with the scroll and the warning. Guards were throughout the halls of the palace. Advisors and noblemen looked haunted and hunted. They made it to the throne room where King Magnus sat on his throne looking pale. Queen Ceola, normally so composed through all events, was pale as well, wringing her hands in her lap. King Magnus held the parchment taken from the cult member, but he was not looking at it.

No one was speaking when Portia and Sergeant Lyren burst in. It was a tableau. Portia did not understand. She stood there, panting heavily, trying to catch her breath from their run through the palace. Then she felt it: a faint rumbling. The rumbling grew, and grew, and grew. Soon, the thrones were vibrating and rattling underneath the king and queen. The chandeliers above were swinging wildly. The noblemen screeched and then were knocked off their feet with most landing on their rears. It would have been funny if it wasn't so frightening. Portia fell as well. Only Sergeant Lyren maintained her footing, standing splay legged and riding the wildly vibrating floor.

The rumbling stopped. All motions ceased, leaving only

the chandeliers above still swinging lazily. The tinkle of a small stone falling from the rear wall pierced the silence. Portia looked around at the white faces of the elves in the court. "What was that?" No one answered her. "What was that?" she asked again, this time more insistent.

King Magnus, his face drawn and pale, looked at her. "The hourglass has run out. The splintering is upon us."